ATONEMENT
CAMP

FOR UNREPENTANT
HOMOPHOBES

ATONEMENT CAMP

Evan J. Corbin

ATONEMENT BOOK, LLC

1

Northern Syria

It was just after sunrise. The call to prayer from the nearby city's rooftop loudspeakers receded as Dr. Michael Donahue's driver left a familiar road for the makeshift trails that led deep into the desert. *One faith bridged to the next*, he thought. Before long, he wouldn't need the light jacket, but he wore it anyway. It was a mysterious quest, and he tugged the jacket tight around his chest.

The jeep bounced over the rough terrain as Dr. Donahue carefully poured hot water from his thermos over his yerba mate leaves. His second mate would be less bitter than the first. Each time he made a fresh tea, the leaves lost more of their bitterness to the boiling water. The same leaves could be used again and again any given morning. It reminded him of his profession. Archeology was the sober study of the forgotten—people who lived, laughed, suffered, and died, their history diluted by each passing year. Dr. Donahue was determined to learn as much as he needed to reanimate their past with subtle detail, adding context to what would otherwise be merely more than a list of dates and details for his undergraduates to memorize before a test.

As promised, a man stood by the still-empty dig site. He was dressed in a Western style—no keffiyeh or other head dressing. With short sleeves and rugged boots, his attire was more practical than fashionable. Dr. Donahue always appreciated utility and function above much else. He acknowledged that his estimation of the man's credibility was thus-far unearned, but he nonetheless felt more comfortable in the company of the familiar.

The site had been Dr. Donahue's home for most of the past year. His team would return after Ramadan. Dr. Donahue's research specialization centered almost primarily around the early Christian era. He took a certain guilty pleasure in casually admitting his atheism each semester to the newest crop of freshman at his university in Washington, D.C. Like all things, he saw it as a learning opportunity. *One is not excused from understanding something just because they don't agree with it*, he'd remind them. The site itself was an early Christian refuge under the Roman Empire. Forgotten by time, but now rediscovered. Painstakingly, he and his team would uncover artifacts and consider what stories they told about the people who made them. Dust from the jeep's tires made a gritty fog that enveloped the air. Dr. Donahue squinted, his eyes already dry. He coughed and plodded through the sand to the man silently awaiting his arrival.

"Dr. Donahue." The professor extended his hand to the stranger.

The man took his hand and smiled. "Thank you for coming. Your research associate mentioned your name last year when he worked with us, and we immediately knew we needed to meet with you."

Dr. Donahue fanned the remaining traces of the sand from his face. "We?"

The man flashed a half smile. "Consider us like yourself, Professor. Archeologists."

"I would assume, but that doesn't answer my question."

The man chuckled. "By the end of the day, I expect that to change. Come. Follow me," he beckoned.

Still confused, the professor followed the man down the makeshift stairs to the dig site.

"We're not certain where it was found," the man said, waving his arm over the site, "but this is likely close and as good a spot as any."

"What, exactly, was found?"

The man frowned. "Technically, it was never lost. Let me be more precise. This is where it will be rediscovered."

The professor felt his frustration growing. "What, and by whom?"

The man turned to face the professor, still smiling. "The oldest copy of the Gospel of Mark ever discovered. I'm what we refer to as a Custodian—a group of people committed to protecting this draft as we have done for more generations than our history may account for."

The professor's jaw dropped. He looked for answers in the man's eyes to questions he could not manage to formulate.

"Every truth has its season, professor," the man said, lowering himself to sit next on an empty crate near an assortment of digging tools. "This region has been plagued with war. We fear that if the artifact is not returned to the world now, it may never be."

If his research associate hadn't already vouched so strongly for the meeting, the professor was certain he would have already left the madman in another cloud of obscuring sand. Instead he asked: "Why have you kept it in the first place?"

"It contains a passage not found in any modern text. What's the American expression? 'One man's waste is another man's treasure'? That's how our forefathers saw it. They saw something worthy of protection until the world was ready for the message. That time is now."

Dr. Donahue smiled. His birthday was the following week, and the realization that his research associate might have set this up as an elaborate practical joke began to seem like the most likely explanation. *It wouldn't be out of character for him*, he thought.

"So, where is it?" he asked, playing along.

The man pointed to a black chest. Taking the bait, Dr. Donahue carefully lifted the lid, expecting some puppet to pop out and exclaim "Happy Birthday!" Instead, the heavy lid creaked open to reveal a scroll bound in plastic and wound over on itself. His smile faded. Even without the aid of his radiocarbon dating equipment, he could tell the document was old. Very, very old.

"Naturally, I don't expect you to believe me," the man said. "That's why I want you to take that back to your lab at the university in Istanbul or D.C. Test it. Once you're adequately assured of the authenticity, you will want to take this to the Vatican. Your research associate has his contact information—Cardinal Rodriquez."

The professor hesitated. "Even if what you say is true, why me? Why not deliver it yourself?"

The man sighed and stood, dusting powder-fine

grains of sand from his jeans. "As fortune would have it, you're here. I have obligations to my order, but no credentials. My job is to watch over what you see before you and make sure it's returned to the world when the time has come. Now, I have."

The professor knelt reverently before the box and resisted the urge to touch the flaked parchment with his hand. "What passage was worth all this secrecy?"

"Most notably, Jesus ministered to a homosexual. Rather than finding sin, he said the man committed no sin, and those who would condemn the man need to atone for their sin to find salvation."

The professor's heart skipped a beat. The enormity of the new revelation robbed his lungs of air as he struggled to his feet.

"Professor, all I ask is that you tell no one how this was discovered, only where. The credit is yours. Your research associate agreed to join our order. He will help you with the rest and follow this to places I cannot."

The professor's mind raced, but he no longer expected birthday balloons or cake. He realized they had dispensed with the party and decided to give him a gift instead.

2

"Ricky!" his mother yelled. "Ricky? Ricky, go get your momma a gravy biscuit."

"Momma, I got you one this morning. I'll heat it up for you."

Rick watched as his mother shuffled down the hall with the aid of her walker, taking small breaks along the way to catch her breath. An oxygen tank waited for her in the kitchen.

"Did you get sweet tea?"

"No, Momma. Doctors said you can't have that. Diabetes."

"Bleh," she spat. "Son, it's hardly living if you can't have sweet tea."

"I made you some hot tea and squeezed some lemon in it for you."

She glared disapprovingly at the steaming cup on the table, but Rick watched her resign herself to sit down and sample it. Her hand trembled as she gently brought the tea to her lips, only spilling a little. "Did you finish that sermon yet?"

"Nearly."

"You prayed on it?"

"Always do."

"Times are different is all, Ricky."

"Oh Momma," he said, setting in front of her a plate with sausage gravy over a biscuit. "Times may change, but the word of God stays the same. Always has been."

His mother raised an eyebrow and rebuked him with her expression. Rick shook his head, reluctant to continue a debate he knew he wouldn't win.

At that, their dog Liberty began to bark furiously. She jumped up from her bed and ran to the door.

"It's too early for the letter carrier," Rick said. "Calm down, girl!"

"That's not the letter carrier. Elder Monroe said he needed to come see you today."

"Could have told me, Momma," Rick said. He took the dog's collar and held Liberty back just as Elder Monroe rang the doorbell.

"Sam, good to see ya!" he said, speaking through the screen door. "Sorry about Liberty. Every time someone comes to visit, you'd think it was life or death for the old dog."

"Oh, that's no problem, son. I can relate to her. At my age, I bet every day could be life or death."

"Now, Sam, I doubt that. Come on in. Let me take your umbrella," he said, shaking the wet umbrella onto the drenched welcome mat. "It's raining like the times of Noah out there."

The two men went inside and exchanged pleasantries with Rick's mother before settling into Rick's father's former study. It was where father and then son would write their sermons and take their solitude. Sam delicately stepped over boxes of books, religious videos, and undelivered pamphlets on abortion, evolution, and every other modern social controversy. Most of the boxes sat untouched since Rick had taken over the church after his father, Pastor Harris Sr., was called home to meet Jesus a few years back. *It was probably best the man didn't live to see such dark days*, Rick considered. Still, the young pastor often thought he was no more capable of taking care of his ailing mother than he could the ailing church his father left behind.

"You know why I'm here, I suppose," Elder Monroe said.

"I suspect you don't want me to give the sermon I've written for the homecoming this week. You'll say it'll offend the delicate sensibilities of the people who have given way to Satan and abandoned our faith. Oh, lest we do that," Rick said, mockingly holding the back of his hand to his forehead.

"Times have changed, Rick. The New Revelation and all."

"But our God hasn't."

"Ever since the pope came out of the closet, the whole world's changed, Rick. Hell, the man may even marry now that they said that's okay too."

"How many translations have there been of books that never made it in the Bible? Plenty, that's how many. The world has lost its damn mind. My daddy would never stand for this, and you know it!"

"People are leaving this church," Sam said. "John Beck will be one of them."

"What?"

"Came to me last week. Didn't want to talk to you about it."

Rick tossed the papers he was holding onto the inherited desk. "Wait, what? Why?"

"His oldest, Ryan. Ryan came out of the closet. His own son is gay, Rick."

Rick whistled and shook his head. "No wonder. I can't imagine the shame he has to feel right now. I should go to him. Pray about it. Maybe we can do something."

"No, Rick," the elder interrupted, grabbing Rick's elbow. "You don't understand. They're already planning a coming out party for him. They're all about it. Like a damn Mexican *quinceañera*."

"Oh, God no," Rick whispered, almost to himself.

"They don't want to be a part of any church that won't recognize the New Revelation and accept their son with the same love Jesus had for gays. They are blessed among all people, scripture says."

Rick stood. "Elder Monroe, you sound like you believe that yourself. You believe that blasphemy? Those lies?"

"I don't know what to believe," Sam spat back. "I just know that over forty percent of this church's revenue comes from his family. Even more if you think of all the food and entertainment they provide at homecoming and the fall harvest party. Not to mention, the live nativity. That just started two years ago, and people come from as far as Ashville to see that every Christmas now! We make five dollars for every car that drives down that dirt road."

Rick glared at Sam but remained stoically silent. He was right, Rick had to acknowledge. Beck's BBQ had started as a family business in Hickory, but John took it to places John's father never could—franchise chains were opening from Charlotte to Raleigh, and plans were underway to expand into Virginia by the end of the year.

"He's turned this church around," Sam continued. "You said it yourself. You like that your momma has all the healthcare she needs? Well, fine. Praise God for that, but thank John. We lose his family and everyone else follows. We close the doors to his family and the church will collapse. Won't need much help to do that either!"

"Let the church collapse then!" Rick's voice thundered as he shoved his chair aside and stood to glare down at the elder. "As long as I'm preaching what the good book says and what my daddy would preach, I'm fine if it collapses on me at the same damn time! Better that than to give in to the evil of these times!"

Sam rolled his eyes. "Too much like your daddy, sometimes. Stubborn. Righteous indignation. That's why your father set up this council of elders—to make sure you don't do anything intemperate."

"I just won't do it, Sam."

"Young man, it would do you well listen to my advice on this. Your father trusted me help guide you on the right path," Sam said, lowering his voice to a whisper. "The other elders spoke to me last night. If you give that sermon at homecoming preaching against homosexuality, there will be consequences. Some of them want to send you off to an atonement camp. Some say we should even consider a new pastor."

"An atonement camp? Those places where righteous men get sent off to for brainwashing? You can't be serious," Rick said, his panic boiling over. "Would you ever tell my daddy what he could preach?"

Sam looked on, stone-faced. His father had passed on, but Rick couldn't stop seeing his shadow. Incensed, he sat across from Sam in an impasse between the adult he became and the child he knew Sam still remembered him as. Rick avoided dwelling on the thought. Quiet moments of introspection only led him to contemplate just how much he grew out of the shoes his mother, Sam, and likely the whole town still thought he wore.

"Come on, Sam," Rick said, "let me at least speak to John about this first."

Sam ran his hand through his hair. "For all the good it will do you, be my guest."

Rick ushered Sam out and climbed into his old truck. The seats still smelled like the bourbon and cigars that charted his father's path to the grave. The truck was part of his inheritance of misfortunes, he thought. It barely ran. Crosses and Bible verses dangled down from the rearview mirror as if in constant intercession for the engine to start. Rick looked at his twisted shrine and said a prayer. Reluctantly, the truck's engine turned over after a few tries.

Rick knew where to find John. Despite his growing enterprise, he still waited tables at the flagship restaurant he'd inherited from his father. They weren't so different, Rick considered—John's church was that restaurant. He dutifully greeted the members of his congregation just as Rick did with his own.

Rick's truck rattled its way into the last parking space in front of the restaurant. It wasn't even lunch time, but Rick knew people scheduled their meals by the time the pork was done smoking, not the hands of the clock.

"John, it's good to see you," Rick said as he took his Campbell University hat off to shake the man's meaty hand.

John offered his hand with an apprehensive smile that told Rick everything he needed to know. "Pastor, it's always nice to have you here. Come to bring some BBQ back to your momma?"

"I'd be remiss if I didn't," Rick said, "but I really came to talk about Ryan."

John's shoulders sank. "I expected you might. Come on back."

The two men walked through the restaurant and

into the kitchen. Rick passed by cooks, dressed in white aprons, who busily chopped pork and set potatoes to boil. The smell of stewed tomatoes and apple-cider vinegar reminded Rick of his hunger. Rick knew the employees were all as much of an institution as John. John grunted as he navigated his weight down on a small chair at a table in a stockroom that doubled as an office. Rick took the seat to his side.

"Let me be upfront, Rick. My boy is gay. Hell, we've always suspected it, so it wasn't much of a surprise."

Rick shook his head. "I'm sorry to hear that, John. But don't give up just yet. We can pray on it."

John laughed until it turned into a cough. "Rick, I think it's too late for that. Times have changed. I have to change with them is all, I guess."

Rick bowed his head. "Heavenly Father, we call on you during this dark time..."

"Enough," John said, gently resting his hand on Rick's shoulder. "We have homecoming this weekend. I'll bring out the food truck and people will love it after church, just like usual. We've been friends a long time. Just promise me you won't preach on the gays this year. Maybe preach on evolution instead, no? People like that sermon. You tell it well."

Rick met the man's eyes and feared his own would betray the sting of John's patronization. *You tell it well,* he repeated to himself, hearing John's mockery in his mind. The moment passed as quickly as it came. Rick regained his composure and forced a smile. Both of them were sons carrying on their fathers' legacies, and Rick understood that pragmatism was often the temporary victor over principle. *Victory doesn't always have a direct path*, he assured himself.

Rick stood and extended his hand once more. "If it provides you and your family any peace, I will gladly defer to your judgment. I'll keep you and your family in prayer, my friend."

Rick dutifully took two pounds of BBQ and a side of biscuits with him as he marched back to his truck. *If only I could talk to Ryan,* he thought. Sitting behind the wheel, Rick barely took note of the ride home, his mind fixated on rehearsing that conversation. Rick was an expert on the topic, but Ryan would never need to know. While Rick had no desire to date women, he was confident that he'd like it just as much as any other man. *Perhaps one day*, he thought. One day when his mother didn't need his constant care and his flock was well tended to. Until then, he assured himself there was no time for such things. Obligations to faith and family were supposed to be joyful endeavors, but Rick felt shame with each passing year as they began to feel more like chains. Friends dated. They married. They moved and then moved again. The more the world changed around him, the more earnestly he devoted himself to the obligations that would justify why he hadn't changed with them.

Long nights in his study surrounded by scripture would occasionally find interruption by a worn poster of his savior shirtless on a cross. *How wicked of the serpent to use that image to tempt me to sin*, he would think in guilty revulsion. He recalled the first time he stained that image in perpetuation of the humiliation brought by the crown of thorns. In doing so, Rick recalled crucifying him again and again, each time feeling less guilt in the moment, but ever more over time.

Other occasions, he would succumb to those temptations and find his way to sites on the internet that would ease the passage of time late at night, after his mother went to bed. For those brief moments, he would indulge in the illusion of companionship with men in chat rooms. Their fleeting conversations were his only windows in the jail cell—serving as light into a world he both feared and envied.

Other times, the mere image of a man acting as proxy for his fantasies would be enough to meet that moment's need. Guilt would always follow. The guilt reminded him of his sin and emboldened him to fasten his chains ever tighter the next time, however weak the links always seemed to be. He decided that if Ryan could only be made to understand that pain was not worth the seductive lie of pleasure's consummation, perhaps he would have a chance to save both the young man's soul and spare his parents the shame before he suffered the same fate. Once temptations were given the air to burn, the fire would always grow, he considered. Dim recollections of his own past were the caged demons that once had license to torment him, but no longer.

I must stop this before it's too late.

3

Rick dabbed the sweat off his brow. *The air conditioning isn't going to fix itself,* he thought. He was halfway through Sunday service, but it was only halfway through the month of August. He knew he'd need a miracle from God himself to raise the money to fix it, though due to it being church homecoming, he might just get that. Rick could always rely on people who grew up in the faith coming down from Charlotte, Raleigh, and everywhere in between. Some truly lost souls even returned home from the north.

Wherever they arrived from, they all drove down the same long, dusty road Rick had taken that morning, the one that led from the highway to the old, southern white church by the lake. Two big doors out front with a porch. A tall steeple with a bell that had broken the first time it was rung—too expensive to take down or fix. It was the same church Pastor Harris had grown up in. Rick looked out over the congregation and counted heads in his best approximation of the biggest collections of the year, second only to Christmas and, sometimes, Easter.

He organized the pages of his typewritten sermon at

the pulpit. The first several versions had been scrapped before they ever left his father's—now his—handmade desk in the old study. Liberty had loyally listened to his impassioned rendition of the subsequent several versions, only falling asleep a few times. Today would need to be better. He couldn't afford to have anyone fall asleep in those old pinewood pews. Not today. Experience taught him that if people were bored, they kept their wallets and purses tucked away. He had railed against abortion the previous year. *Decent revenue*, he recalled. It would have likely been more if the state hadn't just outlawed partial birth abortion earlier that same summer. The ban may have saved lives, but in so doing, he grumbled over how it robbed him of another arrow of indignation to fire into the believers' hearts. How could he raise money if the state already solved half his problem?

In concession to John, Rick looked over his pages. Another sermon on evolution. Frustrated, he forced himself to ignore speaking of the elephant in the pews. He recalled his father's dictate to always preach what the Lord placed on his heart. Still, he tried to resign himself to pragmatism. *To everything there is a season.*

The last refrain of the hymn preluding his sermon began. He looked out over the congregation as they

sang. Most were in their Sunday best, though that term
meant something different to each of them. Men mostly
wore suits or buttoned dress shirts. A woman's elaborate
lavender bonnet drew his eye. Then, John's family. They
occupied their rightful seats in the front of the church.
They'd sit at the altar if they could, he thought, glaring
at them. Ryan sat next to his mother. It wasn't lost on
him that the black sheep had elected to wear a t-shirt
emblazoned with a bold rainbow-flag decal. Ryan's
hymnal sat untouched next to him. He glared at Rick
like a bull challenging a matador. Rick clenched his
teeth, his face flushing purple with suppressed rage.

"Today's sermon is about homosexuality," he said,
disregarding the carefully drafted pages before him.
A few congregants stared at him suspiciously. All of
the "shalt" and "thou" words from the earlier scripture
reading mixed in with its arcane language was likely to
lose a few of them who hadn't already been distracted
by the heat, he thought. Rick fought to temper his
incredulity with sympathy. He knew Hickory was far
removed from the state's renowned universities, less by
geography than culture. A high school diploma was the
terminal degree for most. Work was hard to come by.
Most people in the town had been employed by one
furniture manufacturer or another. That industry left,

but the people stayed. Pride was the town's biggest employer now. It didn't pay much, but it always seemed to be enough.

"Gay people!" he shouted. Another pause. A few confused expressions resolved into widened eyes of understanding. John winced and looked down, shaking his head.

The pastor cleared his throat in anticipation of his lecture. "In case some of you strayed too far from home and forgot, you should know that God Almighty is against it! I'm against it. My daddy was against it!" he said, pounding the podium to punctuate his sentences.

He wiped the sweat from his brow again. "I hope and pray with all my being that you all are against it too!"

His eyes met Ryan's. The boy's expression was cold. Rick trembled with malice and an inkling of regret, feeling on a precipice, like the season's first snowflakes of a mountain winter that may give way to a storm just as easily as they may pass in the wind. He knew it was impulsive. Stubborn. He knew regret would temper him, unless he deprived it the time to take hold.

"There will never be gays in this church!" he declared.
He paused.

"There never was. There never will be." The pastor glared around the room, his eyes following his pointed finger as it swept slowly from left to right, as if to spot another one lurking in the corner wearing leather chaps and a crop top, having left a trail of glitter on his way to the pew.

He squinted. "If anyone in this church has left Hickory and come back gay, I need you to leave. I need you to put down your Bible, lest it burn your hand. I need you to walk out that door, lest this old church fall down around us all. I need you to stand up! Stand up!"

Ryan sat, unflinching.

"I need you to walk out! I need you to never come back, because whatever fate falls upon you is no worse than what God will have in store for you!" he said amid murmurs of approval. *Amen* and the like. He had them hooked now. No one left. No one stood. Silence. The father adopted his son's expression.

"In his letter to the Romans, Paul knew it. He was against it. He knew God would never permit gays in his kingdom. Read your Bibles, brothers and sisters. Read your Bible! Read it!" he said, knowing that the hour they spent with him each Sunday was likely the only time they'd read the good book. The rest of the time, the holy scriptures would just take a prominent space on their shelves.

Adultery, pornography, gossip—these were far more relevant topics based on what the pastor had learned in his role as a marriage counselor. Experience taught him people were more receptive to finding the sin in others, not themselves. One would hardly fill the collection plate and pay for their own condemnation.

"Read Leviticus and see whether God was politically correct. He didn't mince words. He didn't apologize," the pastor said. He adjusted his tie and took the welcome opportunity to pause for a second. He let his words swirl around the humid air and sink in like tea seeping out of a bag into a pot of boiling water. If the words lingered too long, the tea would be too bitter. Too little and the taste would be too weak.

"Let me tell you. If you parents have a gay son or lesbian daughter—if they come out to you—it may be too late. Catch them young. Catch 'em! Mothers always know, they say. If you suspect your son is a little more feminine than the other boys, you have to admit that truth to yourself. Don't overlook it. Stop that behavior!" he instructed. A few men leaped up from the pew at that point and professed their *Amen*. Others knowingly nodded their heads—expressing silent gratitude.

"Don't be blind!" he roared, building on the mounting energy. He had the men where he needed them, but the women were harder to read. Mothers always protect their sons and shy away from the switch, he reasoned.

Rick leaned forward and softened his voice to

persuade those mothers on the fence. "If you don't see it, how can you stop it? If your boy listens to the same music your daughter does, throw away the radio. Break it, if you have to. Don't let it set in like a stain on your shirt. If you don't wash it out immediately, it may never come out!

"Don't condemn him to hell, to AIDS, to a life of misery because you were too timid, too weak, too much in denial to say something about it!" he said, hitting the pulpit with his Bible. The leather slapped against the wood like a belt delivering its discipline to a child, leaving fresh wounds in the stained wood as the cracking sound bounced off the walls. How many times did he sit in the pews and see his father do the same? The pulpit had been abused by two generations of Harris men and the people made better for it, he decided.

"Don't be a complicit co-conspirator in his crime against God!" he shouted. More men stood to join the others who appeared no longer be content merely sitting by their wives. The women seemed uncomfortable but too timid to object.

"Slap that limp wrist! Slap it! If you love him, you'll slap that little wrist lest he damn himself to Hell!" he carried on. Many of the women looked down at the closed Bibles on their laps, resigned to the truth but unwilling to drink tea suddenly steeped too long. He reasoned they needed milk and sugar to cut the bitterness.

The pastor dabbed his forehead again with the now wet handkerchief. More murmurs of approval broke among the crowd. If he was the conductor, his congregation was a collection of instruments. If every instrument played at once, it would be noise, not music. *Even water over fire still takes time to boil. Bring them up. Then, sooth them back down before the big climax.* The timing was the trick and the pastor knew he had the technique mastered. If the collection plate went around when they were in a frenzy, they would give every dollar they had. He was counting on that.

"You all knew my daddy. When my daddy led this congregation, there was this boy. About my age, at the time. His parents were good Christians. Good, good Christians. They worried their son was gay. So, my daddy and that family prayed together. They beat Satan down, and that boy joined the Hickory peewee baseball team later that same spring. Then, he got involved in the Scouts. Eagle Scout, eventually, as I recall," he said, but didn't truly recall one way or the other.

"Oh, this was years ago," he assured the congregation. "But, when that boy reached high school, Satan came back. He lost his faith. He confessed his sin to his parents again, but this time he had already lain with a man in the manner Leviticus warned us about," he said.

Heads nodded in the pews. Townsfolk would recall the story among themselves to break a conversation's silence over sweet tea in the summer. Rick recalled the waitress at the diner near the highway thought she'd heard a more recent story from a truck driver about the young man's fate, but it was casually dismissed as rumor—no doubt conflated with so many other half-remembered stories based on the same event. But they listened to the legend's fresh rendition no less intently, ever eager for a new detail.

"Later, he took up with this older man in Charlotte. Devil had a plan for him, and that boy didn't care what God wanted. That boy got AIDS!" the pastor said, his voice cracking as the jagged word wounded his throat on its way out. That word alone made the congregants shift in their seats and look down at their laps in what Rick assumed to be mournful respect of the harsh punishment, however deserved it may have been.

The pastor took note of the congregants fanning themselves with the church bulletin. "Yes, they may have cured AIDS, but just like the plagues of the Old Testament, there will certainly be another. And another.

For so long as there are gays, there will be suffering—no matter what lies they may dig up in the desert to the contrary."

Rick then looked directly at John and his wife. "Save your children! Save them! Save them!"

The congregation started to murmur again. The same men began to jump back up to their feet, the women nodding their heads. Rick hoped they were growing confident that harsh actions were forgiven by their need to save their children from even greater harm.

The Becks sat in silence.

"For if we forsake our children, do we love them?"

"No!" the people answered.

"And, if we don't love our children, can we expect *God* to love us?"

"No!" the people answered.

"My brothers and sisters, let us fight Satan now and until the scourge of liberalism and homosexuality is ended forever!" he said, raising his father's black leather Bible climactically above his head. Like Lady Liberty's torch, he offered it as the light that would guide them to a righteous path.

Most of the congregation were on their feet now, professing *Amen* and shouting other responsorials of their approval. Having paused only a moment, Pastor Harris gave a gentle nod to the choir. They stood and the organ began with the familiar notes of that old hymn, *Jesus Loves the Little Children.*

"We will take an extra collection today for the upkeep of this church. Please give generously to make sure we can keep sharing God's message. You won't hear this unvarnished truth anywhere else!" the pastor said, shouting above the organ, just before the choir began to sing.

The service ended shortly after the announcements. He announced that the Lewis baby was going to be baptized the following Sunday. Beth Shoemaker went up to meet the Lord and services would be held for her on Wednesday. In Rick's estimation, Beth had been a prudent woman. And faithful. Before age and infirmity stole her mind, she was always involved in summer bible camp and the like. She died with an insurance policy. Pastor Harris talked to her son to express his grievances and asked all the necessary questions. There'd be little hope of her leaving much to the church, but at least Rick could ask the Shoemakers to leave some of the flowers from the funeral for the baptism to follow. *Why let them go to waste?* Only momentarily lost in thought of a memory from long ago, Pastor Harris came back to the present and kicked off what he knew most everyone had really come for.

"I prayed that the good Lord would give us some

clouds today. All I have to say is sometimes God says yes to prayer and other times he says, not yet."

The congregation chuckled. He knew it was less from his joke and more from a pent-up desire to go tend to the picnic. Pastor Rick read the room. He was the weak dam and they were the rising water.

"In any event, John Beck was kind enough to have Beck's BBQ come out and cater our picnic today, so be sure to come join us all in fellowship out back for home-coming. May God bless all of you, and let's eat. Amen!"

The congregation offered some of the most heart-felt praise of the whole service with their responding *amen* as everyone stood up and started to make their way to the exit while the organist played them out of the building.

Rick worried his white shirt was going to be all sweat through by the end. He recalled going to Pen-ny's the other week and buying a nice new shirt with a breathable polyester blend. Slim fit, the tag said. Blessed with a good metabolism, he took pride knowing he looked like he ran and ate well, even though neither were true. He admitted, he looked good in the new shirt. It paired well with his ice-blue tie, which paired well with his matching eyes, he decided. *You have to spend a little money to make money*, he rationalized every time he felt somewhat too close to the sin of vanity. But he certainly liked to look nice, no matter what the occasion. In moments of self-reflection, he thought it was his way of rebelling in some small way against a father whose piety and frugality were much more loved and respected by his congregation than his family.

Rick collected his notes from the pulpit and tucked them away in his father's worn black leather bag. The chattering voices diminished as the congregation filed out. Muffled sounds of children yelling as they ran behind the church crept through the windows, no better able to insulate from sound than the cold winter wind. The children wasted no time getting to the old swings out back. A sandpit under the swings had blown away over time, leaving dirt and rocks where no grass would dare grow. The swing squeaked under the weight of the riders. Rick thought the swing was like a metronome that seemed to keep time over all the years. Rick heard himself in the children's laughter. He had swung on the same swings so many years ago. He was 27 years old now. *Where did time go?*

Rick traded the humidity in the church for a breeze, but the sun beat down with unforgiving heat. *Like the wrath of an angry God*, he thought. Still, the breeze seemed welcome. Rick saw John's wife, Elizabeth, in the distance. She was with the other women pulling the folded legs out from mismatched tables that must have come from the church basement.

Rick was hoping to go count the collection, but there'd be time for that later. His debts had to be paid first. Rick hated when he wasn't behind the pulpit. Small talk would inevitably lead to uncomfortable questions. *Let me introduce you to my cousin.* Or, *A man of your age should be seeing a nice, Christian woman.* Rick had heard them all. His dodges were rehearsed and well-used. Every conversation was a game of chess where Rick always thought two moves ahead, adroitly trying to avoid any discussion that may touch on his personal life. Rick envied his father. The man brought his life to his faith and shared it with the people in ways Rick never allowed himself. Rick preferred the wall over the gate.

Rick dabbed the sweat off his brow with a fresh handkerchief and put on his Campbell University hat to take some refuge from the sun. "Elizabeth! A pleasure to see you! God bless ya. Thanks for coming out today."

The woman's scowl jolted him. "Rick Harris," she said in the same admonishing tone his mother would use. "How dare you, pastor. Our son needs support right now, not your admonishment."

"Mrs. Beck, I love your son and your family," Rick

stuttered. "I was prepared to preach on evolution today, but the Lord put his hand on my heart, and I had to speak my mind."

"Your mind? You've lost your damn mind, Rick," she said. "It's hard enough without you turning the whole town on Ryan. Don't you see?"

"Mom," Ryan interrupted, "these are the last of the tables. Can I just wait in the car?"

Elizabeth rolled her eyes and scowled at Rick.

"Young man," Rick said, "I didn't mean any harm to you. I just needed to preach on this whole situation so we can all pray for you."

"Pray for me?" he asked. "Fuck you. Pray for yourself!"

"Language," his mother warned.

"Mom, it's his fault for not seeing the truth and accepting the New Revelation. His soul is on the line, not mine. Who preaches to him?"

Elizabeth glared at Rick. "He marches to his own drum. Come help me with the potato salad. I can't imagine your father will want to stay here a minute longer than we need to."

Rick shuffled away in hopes of finding a more forgiving audience. *Where were all the people nodding their heads and standing up in church?* he wondered. Feeling like a pariah, he ambled invisibly from one group to the next, his chest tightening with anxiety. He could overhear short bits of hushed conversations as he made his lap around the lawn. *That sermon. The Beck boy. Gay. The bravery. The audacity.* The words stung like bees from a nest he'd unintentionally crushed under his foot. The seed of regret found good soil and finally sprouted.

"Excuse me, Pastor," Billy Martin said, holding his camouflage hat to his stomach. His old high-school hunting-team cap was stained with the same dirt that was under Billy's nails, making the hat unrecognizable to anyone not already familiar with the school. The hat would have been tossed a long time ago, were it not for the nostalgia of simpler times. Times when a winning game was all one needed to be a hero. Life was no longer so forgiving, Rick considered.

"Billy, how are you doing? How's that wife of yours?"

"Oh, she's fine, Pastor. Resting well. She's almost eight months along now. It's just too hot for her, so she felt best to stay home today."

The pastor shook his head. "Well, I'm praying for her and you both. I can't wait to see the little one. Now, you be sure to take some of that BBQ home to her."

"Pastor Rick," Billy beckoned him, just as Rick had started to make his escape. Rick stopped and turned back. Billy's face was pensive, and he clutched his cap just a bit more. "Pastor, with Anne not working and the baby on the way, things are a bit tighter, you know?"

"Now, Billy. You know we're here for you. We're praying for you. Every night, I pray for you both. Times are tough, but the Lord will provide for you if you have faith," he said, clasping Rick on the shoulder. "Now, go fill yourself a clamshell of that BBQ to take home for you both. Take two plates. Tell John I said so."

"Oh, I will, Pastor. I just wanted to know if there might be some help from the church, you know? Rent was due Thursday, and I don't get paid again until the next Friday. Anne was hoping to be able to work a bit longer and all before the doctor told her to stay home."

"Billy, we will see what we can do about that. Things are tight for the church right now. We need some structural work done on the building, and there are just a lot of priorities right now, but come to my office tomorrow and we'll see what we can do. Lots of people put something in the collection today, so I'm sure we can spare something."

"Yes, I was sure to be one of them."

Rick's eyes welled up. "I know, son," he said. "I saw that from the pulpit. Mark twelve forty-one. Jesus said that the poor widow who put in her only copper coins gave more than the wealthy ones who gave much more, but sacrificed so much less."

Billy's family was always a paycheck behind the bills. Billy was a good man, in Rick's estimation. No alcohol. No drugs. Worked hard. Married too young though. An associate degree would have gotten him a lot further than a high school diploma and a wedding ring.

Rick climbed into his truck as the sun began to set, his neck burning even though dusk had begun its encroachment. Between the ticket sales for the fifty-fifty raffle, silent auction, and the collection, Rick thought he had the winning ticket to the lottery. Money always had a way of smoothing things over. Things with the Beck boy would blow over, he assured himself. Elizabeth's shaming had been enough to keep Rick from making eye contact with John at the picnic. He'd speak to him later. *All things in time*, he muttered.

4

"Ricky!" his mother called from the other room. "Ricky?"

"Yes, Momma?" Rick shouted from the kitchen.

"Ricky, go get your momma a biscuit. One with gravy on it."

"Momma, I made scrambled eggs with that low-sodium toast the doctor asked you to eat," Rick said without looking up from the morning paper.

"Ricky, be a good boy and go get your momma a biscuit," she pleaded. His mother's voice got louder as she shuffled down the hall towards the kitchen. Ever since her hip surgery, she relied on a walker. Nearly six decades of smoking had taken as much a toll on her lungs as her voice. She was no longer in the choir at church. She rarely even left the house after the surgery and Rick's father's death.

"Momma, I'll go out and get you a biscuit around lunchtime when I get back from visiting with Elder Monroe."

"Ricky, it's too early for you to be drinking that beer. You going to get me another six-pack? Get me the Bud Light this time. And some Virginia Slims."

The pastor didn't look up from his paper but took another sip instead, having no desire to get her either. Doctor's orders.

"Ricky, Sam told me about that sermon you gave yesterday. These are difficult times for the church."

Rick rolled his eyes. "I preach what the Lord calls me to preach."

"People in this town just love the Becks, baby," she said, reaching for his hand. "If they fire you, we'll get by. Don't you worry."

"They won't fire me," Rick said, pulling his hand away.

"Just be careful, baby. It wouldn't hurt to go along with what Sam and the other elders say. Let things blow over is all."

Rick took the last gulp of beer and crushed the can in his hand before tossing it in the garbage. "Yes, Momma. I know how to handle Sam. I'll talk him down from the ledge. Always do."

The sun started to shine through the glass door to the patio as it made its way higher in the morning sky, its rays illuminating the dust in the air and bathing the kitchen table in light, making it difficult for Rick to see the paper. He put it down in frustration, squinting.

"Well, baby, you let me know. I can call him."

"Momma, I can handle it. Don't get involved—just gonna make things worse."

She pursed her lips, and Rick took it as his cue to leave, lest he linger and perpetuate the conversation. A moment later, Rick was sure she'd bring it up again. She always did, but he never knew if it was persistence or just dementia.

The truck fought him as he coaxed it to start. He pumped the gas and listened to it turn over. He waited. Pumped the gas again. Finally, it roared to life. The idle was uneasy, but at least the starter wasn't broken. It could stall or it could run just fine. Rick could only ever guess. He just didn't have the ear to listen to what the truck was saying, like his father had. His father had taken care of that truck through its first one hundred and fifty thousand miles. Unless the church elders agreed to his request for a raise, it may be his for the next hundred and fifty thousand.

The white-picket fence around the home was blackened at its base from dirt and splattered mud. The flowers in the windows had long since died once his mother could no longer spend her weekends on her knees digging in the soil and watering the plants. Cracks in the driveway had formed, and long-dormant weeds found their way up between those cracks. An old wind vane with a metal rooster suffered too many storms and was bent at each end, catching the wind and scraping against rust as it spun aimlessly, no longer able to find its way. The house stood in stark contrast to the way it shined in the nostalgia of memory. Now, everything was falling apart or dying.

The brakes (or what was left of them) squealed as Rick slowed the truck to a stop outside the church. Billy Martin was already there, waiting on the steps. Rick put on a smile and bounded out of the truck. Billy smiled back weakly, his hat clutched by his waist again. As he and Rick shook hands, he noticed the same dirt underneath the man's nails. The two men made their way to Rick's office and sat down.

"Now, Billy, give it to me straight. How much do we need?"

Billy looked down at the desk. "We have two hundred and fifty for the rent, but need five hundred more. The other bills can wait till the fifteenth, but the landlord already put an eviction notice on our door. If we don't give them the rest by Wednesday, the landlord says she'll have to evict us. Pastor, with the baby on the way, we can't leave that apartment."

"Billy, don't even think about it. Let's pray on this."

Pastor Harris took Billy's hand, and they both bowed their heads. "Dear Lord, please bless Billy and his family. Bless that little baby in the womb. Bless his wife. They're in some awful straits right now, but you've promised us that we don't have to fret and toil. Matthew chapter six, verse twenty-five tells us, 'Do not worry about your life, what you will eat or drink; or about your body, what you will wear. Is life not more than food, and the body more than clothes? Look at the birds of the air; they do not sow or reap or store away in barns, and yet your heavenly Father feeds them.' In the same way, we pray to the Lord to feed you and provide for your family's shelter. Amen."

"Amen," Billy replied, looking up again.

"Times are tough for this church as well, but we have one hundred dollars to give you."

Billy looked stunned and hesitated before he spoke. "Thank you, Pastor Harris. I sure do appreciate that, but what about the other four hundred dollars?"

The pastor pursed his lips and thought for a moment. "Here," he said, pulling out his wallet. "Here's what? Twenty, thirty, thirty-five, forty, fifty," he counted, drawing the bills from the wallet. "This is all I have in my wallet, but you need it more than me."

Billy blushed. "Oh, pastor, I don't want to take from you. You need to provide for you and your momma just as much."

"No, now don't think about it. Don't you worry

about it. You worry about that wife and that beautiful baby you two have on the way. You need food? I can call the food pantry and tell them that you'll come by and pick some things up."

"Thank you, Pastor Harris. I just don't know what we'll do for the rest of it. I was hoping that the church may have enough to help us get by. Maybe a loan? I can pay most of it back on the fifteenth."

"I wish we could, Billy. I wish we could. But we did something better. We prayed on it. If you come here putting your faith in the Lord, then he will provide for you. Have faith and rejoice that he's giving you this chance to have faith in him."

"Yes, I do believe, Pastor Harris. I believe. I'm sure something will come up. We always have miracles to hope for, right?"

"Absolutely! We love an awesome God who performs miracles all the time. Put your faith in him, and I'm sure this will all just work out."

"I have to get back to work. It's only my lunch hour. But I appreciate you, Pastor."

"Amen, son. We appreciate you as well. Now, go on back to work and make sure to stop at the pantry on the way home tonight."

The pastor crossed his arms as Billy walked up the aisle and out toward the parking lot. He shook his head and whispered a prayer to himself as he walked back to the small kitchen to find Elder Monroe there, looking through the church ledgers.

"Pastor, we see him more than we should," Sam said, stretching his back. "'Teach a man to fish,' the good book says, no?"

"We look out for our own, Elder Monroe. As best we can."

The elder raised an eyebrow and turned his attention back to the ledger. "Do we now?"

"I know you're upset about that sermon," Rick said, taking a seat next to him.

"We'll get to that," Sam said, taking off his glasses. "You can't go giving everyone your own money any more than you can give them the church's. Not for long anyway. At least you sent him across town to that food kitchen the Catholics run. Maybe they'll coddle him for you. Your daddy would have never done that, let me tell you."

The pastor's face burned, and he pointed his finger. "Now, Sam, I'll tell you one thing, my daddy would never let someone listen in when he offered pastoral guidance to a member of this church!"

"I couldn't help but overhear," the elder said as he put his glasses back on and lifted the ledger from the table to turn the page. "Your voice carries itself all the way up to heaven. But it tells me your daddy was right to set up a better system of financial management for this church before he passed. He wanted us to keep an eye on you. Make sure you didn't go too soft and ruin all he built here. He always said you were too soft—too much like your momma."

Rick's eyes narrowed. "Don't lecture me, Sam."

The elder snorted and smiled a bit as he met Rick's eyes. "Son, that's the least of your problems. Spoke to John last night. We were prepared to fire you outright after that stunt on Sunday, but the man's compassion for you is still sincere. You have a choice. We fire you, or you go to an atonement camp."

"What?"

"You go to the atonement camp and you pass. You have to earn the certificate. Then you come back to us and never preach against gay people again."

"Or you'll fire me?" he asked. "Are you serious? This is my family's church. My daddy's church. Who the hell do you think you are? These atonement camps—you think they'll brainwash me like all the people who get sent there? Won't work. It's a waste of time and money."

Sam sat, unmoved. "If we fire you, what will happen to your momma?"

Rick struggled for words. "You'd fire me? Sam, I… I can't lose my job. Momma needs me. We've got this house, but not much more. There's no way I could find a job preaching anywhere else. What would we do?"

"We can pray on it," the elder said with a smirk as he raised an eyebrow and leaned back in his chair. "Have you read Matthew chapter six, verse twenty-five?"

"Don't give me that shit, Sam!"

Rick stood up and started pacing the room. Elder Sam Monroe sat motionless, keeping an even gaze on him.

"Here's how it will work," Sam began. "The church will send you off to the camp. You'll do what you need to do. Graduate. Then when you come back you can believe whatever you want. You just can't preach on it. We already have people who've volunteered to come by and check in on your momma every day while you're gone. We even have a plane ticket for you."

"Plane ticket? Where is this?"

"Virginia."

"What? I've never even left North Carolina. Why can't they have this right here in Hickory?"

"I didn't build the place, Rick. It is what it is."

"Let me get this straight. I have to go to some indoctrination camp where they do some homosexual shit to me, and the *only* place it can be done is all the way up in Virginia?"

"Last time I checked, Virginia fought for the Confederacy."

"Coulda fooled me! They voted for the president and *her wife*! Sam, this is madness!"

"Don't be hasty, Rick," he said, his voice softening. "Talk it over with your momma and let me know which way you want to go by this evening. Take a minute for once to think about something before you act on it."

Rick shook his head and stormed out of the church, feeling it was no longer his sanctuary. The old truck rumbled down the road, and Rick considered his long-neglected plan to start a virtual church for lost Christians around the world who would give virtual donations. Being behind a camera had the added benefit of liberating him from suffering their casual inquisitions into his personal life. He chuckled to himself at the prospect and strained to estimate his costs and profits.

He passed children playing basketball in a cul-de-sac. How casually indifferent they were to Rick's world crashing down. He scowled at them. A block away from the house, his truck lurched, and Rick gripped the wheel tighter. The engine light went on, and the accelerometer collapsed as the truck stalled.

"Damnit!" Rick yelled, hitting the wheel. Crosses on the rearview mirror bounced off one another and jangled as they swung on their pendulum. Rick didn't bother trying to turn the engine over. The truck coasted to rest along the street where other cars were parked.

He slammed the door and marched the remaining way home. Liberty barked frantically, happy to see him. He ignored her as he made his way to the kitchen to find his mother staring blankly at a soap opera on television.

"Baby, did you get your momma a biscuit?"

"No, Momma."

He saw her studying him. She would often boast how she could tell if he so much as had a fever, even if she was on the other side of the house. "Baby, that camp wouldn't be so bad. You could make some new friends, maybe? I hope you don't decide to resign from your daddy's church is all."

Of course she knew, he thought. "Momma, they want to send me away to some atonement camp run by the queers. Can you imagine? Me? If they know about me, heaven knows what they'd do to punish me."

His mother looked down and started to pile up the coupons she had cut from the circulars that day. "Could you do marital counseling?"

"Momma, you know I hate that. People promise to stay together, then can't keep their promises. I told them they shouldn't have signed up for it if they didn't mean it."

"Baby, sometimes you need to just listen more. Let them talk it out. Not everything is as black and white."

"Telling me their sex life isn't what it used to be," he said, shaking his head. "Can you believe that? The Bible says a woman should submit to her husband. God never promised someone's intimate life would be prom night forever. See, it's this porn and these Hollywood movies that tell people to expect all that nonsense. Not my fault if they don't want to listen."

"Ricky," his mother said, smiling, "that's just not how a marriage works. People have problems, but the biggest one is not being able to listen to one another."

"Which is exactly why they should start by listening to me," Rick said, growing frustrated.

"I can see your daddy in you," she said, laughing before taking a deep breath from her oxygen tube. "After forty years married to that man, I learned that the trick with someone that stubborn was to get my way and make him think it was his own idea."

Rick scoffed. "I could do that virtual church I was telling you about, maybe," he casually suggested.

"Yes, I suppose you could," she said, distantly. "Medicare doesn't cover all my bills, you know. Take you awhile to make any money off all that."

Rick didn't know what to say, but he knew she was right.

"This place," she said, motioning at the kitchen. "Oh, this old house. Fine to raise a family in, but so big for just the two of us. I could put it on the market. Get something smaller. You've lived in that room your whole life, baby. We still have your toys in there."

Rick rolled his eyes and thought to explain for the last time that the action figures in his toy chest were *collectables*, not toys. But shame sealed his lips after considering how ridiculous it would sound to her. He hated being reminded of his life sentence to that room. He often entertained fantasies of living on his own— having a life that didn't involve shuttling his mother and her oxygen tank from one specialist to the next. Nonetheless, reality reminded him that guilt was his captor and resentment his cellmate.

"We don't need much. House money would help us get by," she said, having organized all of her coupons in an unsteady stack as her shaking hand clamped a paper clip on them.

The thought had never occurred to him, but now it froze him like a blast of cold morning mountain air. The old house was all he ever knew—the last remnants of his father still lingered in every room. Moving was only enticing as a salve in moments of frustration, but the prospect of letting the seas wash away the only stone foundation he could ever call home was unimaginable.

He felt like a person who peered over a cliff for the first time, only to realize in that moment how terrified he was of heights.

"No, Momma," he said, sighing, "we won't be going anywhere. I'll go to the damn camp."

5

Rick was at Charlotte Douglas International Airport with two hours to spare, making sure to leave ample time for traffic and security. No fewer than three people helped him find his gate. In all his years, he'd never set foot in an airport.

"Just no reason to," he explained to the person sitting next to him at the bar, chosen for its line of sight to his gate.

"It's truly the safest way to travel, they say," the man said, scrolling through his text messages.

"If God meant for us to fly, he'd have given us wings. Do you live in Charlotte?" Rick asked, taking a sip from his beer.

"Oh, yes. Moved here from Tennessee to take a teaching job in the city. Been here almost ten years now," the man explained. He put his phone down and surrendered to the conversation.

"Oh, you have my sympathies. I can't imagine how you must put up with all that, especially now with this new administration."

"You mean President Macomb? It's not that bad. I can't find much to say against her."

"Not that bad?" Rick mocked. "You're kidding? In her first hundred days, she convinced the U.N. to relocate back to New York, reestablished the minimum wage, and passed universal health care. Socialist! In just a hundred days she rolled back all the Trump administration's greatest accomplishments."

"I actually support the universal school brunch plan," the teacher admitted.

"What?"

"No, really," the man said, smiling. "The country went from like twenty-seventh in the world for public education and now we're number three. The free brunch makes all the difference. No one would ever get here early enough for breakfast. They'd be so hungry at lunch, they'd zone out for the rest of the day. Brunch really is the best time of day for a meal."

"Ohhh," Rick moaned. "You've got to be kidding me. Seriously? I don't even know what country this is anymore."

The teacher took a long sip of his Diet Coke. "The sex-positive sex education classes took a bit getting used to, I'll admit."

"What the hell is that?" the pastor demanded, slamming his empty glass on the table a bit harder than he'd intended.

"Sex positive, you know. The edict where we make birth control available and let the kids…"

"Ma'am, I'll have another lager, please," the pastor called to the bartender. "Quickly!"

"But the sex communication classroom exercises are helpful," the teacher noted. "I even think it improved my marriage."

Their conversation was interrupted by an airport announcement that was noticeably louder than the others on account of their proximity to a nearby gate. "Ladies and gentleman, Flight Two-Three-Three to Seattle, Washington will begin its boarding process, shortly. At this time, we invite active military members, parents requiring extra time to board with their children, and our African American, lesbian, gay, bi, and transgender passengers to pre-board. Momentarily, we will board our Double Diamond Affiliate members and first-class passengers. Once again, Flight 233 to Seattle will begin boarding, momentarily."

"Looks like that's me," the teacher said as he stood. "It's a long flight out west, and I don't want my husband to beat me to the window seat."

The pastor's eyes widened, and he let out a gasp.

"What the hell?" he whispered to the bartender, just as she returned with his next beer. "Why are they letting the blacks and fags on board first?"

"The *gays*? Careful," she whispered. "I can lose my job if there's hate speech here!"

"Sorry," the pastor said, adopting a sarcastic tone. "I meant to say *the homosexuals*."

She looked around before she continued: "The airport subscribes to the voluntary reparations program the White House proposed. Drag queens need extra time—what with the hair and all. Do you even read the newspaper?"

"Not anymore. Haven't in a while. Why read the living history of the death of a Christian nation?"

Rick finished his beer in one long swig and stared into the empty glass as he turned it in his hand.

"You sound like that guy over there," she said, pointing to another man sitting at the other end of the bar. "He's a minister of some kind. A fundamentalist one. He's being sent up to an atonement camp. Never seen a man so hollowed out."

Rick's eyes widened and he sat erect on his stool. "Excuse me, Miss. I think I should absolutely speak to that man. I was told to find him, actually."

The man in question reminded Rick of a slightly younger version of himself. He must have been in his mid-twenties. The man's suit was a bit too baggy. It reminded Rick of the people he sometimes saw in his church who only wore the same ill-fitting suit at weddings and funerals. *A pity.* He'd look much better with more of a European tailored suit to fit his frame, Rick decided. The young man's blond hair flopped over his toasted-almond brown skin. To Rick, the young man looked more like a surfer than any sort of minister. Regardless, the well-worn letter of instruction from the camp that occupied his breast pocket contained a recommendation to meet him.

"Excuse me," Rick said.

The man looked up from the bar to meet his eyes.

"The bartender over there told me you're a minister on your way to an atonement camp. Is that right?"

"Shh! Lower your voice. It's not the type of thing I thought anyone would share with the whole world."

"Oh, I know," Rick whispered. "They're sending me off to one too. That's why I'm here! Are you Jimmy? My letter said we'd be on the same flight and they booked our room together."

The man's face lit up. "The one in northern Virginia, that's right—Jimmy Simons."

"Yes, I believe it must be the same one," Rick confirmed.

"Oh, gosh," the man said. His eyes started to well up with tears. "I thought I was the only one! You must be Rick?"

"Nice to meet you," he said, shaking the man's hand.

Rick was surprised to feel his eyes also tear up. It was as if they'd been waiting for years for the first excuse to come out. "Christians have always been persecuted for their beliefs. Only now, we've persecuted ourselves. No one else is sane enough to even see what's going on."

"I know! I'm a youth minister. I saw two boys kissing on a mission trip a few months ago. I separated them in different rooms and told our pastor as soon as I got back."

"Good!" Rick said.

"Except, the parents found out and threatened to sue the church. Said I emotionally traumatized their sons. Our church adopted the New Revelation of course, and it was either this camp or I'd get fired. The parents said they'd drop the lawsuit against me and the church if I went to this camp. So, here I am."

"Blasphemy! New Revelation, my ass. Pardon my language. It just makes me so angry! I'm the pastor at my church. Same church my daddy started and preached in his whole life before he passed and put me in charge. He had a council of elders set up and they took control. First, it was the finances. Didn't think I could manage them without my daddy around. Now, they took control over what I preach! Can you believe that? Some lay people who aren't ordained threatening me over what I can say? I'm here to save my job, but I sure do feel like we're being sent to the belly of the whale."

"You know, Rick, maybe we should rejoice being sent to the belly of the whale. It must have been frightening, but God saved Jonah from that whale, and I'm sure he'll save us too!"

"Jimmy, you're right, you're right. I can just tell you've got the makings of a great minister, and we need to get you back to those children!"

Their conversation was interrupted by another announcement. Their flight was soon to board. Rick's stomach dropped.

"I guess it's about that time," he said. "I confess. God is testing our faith. I'm terrified about this camp. I don't know what to expect. What if the rumors are true?"

Jimmy looked at Rick, but his eyes were focused on something unseen in the distance. "Most of the rumors are just internet conspiracy or gay propaganda. Met a guy who knew someone who went to one. He said it was worse. Worse than the things you read. They guy's friend wouldn't talk about it, though. His family found him dead not a week later. Hanged himself."

"Jeessuuus," Rick whispered.

Rick took some solace in knowing his plane was

landing at Ronald Reagan International Airport. The three beers before boarding and a cocktail on the flight helped him calm his nerves as much as he could without taking one of his mother's nerve pills. He'd managed to bring a few with him, but he regretted packing them in his checked luggage. *They do me no good here*, he thought.

Rick grabbed the seat handles tight enough to make his knuckles white for the last ten thousand feet of the flight. He interpreted the captain's acknowledgment of a "final descent" a bit too apocalyptical, and felt lucky to be landing at all. Despite the rain pattering down an angry torrent against the plane, the pilot managed to land without incident. The tires screeched on impact with the tarmac, and Rick gasped for the last time on the flight.

"Praise be," Rick whispered.

"Amen to that!" Jimmy said, smiling and unbuckling his seat belt before the plane reached its gate. "Shortest flight I've been on. Didn't even have time to watch a movie on my phone. You did all right though! Ready to do it again?"

Rick's eyes caught his. "I may end up just driving back home."

After what felt to Rick like a disproportionate amount of the trip, the plane finally inched up to the gate, and passengers at the front started to exit. Rick sighed as loud as he could and looked at his watch for the fourth time in a minute.

Jimmy glanced over to him and raised an eyebrow. "This is the worst part, Rick. Takes forever."

"They went through the whole lecture with us. The plane has four doors. Look here," he said, drumming his finger against the now-memorized emergency exit brochure in the seat pocket.

"I know. You read it at least twice on the flight."

"Four doors and we only use one to get out? They were in such a hurry to put on us on the plane, yet no one seems to care when we leave. Hot as Hades here," Rick said, futilely twisting the air valve above his head. "Can that young woman bring us more water? I wouldn't mind a cocktail. For the nerves. I don't like to drink, of course."

Jimmy laughed. "Best we can do is just wait our turn."

At long last, Rick and Jimmy made their way off the plane and into the terminal.

"This way to the baggage claim," Rick said, observing the sign by the gate.

"So, you're a regular expert now?" Jimmy asked, rolling his eyes.

It was all Jimmy could do to keep up with Rick as he power-walked through the terminal. Rick's black wheelie bag would occasionally take flight when Rick determined a burst of speed was necessary to swerve around a slow walker. The bag's tiny wheels couldn't keep pace any better than Jimmy.

"What the hurry?" Jimmy asked breathlessly, lightly jogging to keep up. "Even if we're the first ones in the baggage claim, I think we're still gonna be in Virginia for two weeks."

"Jimmy, the Lord spoke to me just now."

"Oh?"

"We're supposed to be here. We were called to be here, understand?"

Jimmy looked puzzled as he barely avoided a collision with a speeding cart.

Rick came to an abrupt stop. "Jimmy, I believe the Lord called us here so we can spread the Gospel to these homosexuals. We can preach at them and have them step out of the darkness and find their way with the Lord! We're blessed to have this opportunity!"

"Oh, I suppose so. I hadn't thought of it that way," Jimmy said, appearing lost in thought.

"Let us rejoice and be glad in Him!" Ricky proclaimed to an audience of anonymous passersby who either couldn't hear him or chose not to. At that, he bounded off again down the busy corridor.

They were indeed the first ones to the baggage

claim. Rick glared at the motionless conveyor belt, almost as if he could will it to start moving. Jimmy returned to his side a few minutes later, having picked up a drink and gone to the restroom. He found Rick exactly where he'd left him, standing at the mouth of the still-empty conveyor belt.

"How many bags did you bring?" Jimmy asked, looking at the over-sized luggage cart parked next to Rick.

"Three," Rick said, not taking his eyes off the conveyor belt.

Out of the corner of his eye, he saw Jimmy's eyebrows shoot up as he took a measured step back. "Oh, I only have the carry-on and one duffle bag."

Rick turned to face him. "What? We're there for two weeks. That can't be enough clothes for two weeks!"

"Didn't really think about it. I imagine they have a laundry room or something for us."

"Who knows what we'll find in that snake pit. I wanted to make sure I brought my clothes for church, assuming they have churches wherever those godless queers are taking us."

He noticed a few heads turn with admonishing glances at his choice of words. Just then, the conveyor belt lurched to life. After several more agonizing minutes, Rick pulled the first of three identical suitcases from the belt. Each white, hardened-plastic suitcase was the size of a small stove. Eventually, Jimmy picked up a black duffle bag that looked like it had lots of space to spare.

Rick started to fumble again with his Letter of Instruction for the Atonement Camp, "It says here that we go to the elevator in baggage claim and find the representative holding a placard with our name on it."

"Uh, I think I found it," Jimmy said.

Rick looked up from his paper. "*Jesus*," he whispered as the two men made their way.

"Oh, you must be one of them? Which one is you?" the woman asked, looking down at Rick. She was about seven feet tall if measured from the base of her nine-inch heel up to the top of her French-twist hair pinned in an up-do. Her black skin and blond hair were as unnatural to Rick as her breasts, each of which would have likely have counted as carry-on baggage.

"Uh, excuse me? Ma'am? Or sir? What is it?" Rick asked.

"Lord, Marilyn. This one's gonna be work," the other woman said. She was equally as tall, but with a fair complexion, light green eyes, and a long, flowing gown that looked more appropriate for a state dinner held at a carnival than any other occasion.

"Ma'am will work just fine. I'm Marilyn Man Hoe. This is my esteemed friend and co-worker, the indelible

Eileen Right," she said, pointing to the woman beside her. Eileen curtsied.

Marilyn offered her gloved, ring-adorned hand. Rick lightly gripped a few of her fingers and wagged his hand with hers for the slightest moment, an approximation of a handshake.

"Uh, ma'am sir, I'm the Reverend Rick Harris of the First Freedom Church of the New Revival from Hickory, North Carolina. This is my colleague, Jimmy Simons, youth leader. Now, tell me, are you one of them drag queens or one of them people who thinks they're a woman trapped in a man's body?"

"This is drag, honey. I assure you, I'm all man underneath, and if circumstances present themselves, I'd be happy to prove it," Marilyn said.

"You see there, Jimmy, this is an abomination. An *a-bom-in-ation*!"

"Oh, yes, Rick. Sure is," he agreed.

Rick pointed his finger at Marilyn. "Do your parents know you go out in public dressed up as a woman?"

"Oh, baby," Marilyn laughed, "who do you think lent me these shoes?"

"Whole family of sinners! Jimmy, the devil has a hold on the whole family!"

"Marilyn," Jimmy began with a tremble in his voice, "Miss Marilyn, have you been saved?"

"Honey, at this point, the most I can hope for is being salvaged."

Rick jumped in: "Ma'am sir, you probably think we hate you. We don't. We just don't want you to burn in Hell for eternity with maggots and gnashing of the teeth."

"If all the gays are in Hell, Rick, I'm sure we've at least doubled the property value since they opened the place. It'll be the club all the angels wanna get to. I bet they'll call the gay bar Fallen Angels," Eileen mused.

"Rick, you have some surprises for us?" Marilyn said as she marveled at the stack of suitcases that rivaled her height. "I don't even have that much luggage, and I suspect I'm the only one with three wigs and a latex bodysuit. Or am I?"

Rick blushed. "Oh, no. Ma'am sir—I just like to be prepared for anything."

"Baby, you prepared for all four seasons and a moon landing," Marilyn marveled.

"What have we here?" Eileen asked. She studied Jimmy. He had taken off his suit jacket during the flight. Even though the white, button-down shirt was a size too large, his shoulders and arms filled out the sleeves, and Rick could see more than a suggestion of the contour of his well-defined chest underneath.

"Myyyyy, yes. Jimmy, it's like you do everything you

can to hide the fact that you're a beautiful, hot young thing! I'm single, by the way," Marilyn said.

"Uh, guys, I'm a Christian man and I'm sure I'm not what you're after."

"Oh, I suppose you're not," Marilyn said, dismissively.

"You'll have to forgive me, Jimmy. It's my first time as well," Eileen explained. "Two months ago, I was working for strangers to throw dollar bills at me on stage at a bar in D.C. Now, I'm getting a tax-free, six-figure salary to be a camp counselor."

Marilyn interrupted, "She's my understudy, but don't worry. She'll be *amazing*. Let's get you two in the van so we can get you all checked in. You must be exhausted from the flight! Sweetie, look at them. So frazzled!"

Reluctantly, Jimmy and Rick followed Marilyn and Eileen as they left the baggage claim. Rick sounded like a one-person marching drum line as his luggage cart banged and bounced against the pavement. Their escorts didn't even slow as they approached the street leading to the parking deck. A car made an abrupt stop to avoid hitting them in the crosswalk. The crossing guard furiously blew her whistle at them, but the drag queens ignored it like the sound of birds chirping in a tree.

Rick's stomach sank. He saw the van he was being led to long before they got there. He should have known. The van was low to the ground, and it was painted with long stripes of the rainbow from the roof down.

"Oh hell no," Rick mumbled.

"I agree with you, darling," Eileen said. "I wanted the convertible, but it's just as well. With all that luggage, we would have never been able to fit you in."

Marilyn opened the double doors on the back of the van. Rick noticed two bottles of champagne protruding from ice buckets between the seats in the back. Marilyn twisted a cork out. Jimmy jumped at the popping sound as it echoed in the parking garage. Eileen took champagne flutes from a picnic basket and held them for Marilyn to fill.

"No good road trip ever happened without a little bubbly," Marilyn said, handing Rick a flute.

"I don't drink," Rick said, looking at the glass with disdain.

Eileen rolled her eyes. "Bullshit."

"I hope you two aren't going to drink and drive," Jimmy said with an accusatory tone as they swallowed their entire glass of champagne in unison, like they were taking a shot.

"Baby, I've been drunk since nine thirty this

morning," Marilyn confessed. "Don't worry though, I'll sober up as we drive. Buckle up though!"

Rick buckled himself into the "captain's chair" in the second row of the van with a belt bedazzled with rhinestones. Thoughtfully, a champagne-flute-sized cup holder was affixed to the seat. Rick and Jimmy exchanged wide-eyed glances at one another, but any attempt to give further voice to their frustration was immediately drowned out from the van's custom speakers, blaring the bubblegum-pop hit of the day.

Marilyn effortlessly tossed in Rick's luggage and joined Eileen in the front seat. Rick sipped on his champagne. It tasted good enough to overpower his spiteful protest. Rick shook his head in disappointment while Jimmy refilled his flute. Jimmy turned and refilled Rick's flute. Rick surrendered with a sigh and decided it would make the day easier to survive.

The playlist transitioned to EDM. Its rhythmic patterns, combined with the alcohol and the van's gentle rocking on a long stretch of highway, was all Rick needed to close his eyes. He opened them occasionally as he fought the temptation to sleep, but, like with all temptations, he allowed himself to eventually give in.

Marilyn gently shook Rick's shoulder. "Baby? Baby?"

He woke up, startled. "What? Where are we?" he stammered.

"Looks like we're here," Jimmy said, looking out the window.

Rick looked around. They were on a dirt road that led to a sprawling complex surrounded by fields. The beige buildings were between one- and three-stories high, each with only a few windows. Covered walkways connected each of the buildings in the annex. The entrance was conspicuously encircled with American flags interspersed with rainbow flags on poles.

Crestfallen and still too disoriented to protest, Rick stumbled out of the van. A young, shirtless man in a bathing suit was standing by the van with a luggage cart.

"This is John," Eileen said. "He's one of the pool boys. They're here to help you with anything you may need during your stay."

"At least there's a pool," Jimmy said.

"Oh, no. No pool," Eileen said as she started helping Marilyn unload the van.

"How many people are here?" Rick asked as he surveyed the compound with his hand above his brow to shield his eyes from the midday sun.

"There will be about thirty people in your cohort. All men. We run a separate camp for women in Arlington. Currently, there are five cohorts at any time. We're always expanding, though. Each cohort has two camp counselors like us. Think of us as your fairy godmothers," Eileen explained.

"Whew, thank you, baby," Marilyn said as John helped her unload the last suitcase. He struggled considerably to move the luggage cart. Clearly he hadn't been hired for his upper-body strength, Rick observed.

"Now the fun begins," Marilyn declared, raising her arms. Her studded gloves glistened in the sun. "Honey, let's lead them to their rooms and let them settle in so we're not late for orientation. Can't have Mother come down on me for being late again. Wasn't my fault there was a sale at Coach at the outlet mall on the way over last week."

"What's orientation?" Jimmy asked.

"Damn, girl," Eileen said, pushing up her breasts, "this one doesn't even know his orientation. It's like showing up at the club before six with this one."

"You get your itinerary," Marilyn said as they continued to the doors. "There's a whole schedule of events every day. Do what interests you. Open bar. All you can eat too. Cafeteria never closes."

"Sounds like a cruise my family went on," Jimmy said.

Eileen stopped to put her hands on her hips. "Well, that's the point! What sort of thing were you expecting?"

"Geez, I don't know. I thought you'd try to make us gay or beat us for what we've done," Jimmy admitted.

Marilyn stopped and turned around. "Oh, no, baby. Whoever let you think that? You was born the way you was born. We celebrate that. You on vacation, henny!"

Jimmy smiled and breathed a sigh of relief. Rick noticed the color starting to come back to Jimmy's face for the first time since they met.

"Careful, Jimmy," Rick whispered. "Satan knows how to tempt mankind. He's done that since the Garden of Eden. I don't care how nice they may seem. They want us to accept their wicked lifestyle. Marilyn Man Hoe. See? That man took a perfectly good, Christian name his parents gave him and perverted it to glorify his debaucherous, sex-obsessed, wicked lifestyle. God will burn this place down in His judgment!"

"I suppose so," Jimmy said, frowning.

6

The Pride flags of the honor guard flapped tauntingly, or so it seemed to Rick as he made his way into the entrance pavilion. They were, however, well organized, he grudgingly admitted. Rick glumly accepted the laminated itinerary he was given at the reception.

"Name?" a drag queen with green hair and leopard-print fingernails asked him as he took his turn at the next table.

"I'm the Reverend Rick Harris of the First Freedom Bap—"

"Pronouns?" she interrupted.

"What?"

The woman looked up from the registration roster. "Your preferred pronouns," she repeated in her nasally New York accent. "He, she, they, them. You know?"

"No, it's only just me."

She sighed loudly enough to make a statement and jotted it down. "Now, take this paper down to get your photo for the ID."

Rick looked around. "Wait, where?"

She abruptly turned her attention to the next person in line. A man waved at him from the next table. The camera booth was another giveaway, Rick thought, feeling disheveled and somewhat bewildered.

"Okay, my friend. Let's see what you have here," the bald man with a slight frame said, taking Rick's paperwork. "Oh, good—you're from North Carolina. I went to school in Chapel Hill. Always nice to see a neighbor!"

Rick puffed up his chest. "I've never set foot in Chapel Hill."

"Here, look at the camera. In three, two, one…"

The camera flashed, and a machine instantly started printing his ID. The photographer handed the card to Rick. It was still hot to the touch. On inspection, Rick saw his grimace reflected back at him in the photo. *Looks just fine,* he thought.

He hung the ID card limply around his neck with a lanyard. Rick was told it would open all the doors he had access to, including his room. Rick immediately felt suspicious of the rooms he wouldn't have access to and why. The resort now felt more like a minimum-security prison. *Were not the best prisons those who lulled the captives into the belief they were free?* he thought.

"Last thing," the camera man said, "just need you to sign this release."

Rick numbly took the document. An inked *X* marked where he was supposed to sign. His eyes glanced over the small font, and only a few passages caught his attention.

> *Campers hereby consent to and assume risks appur-*
> *tenant to the use of glitter, hot glue, brunch, fashion*
> *crimes, humiliation, binge drinking, light bondage,*
> *playful sadism and/or masochism, and role play (col-*
> *lectively, the "Assumed Risks"). Campers hereby release*
> *the Camp and its instructors, officers, employees,*
> *and shareholders of any liability related to the As-*
> *sumed Risks.*

Jesus, Rick thought as he scribbled his name.

"I'll let you boys settle in. Your luggage will arrive in a few moments. You've got an hour before we all meet in the auditorium, so feel free to freshen up. Each room is appointed with an en-suite bathroom, naturally. The bunk beds may be a bit Boy-Scout chic, but don't let it fool you. There's a seven-hundred-thread-count sheet set on each of them," Eileen promised.

With that she retreated, closing the door behind her. It clicked and automatically locked. Jimmy and Rick stood in silence for a moment, taking in the room. It reminded Rick of a college dorm, except much nicer. Next to the beds were two adjacent desks. Amber-colored hardwood floors. Real wood by the feel of it, Rick reasoned as he stepped further into the room. The smell of fresh-cut lumber still lingered in the air—a telltale sign that the whole facility was as new as it looked. A giant TV hung on the wall. The room reminded Rick of pictures of nice hotels he'd seen in magazines. Aside from the occasional motel on the side of a numbered highway he'd stay at on his way back and forth from a regional church convention, he'd never had the occasion to sleep in one before. He just knew this was better than most would expect. *How much did it cost to send me here?* he wondered.

"Top or bottom?" Jimmy asked.

"What?"

"Do you want the top bunk or the bottom one?"

"Oh. I don't know. I've never done it before," Rick confessed, still preoccupied with the light-dimmer switch he discovered.

"Wait, you've never been in a bunk bed before?"

Rick crossed his arms. "Oh no. Only child. Never had to."

"Never at camp or college?"

"Never went to camp. I had my own room in college. Never shared it with anyone. My momma is the only roommate I've ever had."

"Well, okay. How about I go on top then. The bottom might be more familiar for your first time," Jimmy offered.

"Yes," Rick said, lost in thought, taking off his

shoes. "I'm sure it'll be easy enough for me to be on the bottom, unless you don't like being on top."

"Don't mind at all." Jimmy swooped into the bed. It creaked as he shifted his weight, but it still seemed sturdy enough to offer Rick some reassurance that Jimmy wouldn't crash down on him in his sleep.

Rick fumbled for his cell phone. It was a good time to call his mother and at least let her know he'd survived the flight. No signal. The call failed. He scanned for Wi-Fi signals. He watched the phone search fruitlessly.

"I haven't had signal since we got here. You?" Rick looked at Jimmy, only to notice he was softly snoring on the top bunk, shoes still on his feet.

Rick began to explore. Perhaps a password was scrolled on something nearby. He frowned when he couldn't find a Bible in the dresser drawer. Rick had brought his own, naturally. *Godless gays*, he mumbled to himself, picking up the room service menu, then walking into the bathroom.

He turned on the light. Not only did it illuminate the bathroom, but it lit the bulbs that circled the perimeter of the massive mirror surrounding the dual sinks. Two shower stalls were positioned to his left. Each had a curtain, but the stonework around the shower otherwise left no divide between it and the rest of the bathroom. A giant tub in the right corner warranted

Rick's closer inspection. He surmised the holes in the tub were for air or water. *A Jacuzzi*, he noted. *That's another first.*

A bucket with ice resting on a ledge by the tub held yet another two bottles of unopened champagne. "*Jesus*," he whispered to no one in particular, wondering whether anyone was expected to stay sober here.

Rick turned the itinerary over in his hand, still searching for a Wi-Fi password. As Eileen had mentioned, the afternoon had a kickoff event at four in the auditorium. Helpfully, a map was included. He looked ahead to the other upcoming events for the evening.

4:00 PM -- Welcome to Your Orientation with Drag Mother Missy Bottom

4:45 PM -- Love Yourself as you Love Others breakout sessions

5:45 PM -- Cocktail Hour -- Grand Ballroom

6:45 PM -- Dinner. Resort casual attire

Rick was interrupted by a knock at the door.

The pastor tiptoed there. "Ah, who is it?"

"Pool boy. I have your luggage, sir."

Rick opened the door. Another thin, younger man stood at the door. He couldn't be a day older than eighteen, Rick guessed. His shorts were a different blue with white stripes, but he otherwise looked identical to the other shirtless blond man who had met them at the van. The pool boy grunted and strained a bit to budge the top suitcase from the stack.

"Here, let me help," Rick said, with no lack of frustration in his voice.

"Thank you, sir. May I get you anything? A cocktail?"

"No," Rick hissed, regretting it somewhat as the idea sank in.

"Maybe just a snack to tide you over before dinner? Wine and cheese? A charcuterie plate, maybe? Low-carb baguettes?"

Rick rolled his eyes and sighed. "If it's not much trouble, I wouldn't mind having a drink. Maybe a mai tai?"

"Of course! May I suggest a chicken satay snack to go with that? No carbs. No gluten. No sugar, I promise!"

Rick almost pitied the man. "That will be fine, yes." Rick dug in his pocket and took a dollar from his wallet, hoping it would be enough to entice the young man to prance off.

The pool boy looked at Rick quizzically for a moment and then tugged suggestively on the side of his shorts.

Refusing the invitation to use the man's loins as a piggy bank, Rick hastily put the dollar on the cart and closed the door, only to suddenly open it again. "Hey, do you know the Wi-Fi password here?"

The boy blushed. "I'm sorry, sir. There's no Wi-Fi. No internet. No cell signals either. We're too far out in the middle of nowhere. They'll cover all that at the orientation, I'm sure."

Rick mumbled his disapproval and closed the door again, feeling a twinge of anxiety at the thought of his mother not being able to reach him. Resigned to his immediate circumstances, Rick settled into an ergonomic chair, wishing it weren't *so* comfortable. He turned on the TV, careful to keep the volume low enough not to wake his roommate. He started to cycle through the channels. *What is this shit?*

A home and garden station, a music station, another music station, some pop-culture interview show, a drag competition, a game show, another home remodeling station. Rick sighed. The reality sank in: There would be no televangelist station. No Christian station. Just smut. He impatiently clicked to the next channel. It was an old film, but Rick recognized it instantly. *My Fair Lady* with Audrey Hepburn. Rick smiled and set down the remote. The last time he'd seen it was with his mother years earlier, when he was still in high school. They'd stay up some nights when his father was traveling for the church and watch old movies together. This was one of his favorites.

Two mai tai cocktails, a skewer of chicken satay, and half a cheese board later, and just as Higgins asked Eliza where his slippers were, Jimmy began to stretch and wake up. Rick turned off the TV, and the two made their way toward the auditorium. The halls were busy, drag queens running here and there. "Places!" one yelled to the others.

There was music playing somewhere, but it was drowned out by the commotion in the hallways, where voices ranged from confused to angry. Some the men in his cohort wore suits; others were more casual. Jimmy had used the occasion to change into jeans and a tank top. The drag queens kept doing double takes of him and smiling flirtatiously.

Rick crossed his arms and sighed. "You sure do look comfortable."

Jimmy fumbled for the paper in his pocket. "The itinerary said dinner will be 'resort casual.'"

Rick tugged at his suit jacket. Two of its three buttons were neatly buttoned. "All the more reason not to. I reject their lifestyle. I reject their 'resort casual,' whatever the hell that means. I reject this whole damned place!" he said a little too loudly.

"Couldn't agree more," a somber voice said from behind him. Rick turned to face an older priest with a military-inspired buzz cut and a black shirt with his Roman collar.

Wearing a stoic expression, the priest extended his hand. "Father Henry," he said in the consolatory tone reserved for funeral-home directors and nightly news anchors reporting on the most tragic of events.

"Reverend Rick Harris. Call me Rick. It's a pleasure to meet you."

Shaking his hand, but ignoring the pleasantries of further introduction, the priest continued: "I was in Cambodia working with a human-rights commission focused on human trafficking. I spent the last three years sleeping on a mat in what was barely more than a mud hut. I'd shave with just the water I'd boil and a blade I'd sharpen on a rock. It was all I ever needed, that's for sure. Now, I'm here?"

Jimmy's forehead creased. "How'd that happen?"

Father Henry looked off into the distance. His jaw clenched. "Messenger came. From the Vatican. Told me to be here. So, here I am."

Rick nodded. "The world has gone insane. All we need now is a rabbi and we've got the setup for a great punchline."

The men walked into the auditorium. Someone

had set up bars in the corners, and the rest of the space hosted circular tables covered in black tablecloths. Pool boys circled the room, pouring drinks. Each one had a tip jar on his tray. The room was filling up from the back. Rick took a beer from an ice bucket and followed Jimmy and the priest to a row of seats near the middle of the auditorium. The stage was too big to be wasted on just a single podium in the middle, he thought.

Rick looked at his watch. Some twenty minutes had passed from the dictated starting time. He swirled what was left of his second beer. He decided not to have a third—a decision motivated in part by laziness, but mostly the fear of having to find a restroom. How much had he drank since the airport today? He'd lost track.

Without any notice, the lights dimmed and the music in the background faded out. The voices in the auditorium responded in kind. As whispers passed through the crowd like the breeze through a pile of autumn leaves. The moment of silent contemplation was replaced by drums. Not a recording, but live. The *rat-a-tat-tat* of a snare drum followed by the bellowing accompaniment of larger bass drums signaled the event was to begin.

One by one, a band marched across the stage, each member more flamboyant and colorful than the last. The first marching drag queens carried drums. Then one came with a metal triangle used with no particular deliberation. It appeared more as an accessory than an instrument, swung lackadaisically back and forth in her hand. A queen clacking her fan came next. Then one playing shrill notes on what seemed to be a recorder or a flute.

At last, the dozen or so of them came to a synchronized halt. The music stopped. A spotlight flared to life, and the queens parted down the middle of their line to make way for the tallest of all the drag queens to walk from the back of the stage toward the podium.

Her wig was a green afro. She wore an over-sized orange Mad Hatter's hat and a rainbow-colored suit over her comically large breasts. Her face was painted white, except for red eye shadow on her right eyelid and blue on the other.

"Gentlemen, drag ladies, and those in between. Men dressed as women and men dressed as themselves. Welcome! Welcome, welcome, welcome!" she said. "I am Missy Bottom, drag mother extraordinaire! I gave up my life as a playboy socialite to run this camp. You're all quite welcome. I hope by now you've met all the camp counselors, my daughters."

She motioned to the drag queens to her right and left. Rick recognized Eileen and Marilyn among them. "I'm sure you have questions! But questions that get answers only provoke more questions, no? Seems like a waste of time. We'd be here all night. So let me just tell you what you need to know now and we'll figure out the rest as we go!"

Rick rolled his eyes and sighed loudly enough for Jimmy to hear.

"This will be your home for the next two weeks. We will try to cater to your every need. You're our guests!" It appeared to Rick as if Missy was scrutinizing the doubtful expressions in her audience. "This is about atonement, not retribution."

She paused, allowing her words to sink in. "You are all said to be among society's most unrepentant and terminally incurable homophobes. Priests, pastors, teachers. While our guests' identities are held in the utmost confidentiality, I can say we've even had a former vice president of the United States, one current U.S. senator, a few congressmen, and countless members of law enforcement. They were all like yourselves and each one made it home with their certificate of attendance."

Missy adjusted her hat. "Binary gender subscribers. Trans deniers. Hypocrites, sinners, and fools. Honestly, I don't care who you were before you came here. I only care about the people you'll be when you leave. No one is hopeless. No one is beyond redemption."

She cleared her throat. "Now, each of your cohorts

will be going to an organized activity before dinner. I hope all of you enjoy the experience! The next two weeks will be fabulous! Absolutely *fabulous*! Each day, our beautiful pool boys will slip a new itinerary under your door. Some days will have structured events, but don't worry. There are plenty of opportunities to take electives. Follow your hearts, loves!"

The invitation was met with confused silence. Rick exchanged a concerned glance with Jimmy. Father Henry remained poised, his face giving no indication of his approval or disdain. His eyes fixed on the stage, scrutinizing every detail.

"Some of you may have noticed that there's no cell service here," Missy said with an overexaggerated frown. "I sympathize, sweeties. It's hard for me too. But outside influences only interfere with the good work we're doing here. So don't worry. Your work will keep until you get back. Our automated system will leave messages with your emergency contacts to let them know you're all tucked in here."

Rick's face reddened. He crumpled his beer can ever so slightly in his hand as the invisible fence marking his captivity's metes and bounds grew ever taller.

After various announcements about the grounds, the chef's culinary resume, an on-site stylist, and other things Rick ignored, they were finally dismissed. Based on their badge color, Rick, Jimmy, and Father Henry were all in the same cohort. As instructed, they left the Milk Building and walked across the covered walkway to an adjacent building where they met Eileen and Marilyn standing outside double doors.

"Oh, I'm glad you three have met!" Marilyn said, smiling at them. "The very first thing we need to do is…"

"The first thing we need to do is call home. You can't keep us here like prisoners! We have rights!" Rick's cheeks went from pink to indignant violet. "You bring us here, control what we do. When we eat. Subject us to this satanic music and that awful, awful performance!"

"You know, Marilyn," Eileen said, "he is right—our band could have used more practice."

"Not our finest," Marilyn conceded.

"That's it!" Rick took two steps toward Marilyn. "I want to leave. Take me back to the airport. Right now. Right. Damn. Now!'

"Sweetie," Marilyn said, softening her tone, "you can leave anytime you'd like. It's a thirty-mile walk to the nearest town, but if you leave now, maybe you can get there by morning."

"Have one of those pool boys drive me then."

"Are they old enough to drive yet?" Eileen asked Marilyn.

Marilyn's smile dissolved into a scowl. She stepped

forward and looked down at Rick, balancing herself with a hand on the wall a foot above his head. She spoke in the deep, gravelly tone of her natural voice. "Listen, Pastor, you don't want to make me mad. You best not test me. Not tonight. You've been here barely two hours. If you still feel this way tomorrow night, you and I will chat. You good, child?"

Rick sighed and relaxed his shoulders a bit. "Fine."

"Oh, good!" Eileen exclaimed to the group assembled around them. "Marilyn, we have all the most attractive men in our cohort!"

Marilyn's smile flashed back, velvet returning to her voice. "Oh, I love men! This is gonna be a good group!"

"Sweeties, darlings. Our first day's lesson is: You have to love yourselves! That means you need to take care of yourself. Pamper yourselves! You deserve this!" Eileen said.

With that, Eileen pushed open double metal doors behind her and revealed a room with rows of reclining chairs, each with a small tub at the foot. Women in black blouses and black jeans, each devoid of any ostentatious style, stood smiling in anticipation at the back of the room.

"Mani pedi time!" Eileen exclaimed, jogging into the room as best she could in heels—each step pattering only inches forward, her jazz hands waving at her sides.

The men followed Eileen and Marilyn. It looked to Rick as though the men walked tentatively, like they were taking their first steps on the moon. The room smelled of overpowering lavender, and soft windchimes sang sleepily in the background. The room was dim with shaded pillars of lamplight in the corners. Lush houseplants occupied the spaces in between each chair, giving a bit of privacy to the experience.

Rick positioned himself awkwardly next to one of the chairs. "You're going to cut my toenails in this thing?"

"No, sweetie," Marilyn said, "she is."

Rick looked at the younger woman who had taken a seat at the end of the chair by a small tub. On close inspection, Rick couldn't differentiate between any of the women. To him, they all looked identical.

"I'm not letting her touch my feet!"

"I agree with the reverend," Father Henry said. "Just give me a pocketknife. I'll do it myself. Always have."

"Boys, it's actually quite nice. See, Jimmy gets the idea," Eileen said, pointing at the chair next to her. Jimmy rolled up his pant legs and took off his shoes. He placed his feet expectantly in the small tub for whatever came next. He seemed startled by Rick's wide-eyed stare.

Marilyn put her hand on Rick's shoulder. "There's

nothing to be nervous about. It's not gay. You know, Jesus practically invented the pedicure."

"Blasphemy!" Rick spat.

"No, sweetie. What was that story from the Bible about how Jesus washed his disciples' feet? That happened, didn't it?"

"Well, yes…"

Marilyn cut him off. "Then if the disciples can do it, why can't you?"

"She has a point," Jimmy said. Water filled his tub as an attendant added a bubbling soap with a perfumed smell that wafted to Rick.

"Listen, baby," Eileen added, "if everyone went around not letting people love them, then how could people love one another? Sometimes, you got to accept love if you want people to give it, no?"

Whether by persuasion or just resignation, Rick slid into the chair, took off his shoes, and rolled up his pant legs as Jimmy had done, gripping the armrests of his chair like he had when the flight took off. He looked squarely at the young woman at the end of the chair, who had started running warm water over his feet.

"Who are you?"

"Melissa," she said, adding the same soap to his tub.

"How'd they bring you here? You're not a drag queen. Are you a butch?" Rick asked.

She smiled patiently. "No, but I do have a sister who's lesbian. I'm an aesthetician. I used to work in Arlington, but I've been on staff here since this place opened. Honestly, I've never earned more. It's actually a great place. You'll love it, I promise."

She winked and started to rub his calf with a gritty gray lotion that smelled of damp clay. Rick wasn't expecting that texture. He hadn't realized how much his feet were hurting. It had been a long day, and he'd been wearing his dress shoes for most of it. The massage was nicer than he expected, and he let out a moan. He blushed and felt immediately embarrassed. He looked to his right and watched as Father Henry compliantly submitted to the same treatment. His face was just as expressionless as before.

Rick found the chair's vibration settings, then he permitted himself to close his eyes. Small motors in the chair hummed softly and kneaded his muscles while Melissa was busy pushing back his cuticles. He giggled once she started to shave off his calluses with her pumice brush.

"Excuse me, Mr. Harris?"

Rick opened his eyes. A pool boy stood beside him, weight shifted to one leg and holding a silver serving platter. He handed Rick an almost-overflowing glass of straw-colored champagne, its tiny bubbles furiously rising to the top. Rick accepted the gift, too resigned to protest.

"I also have this for you," the boy said, handing Rick a sealed envelope.

"What is it?"

"I don't know. It was just in your mailbox. We're to deliver the messages we find in the mailbox," he explained, walking off to deliver the next glass.

Rick opened the card-sized envelope. The front of the card was blank. He turned the blanched cardboard over and read the handwritten message on the back:

THIS PLACE ISN'T WHAT IT SEEMS. I knew your parents. We'll talk when the time is right. I need your help, and I can return the favor with your troubles back at home. Check your mail in three days' time. I can't risk Missy intercepting my message. The pool boys can't be trusted to send mail. Tell no one.

7

Rick flipped the note over and hastily shoved it back in the envelope. He looked around to check if anyone had seen. Sobriety seemed to rush back to him, and his mind started to clear. He stuffed the envelope in his suit-jacket pocket. His heart was racing, but Melissa didn't seem to notice. She was rubbing a hot stone on his calf, the warm sensation punctuated by pain as the rock rubbed off the occasional hair. The experience was growing less agreeable.

Suddenly, a two-note xylophone tone sounded over a speaker. It was followed by a soft-spoken announcement: "Ladies and gentleman, access to the west corridor is temporarily restricted. All program doors are now locking."

Rick heard an automated system lock the solid metal double doors leading out of the room. "What's going on?" someone asked. The room erupted in conversation. Startled, Rick instinctively started to pull his feet out of the washing tub. Melissa softly urged them back in. The once-hot water had cooled over time, making this new baptism less welcome.

Marilyn sat up from her own reclined chair and,

using her dangerously over-sized nails, carefully took the cucumber slices off her eyes. "Gentleman, there's no need to be alarmed. Happens all the time. Get used to it. Another cohort's graduating today. We don't let cohorts at different parts of the program mix. Once they pass down the hall, the doors will unlock."

"Why?" Jimmy asked.

Marilyn rolled her eyes. "Baby girl! Remind me never to take you to the movies. You must be one of those who ask questions halfway through the damn film. Wait, child—just wait."

Eileen raised her hand. "I'd still take him to the movies—yes, girl!"

"Mmmm, mmm, mmm," Marilyn said before popping her lips. "Only if he pays, though."

Rick heard the door unlatch. This was almost immediately accompanied by two more chimes, followed by an announcement: "All clear." Rick breathed a sigh of relief. His feet felt lighter somehow as he was escorted to the nail station. There he received a back massage. Another first. Then, a steaming towel was wrapped around his face. He leaned back and gave into the hand massage. His muscles started to feel like warm clay in a potter's hands. Somewhere between the kneading, the champagne, and warm towel, he surrendered himself to sleep. By the time he woke, the towel was being peeled off his face, and he became aware of the room getting ever so brighter.

Still unsure of themselves, the cohort filed out of the room and back to the recently restricted hallway, which Rick inspected as if it had somehow changed. Nothing seemed any different.

By now, the sun was starting to set. He should have been hungry despite his earlier snack, but he had no appetite. The note tucked in his pocket brought on an urgency more insistent than any hunger. They were led to another room back in the Milk Building. Round chairless tables were scattered like polka dots around the room. The cohort was greeted by crisp jazz music and pool boys bearing *hors d'oeuvres* and wine spritzers. Rick ignored them and made his way over to Jimmy and Father Henry, who had taken refuge around a table in the far corner.

"We need to talk!" Rick said, grabbing Jimmy's shoulder.

Jimmy and the weathered priest wore numb expressions. Fatigue. Resignation. Intoxication. Rick couldn't tell and didn't care.

"When we were in the room. The room with the foot washing, a boy came in. One of them pool boys. He had a note for me," Rick said, spitting out the words between breaths. After looking over his shoulder, Rick took the card out of his breast pocket. His hands were shaking so much it was hard for him to extract the note from its envelope, much less hold it still enough to read. Jimmy and the priest leaned in. Rick read it to them in a hoarse whisper that came out like air escaping a tire.

Jimmy took the letter from Rick and insisted on reading the words with his own eyes. "What does it mean?"

"My daddy was a preacher," Rick said. "He passed years ago, but he'd have none of this. None of this wretched sinfulness. If there's someone here who knew my parents and is warning us that this place isn't what we think it is, it means whoever wrote it is in trouble. It says he needs help."

"So are we," Jimmy said, his own voice now barely a whisper.

Father Henry rested a consoling hand on Rick's shoulder. "Son, if you're right, then the person probably came from your hometown. Do you know anyone else who might be here? Anyone else who may have just disappeared and went missing before you came here?"

"No, no. Not that I know of." Rick took a mental inventory of every bigot and homophobe he knew. The list was empty. These days, anyone else who felt any animosity toward gay people had the good sense to keep their mouths shut. John Beck had been at the top of Rick's list of God-fearing Christian men who didn't care about political correctness—or he *was*, until he became responsible for Rick's internment.

Jimmy scratched his head. "What do you think they're doing to them? They wouldn't even let us see the ones that got here just two weeks ago!"

"I think I know, dammit," Rick said, suddenly much less concerned with anyone hearing him. "I think they're trying to get us all drunk to make us into queers! It's why there's alcohol in every place we get sent to! Every damn pool boy has it. Even in our rooms!"

"What?" Jimmy asked. Father Henry drew his eyebrows together.

"They used to have conversion therapy," Rick said. "My daddy talked about the places they'd send the gays. Before they outlawed it. If they can make someone choose to be straight, maybe they think they can brainwash us to be gay! I don't know. I just don't know!"

"Maybe they'll just kill us," Jimmy said, his shoulders slouching under the weight they now carried.

"Most of the saints were martyred," Father Henry said with less apprehension than Rick would have preferred.

"Are these pool boys even legal?" Rick asked. "Is this just sex trafficking? We need to find this man who needs our help and expose this place."

"Excuse me," an older man said, approaching their table. "I couldn't help but overhear. I'm Bob. Bob Wilson. This place creeps me out—wouldn't be surprised if someone's held prisoner here."

"Didn't the note say not to tell anyone?" Jimmy asked.

Rick looked frustrated. "It says not to tell anyone, but it's too late. I told each of you. Now, Bob."

"I think we need to respect that from now on until we know more. This person may be in even more danger if we draw attention," the priest said.

Jimmy recounted the story about the person he knew who killed himself after returning from an atonement camp. Bob looked skeptical. "I was told it was sensitivity training. All that bullshit. Talk about feelings—I didn't expect this. These places sprung up all over the country. If people were being murdered here, we'd know about it."

"What's your story, Bob?" Jimmy asked. "How'd you end up here?"

Bob let out a long sigh. He rubbed his scalp where hair once grew and adjusted his round, thin-rimmed glasses. Deep canyons under his eyes betrayed a fatigue that sleep could no longer remedy. "My wife. My son came out as trans, and now he's a she. I'm at the end of my rope. I'm not particularly religious—no offense, Father. I just don't understand it. The wife told me it's either I go here or we're getting a divorce. We tried counseling. We tried everything. I just don't understand it."

In his younger years, Rick thought Bob might have been dashing. But now crow's feet around his eyes further compounded the insult levied on him from his hair loss. Hair still grew all around the sides and back of his head, as though taunting him with a reminder of what he'd lost. Fluorescent lights in the dining room left their glare on his lenses. Frustrated, he whipped them off his face again and buffed them with the bottom of an untucked dress shirt made tight by his girth. Futilely, he tried to wipe away some unseen smudge that still clouded his vision. "Men are born men and women are born women. Period. I'm not about to have my son injected with hormones for some fad or mental illness. What if he regrets it and can't get rid of the tits when he wants to play football in high school. Am I right?"

"We live in sinful times, Bob," Rick sympathized. "The devil has a hold on our society. Wouldn't be surprised if people end up being murdered here."

"Murdered?" Eileen exclaimed, walking to the table with a cocktail in one hand. "Was the pedicure really that frightening?"

Rick squared his shoulders and looked up to meet Eileen's eyes. "We have some questions about what goes on here, and I demand some damn answers!"

Eileen raised an eyebrow, indicating Rick should continue.

"Are those young, half-naked young men here by choice? Do you all lure them here for sex? Blackmail?"

"Honey, Marilyn says she can't get them to leave! I know they're young. None of them are younger than eighteen. Most of them are gay. They come from all over. Best paid summer jobs anywhere, I bet. They have their own lodging here. I can't begin to imagine what they do with one another, but a lot of them are back for another season—so as long as they've had their shots, use condoms, and don't cause trouble, I certainly don't care."

"What if I wanted to send a letter or a postcard, you know?" Rick asked. "I should write my momma. Let her know I'm okay."

Eileen shrugged. "I'm sure they have stamps at the front desk."

"Is there a mailroom?" Jimmy asked, following Rick's lead.

"I believe so. Why?"

Rick answered before Jimmy could. "I'd just like to mail it myself is all."

"Ask the front desk. If they can't help you, let me know, baby."

Bob stepped into the conversation. "So, what's this place all about? Like—are we going to just get drunk for two weeks and go home, or do some touchy-feely therapy? Or what?"

"Oh, sugar," Eileen said with sympathy as overdone as her makeup. "I don't want to spoil any surprises… but, of course, there's some of that. Isn't it nice to talk about feelings and learn we're all not so different?"

Bob, Jimmy, Father Henry, and Rick were eventually led to the dining room with the rest of their cohort. They made their way to one of the tables, all of which were covered in crisp white paper. A dinner buffet ran along the back wall. Carving stations were positioned around the room. The men began to take clean plates from a stack. Rick observed that men of a certain age had all by then learned the silent customs of the buffet, be it from the marketing convention, the awards dinner, company retreat, or the budget wedding. *At least something seems familiar*, Rick thought. The plates were warm to the touch, but this was also expected. Bob asked for an extra slice of ham, and it was dutifully carved.

The four men sat down together. Rick's plate was nearly overflowing with food. If it were a contest, Jimmy and Bob would be nearly tied with him. Father Henry sat with a glass of water (no ice), a slice of untoasted bread, a baked potato, and three olives.

"Father, if they wanted to poison us, I'm sure they wouldn't have gone through all the effort so far," Jimmy said, pouring gravy on his mashed potatoes.

"This is the most I've eaten in one meal after nearly three years in Cambodia," the priest said.

The others looked down at their plates and sat in silence for a moment.

"Let us pray," Rick said—almost as an after-thought—holding out his hands. The other men joined hands around the table. They bowed their heads.

"Heavenly Father, though we walk through the valley of death in this forsaken place of wretched sin—this place that celebrates defiance of your truth while these wretched homosexuals soak in the souring filth of their own unrepentant sin—this place obscured by a long shadow of darkness that has fallen over this valley—the—"

"Pastor," Bob interrupted, "no offense, but my food is getting cold."

Rick opened his eyes to scowl at Bob. He cleared his throat and closed them once again. "We ask that you watch over us and deliver us from this place. With our certificates of attendance. Amen."

The others muttered "Amen" and began eating.

"Children!" Marilyn said as she strolled over to the table, clasping her hands to her chest. "You all survived your first day! I'm so proud of you! Rick, now tell me you didn't like that pedicure."

Defeated, Rick stirred his food and chopped at it with his fork. "It was fine."

"From someone so miserable, that's the closest thing to an endorsement as we can best hope for," she gloated. "Now, I spoke with Missy. She can have a car ready for you in the morning."

"What?" Rick asked.

"A car, baby. You can't walk to the airport! You said you were done and ready to get out of here."

Rick thought about the piece of paper in his pocket. "No, ma'am sir. I think I might as well stay a little longer."

Marilyn arched her back. "Oh! Miracles do happen! Maybe you religious folk are right about that after all. Missy will be absolutely delighted!"

Rick didn't look up from his plate. Evidently, his food needed to be stirred that much more.

Marilyn mercifully left the men to their food, delighted to share the good news with everyone who would listen as she mingled with the crowd.

Bob leaned over the table, giving his voice less

distance to travel in whisper. "You know, every place has a mailroom. I'm sure that's where the pool boy got the note from. If we get in there in three days, maybe we'll find another?"

"That's a good point," Jimmy said.

"Why three days though?" Father Henry asked, staring at the table with his brows knit in thought.

"Maybe he can't risk being caught. Maybe that's the soonest he can sneak another letter," Rick added.

After coffee and dessert, Rick and Jimmy made their way back to their room. Rick sat down on his bed and opened his Bible. The book was his shield and his weapon. Despite the dizzying collection of sinful things he'd seen and the blasphemy that sent him to the camp, he reassured himself that the words in the book were unchanged. That familiarity brought comfort.

Jimmy was making his top bunk bed and unpacking his single, crumpled duffle bag. His body occasionally bumped into the bedframe, which rattled. Rick watched from his bottom bunk as Jimmy's tank top rode up over his navel when he stretched for something unseen on his top bunk. Jimmy's abs were as defined as his chest, reminding Rick that the only weight he had lost with his own gym membership came when he took the money out each month to pay for it. Rick's eyes followed a twisting, curving line that seemed to trace his muscles.

It ran over his chest, defining its contours, stretching around his shoulder and across his triceps. His muscles pulsed with each twitch. Jimmy gave off a faint smell of sweat and vodka brought on from the long day.

They'd been nearly inseparable since they met at the airport. How could that have been just earlier that day? Rick's heart started to beat faster. He turned away and flipped the page. The book was open to Leviticus, but Rick's eyes couldn't focus on the words. He resisted the temptation to look back at Jimmy, but only for a fleeting second. And he regretted that lost second. He would give his life and soul to have that second returned to him. How many seconds pass unnoticed over forgotten minutes, hours, and years? Seconds wasted on doing no more than merely getting from one to the next. But was that not life? Long expanses of the unremarkable punctuated by the unforgettable. Moments that change life in an instant. Rick mourned over that second's passing. That was one second he didn't have to watch Jimmy, knowing that he could do so without the risk of being seen.

Dim, nearly forgotten memories returned to haunt him—memories that warned him—memories that cut with a knife not dulled by time.

8

Twelve Years Ago

Rick's bike bounced over the curb and traced a track through the freshly mowed lawn. In a practiced dismount, he jumped off and let the battered ten-speed fall to the lawn as he bounded toward the garage.

"Ricky!" his mother yelled. "Ricky! Take that bike off the grass. You know better!" She shook her hedge trimmer at him as she stood up from the moat of bush trimmings that were collecting around her in a prison of her own making.

"Sorry, Momma!"

"Be quiet. Your daddy is writing his sermon. He doesn't want any noise. Not a peep!"

Rick rolled his eyes. *Writing his sermon* was more often than not just code for his father being on the bottle. It was a Monday, after all. He never wrote a sermon on a Monday. The drunker his father was, the more his mother would insist on tending to the lawn. If the meticulously leveled hedges and fresh sod in what would soon be flower beds were any indication, he must have been working particularly hard on that sermon, Rick thought.

The long mountain winter was just starting to give way to spring. This in-between season was the time of year when Rick would wear a jacket to school in the morning and shorts in the afternoon. It was as if the season didn't know itself. Even if winter resigned itself to the inevitability of spring, it wouldn't surrender yet. Like any truth, time would reveal the reality despite the most earnest fight to suppress it.

Rick stealthily passed through the door, the latch locking softly behind him. He bolted up the stairs to his room, careful to only step on each stair on the side closest to the rail, lest a creak betray him to his father.

His room was as he'd left it that morning. Bed unmade. A stranger might assume the room had two occupants instead of one. The first was the fifteen-year-old sophomore who listened to a radio and longed for his parents to get him a car for his birthday, but knowing there was no way in hell it'd happen. The other person was the ghost of his ten-year-old self—long-neglected balsawood planes powered by rubber bands still suspended from the ceiling. An old toy box was used to collect the clothes piled on its dusty top. The secrets of an almost-forgotten boyhood remained packed inside.

There were comic books in clear plastic bags stacked

in a corner. A very used t-shirt helped him discover his manhood. The rusty stained shirt was buried deep enough under his bed to escape his mother's periodic cleaning tirades, but not so deep that it couldn't be retrieved as needed. But Rick wasn't interested in any of that today. Instead, he changed into a pair of shorts and made his way back outside as silently as he'd arrived.

"Where are you going?" his mother asked.

Rick picked up his bike from the spot he'd abandoned it. "Just hanging with friends. Be back by dinner!"

"Don't go 'round that Garrett boy! You know your father doesn't approve! Boy's family is wrought with trouble!" she warned, her attention returning to the shrub with renewed dedication.

"I won't, Momma!"

Of course, that was exactly where Rick was intending to go. Garrett had the new *Grand Theft Auto* game, and Rick couldn't wait to play. *Too violent*, his father would no doubt say. His father would say a lot of things, Rick admitted to himself. Garrett's family were members of the congregation. Perhaps it was their proximity to the pastor that informed his father's opinion. Rick suspected his father's opinion of a family's piety seemed suspiciously aligned with their pecuniary contributions to the collection plate. They never gave much to the church and lately gave even less.

Caught between two parents in a divorce that became the town scandal, Garrett was the first of his friends to get any new game. His DVD collection rivaled the Blockbuster Video downtown. His parents' guilt grew the collection by the week, as though the games and toys might somehow distract him from the fact that his father was moving out and the whole town seemed to know why.

Garrett's house was hard to miss. The tiny mansion was newly built in a subdivision. Nearby dirt lots signaled the soon-to-be developed fourth phase, or so read the signs along the freshly paved black tar roads of the neighborhood. Here, trees were planted according to the developer's plans, still too young for nature to find its own way.

That was the first house Rick had ever seen with three floors and an intercom system. Garrett's dad owned a few car dealerships downtown. His mom spent most of her time in therapy or with whomever she was cheating on his father with. Unsurprisingly, there were no cars in the halfmoon driveway in front of the home. The garage doors were closed, but Rick remembered they were too full of moving boxes for any car to find space inside. Rick dismounted his bike and then pushed it behind the house on his way to the unlocked patio door on the empty deck that wrapped around the back of the house.

"What took you so long?" Garrett asked. He was sitting at the kitchen table when Rick made his way through the sliding glass door.

"Had to change clothes. Play it yet?"

"Yeah. One player sucks though. Hungry?"

"Starved," Rick admitted.

It was more of a rhetorical question. They were both always hungry. Garrett would have taken the chips and dip out anyway. It was amazing that Garrett could have abs and still eat constantly, Rick marveled. Abs must have been gifted to him from all the running on the baseball team, he reasoned.

Rick was never into sports in the same way. *Asthma*, his mother would always remind him. One pitch in the wrong spot and Rick would probably break a rib. The pediatrician had his mother make him a chocolate milkshake with two bananas every morning to help him put on at least enough weight to keep his feet down when the wind blew.

With bowls and bags in hand, they rumbled up the stairs. Then, more stairs. At the end of the hall on the third floor, they found Garrett's room. Along the way, they dodged past and jumped over half-packed boxes and rolls of bubble wrap. Garret said his mom would keep the house. His dad would be moving to Charlotte. But Garrett rarely spoke of it. Rick never asked.

Garrett's room was the only oasis of normalcy in the house. Despite the chaos around it, the room was untouched by change. Rick marveled at the eclectic collection of neatly catalogued National Geographic magazines, college-level calculus books, indistinguishable soccer trophies, and everything else that made Garrett the most unique person Rick had ever met.

"Wanna play?" Garrett asked, handing him a controller.

"Not yet. Let me figure out how the controls work," Rick said, flipping through the pages on the instruction manual.

"I can show you faster than you can read about it," Garrett said with a half-smile.

Rick was lost in thought as he studied the words in the manual, committing as much of the controls to memory as time would permit. "Nope, I'll remember it better if I read it."

"Such a weirdo," Garrett said, reaching for another chip.

"You might actually learn something you don't know if you read sometimes," Rick said, not looking up.

"Dick," Garrett said with a laugh.

"Fag," Rick said dismissively.

"Retard."

"Shit stain."

"Jock strap."

"Momma's boy."

"Oh, there's no way *I'm* the momma's boy. Your momma probably knows how many times you shit every day and what color it is," Garrett said. Rick couldn't say he was wrong.

Rick laughed. "At least my momma can tell me apart from the shit."

Garrett laughed and jumped on Rick, pinning him down on the ground. Rick laughed and knew there'd be no way he could overpower him. Instead, he rolled over and knocked Garrett off balance. Even though their gym teacher would always warn the boys not to lift weights before getting a little older and growing a bit stronger, Garrett's dad didn't seem to care. Garrett would work out with his dad a few times every week. If the baseball team was going to make regionals this year, it would rest on Garrett's ever-growing shoulders.

The extra work in the gym showed. Garrett effortlessly rolled himself back on top of Rick, pinning Rick's arms behind his head. They were both laughing so hard they needed to stop and take a breath. He could feel both of their hearts racing. Rick was the first to move. He strained futilely to get out of the grip. Garrett smiled, and Rick knew it was a challenge. Garrett's grip was loosening on account of his suddenly sweaty hands. Rick thought he might be able to struggle free. But why?

Rick could feel Garrett's warm body pressing against his own. Garrett's eyes were the lightest green Rick had ever seen. After headgear in elementary school and braces in middle school, his smile was as perfect as the rest of his body. Rick made a few deliberately feeble attempts to squirm away, but he wanted to be caught more than he wanted to escape. He wanted to be Garrett's prey, his captive.

Garrett's taunting eyes flashed with mischief. "You better do better than that."

Rick made a few more feeble attempts, silently daring him to do his worst.

Garrett started to suck his teeth. He cleared his throat. Rick knew Garrett was about to spit. Rick braced himself. Instead, Garrett let thin wisp of drool slowly escape his lips. With each passing second, the thread of saliva got further from his mouth and closer to Rick's lips. It was like molasses dripping off a spoon.

"Dude, that's gross," Rick said, squirming and pursing his lips closed. Just when the spit was about to touch Rick's lips, Garrett sucked it back into his mouth and laughed.

"You almost had my spit inside you," he laughed.

"Just let me go, man."

"Find your way out," he challenged.

Rick struggled against the thing he wanted most. He feigned an exhaustion his heartbeat betrayed. Garrett tightened his grip. Eyes wild, he leaned in again, close enough for Rick to smell the chips and salsa on his breath. He must have been wearing a body spray, one Rick decided he had to find and steal for himself. Garrett's crotch was grinding against Rick's as his lips stopped just inches from Rick's mouth.

"God, get off, dude," Rick protested as convincingly as he could.

Garrett responded with another trickle of spit. As before, it started at his lips and made its way on a journey that Rick wanted more than anything to end on his own lips. Would he fight it? Or would he welcome it with an open mouth, taking in all Garrett would give him. Rick didn't know. His mind was reeling between the two extremes. Closer. Closer. The thin stream of spittle danced in the air as Garrett's lips twitched from the smile he was working so hard to suppress. Rick pursed his lips and squeezed his eyes shut.

Garrett released his grip and rolled off Rick's helpless body like he had suddenly been electrocuted. "Dude, what the fuck!"

"What?" Rick asked, opening his eyes and fearing he already knew the answer.

Garrett started to say something but stopped. He smiled instead. "Dude, if you don't know, I'm not telling you."

Rick didn't need to be told. Instead, he acted naive with the sincere hope that he could plausibly blame it on the keys in his pocket or some other innocuous bulge. Perhaps it was a lie he could tell by implication, neither of them believing it to be true, but neither of them any more willing to know the truth.

Rick picked up the abandoned controller. "Whatever, man. Just play the damn game."

Rick sat and tried to focus on the game, but his mind was still fixated on the one they had just played. He wanted more than anything to provoke Garrett. Have him pounce on him again. Hold him down. Spit on him. In him. It didn't matter.

Garrett wouldn't take the bait. Eventually, the ecstasy of the moment subsided. Dread followed close after. *What have I done?* he wondered.

9

The days were getting longer. Cold mornings with heavy winter coats became warm afternoons that invited shorts and a t-shirt. Rick waited impatiently for spring to give way to summer. Change was always too slow for him. Before long, school would be out. Summer meant Bible camp. And Bible camp usually meant dread. Long days in a hot building doing anything but playing at the pool was torture. *But, not this year*, he assured himself. This year, Garrett's parents had insisted on sending their son to Bible camp as well.

Rick's father was reluctant to permit it, but they'd paid his tuition in advance, and he was hard-pressed to say no. Nothing had transpired with Garrett since the time they were alone at his house. Despite Rick's best attempts to recreate the encounter that now possessed him, some short-lived horseplay was all he'd managed. At the same time that he wanted to feel Garrett's crotch against his own, he also wanted to forget anything had happened. Bury the shame. The sinful thoughts. *It was an experiment*, he reasoned. Nothing more. Natural. All boys would get hard under such circumstances.

Rick crouched down and stared into the concrete

pipe in front of him. "Where does it go?" He knew it was the same pipe that discharged the water runoff from the storm drains on the street. When summer rains fell, he and Garrett would run to the pipe and watch the ditch in the park near their school fill up with water. Eventually, with enough rain, water would gush out of the pipe. The usually dry ditch became an artificial river that served as the setting for their action figures' perilous adventures. But, that day, the long canyon ditch was dry. They stood in the empty pit, staring into the pipe's dark void.

"I was out here yesterday," Garret said. "It goes under the road, and then there's a drain it leads to in the parking lot."

Rick climbed out of the gorge and looked across the basketball courts, over the road, and across the street to the gravel-ridden lot that was somewhere between an abandoned parking lot and an abandoned building project.

"Damn, that's far," Rick said.

"It's not that bad. It took me like a half hour to get there yesterday. Less today, though. We can ride our skateboards on our stomachs and get there a lot faster, I bet."

Rick imagined the plan, and it seemed reasonable. The pipe was big enough for him to comfortably slide inside. Still, he hesitated. What about rats? Then again, the unknown inspired him. What mysteries did it hold? A secret passage under the ground was a tantalizing quest.

Rick weighed his options, but the scale was too evenly balanced. "I don't know, man."

"Rick, don't be a pussy."

"It's just… what if we get stuck? Does the pipe get smaller as you go deeper?"

"A little."

Rick bit his lip. "What if we get stuck?"

"We won't."

"But what if we do?"

Garrett sighed. "Then we turn around and head back. I've got a flashlight."

Rick's heart was racing. "I don't know."

"Look," Garrett said, "let's try it for a few feet. See what you think. If you don't like it, we'll turn back. I promise."

Rick peered deeper into the blackness. Cool air gently met his face as he got closer to the pipe. It smelled dry, and all he could hear was his own heart in his chest.

The scale tipped. "Fine, but, just a few feet. We'll see if your skateboard idea works."

Garrett smiled, and his eyes lit up. Rick couldn't help but return the smile. Garrett laid his skateboard down on the concrete tube and secured a flashlight to the front with rubber bands. To Rick's relief, the light illuminated the pipe, which was just the same bland gray concrete as far as his eyes could see.

Garrett fumbled with the skateboard as he centered his weight on the contraption. Once he was satisfied with his position, he gave himself a push, and the wheels rumbled over the concrete. "Your turn!" he yelled, his voice echoing off the walls.

Rick centered his skateboard at the base of the pipe, just as Garrett had done. He could see the other boy just ahead. His clammy hands met the cold, gravely wall, and he pushed off. The skateboard rumbled behind Garrett. Garrett gave himself another push. Rick followed. Looking ahead, Rick could only see more of the same. His confidence growing, Rick pushed himself a little harder. They went a little faster. They kept up their speed. Pushing. Gliding. Pushing. Gliding.

Rick laughed. So did Garrett. Occasionally, a bump in the concrete where one section of the tunnel met another would make their boards jump a little.

"Not so bad," Garrett commented.

"Why are you slowing down?" Rick asked just before his skateboard came to a sudden stop as his hands crashed into Garrett's legs. Garrett laughed, and they pushed off again.

"The pipe is getting smaller," Rick said. His comment was less an observation as it was a subtle suggestion to turn back.

"I know," Garrett said. "Don't worry about it."

Eventually, the pipe's diameter narrowed to the point Rick couldn't push himself off the sides of the pipe. Instead, he and Garrett reached out and pulled themselves forward. The rumbling of wheels against concrete softened as their progress slowed. Rick could hear a basketball dribbling above. Sneakers rubbing against pavement.

"We're probably like halfway there now," Garrett estimated.

"It's getting hard to move with the skateboard," Rick said, hoping Garret would pick up on his subtlety this time.

"Yeah, I know. We may have to ditch them and come back for them later."

"Maybe we should turn back," Rick finally suggested.

"Why? It'd take us just as long to get there as it would to get back."

Rick considered the situation and reasoned it would be hard to turn around or crawl backward, so forward was probably their best bet. Just a bit farther.

"Okay," Rick said, sliding off his skateboard. It

rolled backward into the darkness behind him. The air was becoming warmer. Moister. Occasionally, they would crawl over puddles of water that must have never quite dried from the last storm. But Rick admitted to himself that it was easier to move without the skateboards underneath them.

They crawled farther, and the sound of the basketball was replaced with the sound of traffic. *We must be closer to the road now*, Rick thought. *At least we're still going in the right direction.*

Rick cursed to himself after scraping his palm on the rough concrete. "Damn, this is tight."

"You trust me, right?"

At that moment, they both stopped. Rick was panting. Thirst had come to him. He had forgotten his inhaler, despite his mother's admonishments about his asthma. *Calm down*, he told himself.

"Yeah, I trust you," Rick said.

"Good. It's going to open up soon—once we get to the street."

Rick didn't know what lay ahead; he just knew he trusted the path Garrett had taken. Blindly, Rick put his faith in Garrett—the boy he loved. Rick crawled on, just inches behind. The pipe was just wide enough for them to move through, his arms and back rubbing against the walls. Inch by inch, they kept going.

Inches turned into feet. Eventually, feet turned into their next waypoint.

The traffic sounded much louder now—almost over their heads. The air was getting refreshingly cooler. The breeze returned, and Rick realized he was sweating heavily.

"Right up here!" Garret said.

Dim light beckoned them. In a few more feet he saw what Garrett promised: a wide opening near the road. Their small, concrete tunnel gave way to a deeper rectangular chasm. A ladder led a few feet down from the pipe to the bottom of the chasm. The ground was covered in moist leaves and layers of newspapers that had been carried down with the runoff from the road. A dank smell of decay. Another ladder led up to the pipe that would take them the rest of the way. For now, they took refuge in the cool air and the open space. A shadow dimmed the light from the storm drain above them every time a car would drive past on the busy road above.

"It's as good a place as any to take a break," Garrett said, resting against the wall.

Rick climbed down the ladder and leaned against the wall beside him. *Whatever filth and vermin are underneath the layers of old newspaper are well enough left alone*, Rick reasoned.

Rick broke the silence. "Did he move yet?"

"Nah," Garrett said, looking up at the ray of light above them. "August, maybe. I don't know. They talk still. Argue still."

"So it's really happening?"

Garrett sighed. "Yeah, man. It is."

They listened to a few more cars pass above.

"I'm sorry, man," Rick said, then, as if to punctuate his sentence, "I love you."

Rick blushed and was glad to hide in the dark shadows. He regretted the confession as soon as the words fell out of his mouth, but he couldn't stop himself. It was too late. Garrett showed no sign of emotion. No acknowledgment or judgment. Just silence. Rick searched for something to say to change the topic and pretend it never happened, but his voice was silenced by terror.

Garrett swung around just as unexpectedly as the words had left Rick's mouth. He grabbed Rick by the shoulders and sealed his lips against his own. In that moment—in that instant, Rick found the rebuttal to all his feeble self-denials. The monologue in his head that said with practiced repetition, *just a phase, bisexual, only curious*—was reduced to surrender.

Garrett's lips were tense. Then, they softened. He pulled away from Rick's lips ever so slightly, only to return and caress them once again with his own. Rick listened with his body and did the same. His first kiss immediately became his second. His third. His fourth. He stopped counting. They breathed heavier, and their hands became less shy. First the shoulders. Then the back. Then the waist. Then they stopped. Thunder rumbled in the distance, and they jolted away from one another. Rick thought it was as if God called down his condemnation, his anger rumbling the sky.

"Shit, man!" Rick said, not certain what he was reacting to.

Garrett's eyes filled with fear, either of the sound or the wrath—Rick could not say.

Garrett peered at the sky with squinted eyes from under the curb to the street. "It wasn't supposed to rain today."

Rick's voice quivered. "Fuck, this time a year it rains every afternoon."

"We can't get out here. Cars would hit us. Too much traffic. We can't go back. We're a lot closer to the other side. Let's go!"

Not waiting for Rick to agree, Garrett climbed the other ladder, skipping every other rung. He dropped his hand and helped Rick up into the new pipe. Rick wasn't sure if his feet even touched the ladder. *What just happened? What did it mean? Will we ever make it out?* The thought of his parents being called by the fire department terrified him more than the image of his drowned, bloated body washing out of the main discharge pipe into the ditch. His hands were scraped and sore from the concrete. He was breathing faster. *Dammit*, he thought, *why didn't I bring my inhaler?*

He could hear Garrett scraping his hands on the pipe as they wormed their way deeper, going as fast as circumstances would permit. Thirst gave way to dehydration as the air became even hotter. The light dimmed to darkness behind him. Flashes of what lay ahead appeared in strobe as Garrett's flashlight bobbed up and down. Drizzle started to fall. Tires sloshed over the wet road above them.

Rick wanted to gasp in air, but shallow, sharp breaths were all his lungs would allow. Sweat dripped into his eyes. He took a second to wipe his burning tears out and then made up for lost time with a burst of speed. If his hands still hurt, he couldn't feel them by now. The rain was getting steadier. It was falling harder.

"Not much farther," Garrett said, his voice bouncing off the walls.

Life was simpler just an hour ago. At that moment, he would have traded anything to have that simplicity back. Video games. Bike rides. He wanted to be warm. Dry. An unremarkable day.

"There!" Garrett said, aiming the flashlight ahead. Rick followed the beam with his eyes. Another opening, "That must be it!"

"Must be?" Rick asked.

Garrett hesitated. "I didn't get all the way to the end last time."

"What the fuck, man!"

Rick's hands splashed in a trickle of water making its way down the pipe from run-off from the road. He lunged out for his grip to push off against the concrete, but his hand slipped in the water and his chest splashed into the stream that had suddenly grown swift. He pounced up and scurried faster through the splashing water just as a thunderclap boomed above him. Unsettled by the omen, Rick believed God's wrath was unrelenting.

Garrett didn't slow down. "That must have been close!"

Rick said a silent prayer and hoped they wouldn't be his last words. His knee hurt. It must have been cut. The light was getting brighter again, just as before.

Garrett thrust his arm forward and pointed into the distance. "Ladder!"

Before long, Rick caught up to him. Gushing water poured through their escape—a small gap between the pavement and the metal storm-drain cover.

Garrett set both hands on the ladder. "You first. I'll push." The fear in his voice rattled Rick's resolve. The chasm was filling with water, and before long the flood would overtake the pipe completely and the water would start to gush out.

Rick was barely more than a skeleton with torn clothes and cut hands, so it made sense to him to go first. He jumped in the pool of rising water and waded hip-deep over to Garrett. For a moment, they locked eyes. Rick saw Garrett's urgency. His concern. Garrett waded to Rick, grabbed his cheeks, and pulled him into a kiss—more passionate than the first, though it only lasted a second.

Garret hoisted him up by the hips. "Go!"

Rick could feel the cool spring air rushing over his face. So close. He took a deep breath and pushed his head through the gap with water rushing around him. His head slid out, and he grabbed the broken pavement outside. He pulled. Garrett pushed. His wet body slid out easily, and he rolled to a stop. He squinted in the light. The rain was already washing the filth off his skin.

He dove back down to the gutter and reached his hand into the darkness. Garrett grabbed it and he felt him jump up. Garrett's head was tilted to the side as he struggled to escape through the small gap.

"Fuck," Garrett said, spitting out the water that now filled his mouth. "You gotta lift it up!"

Rick braced himself in a squat and wrapped his hands around the wet metal. He strained. The slippery cover didn't budge.

"Dammit, Rick—lift it!"

Rick got behind the grate and lifted from another angle. Garrett pushed up from inside. The metal scraped against the concrete, and it started to budge. Slowly at first, then more. Rick saw Garrett's hair. Then, his cheek. He knew if he let go, the metal grate would slam down with enough force to kill him. He strained harder. He wouldn't let go. He'd die first.

Garrett reached out for the concrete jutting up from what was once a parking lot. The broken stone broke off and he started to slide back into the abyss. Just as quickly, he reached out again. This time, it held. He pulled himself out. Hips. Legs. Just then, the water made Rick's grip slip and the metal grate crashed back down with a clang that echoed in the air with the thunder.

Garrett rolled into the pavement and came to a stop. Rick prayed his thanks to God for sparing them. *A warning, perhaps.* Soot washed away in the pouring downfall, but Rick lamented that its cleansing was only skin deep. The filth on the inside was not so easily washed off. It festered like rocky sand in Ricks shoes, growing ever more painful with each step.

"Are you okay?" Rick yelled, rushing to his side.

Garrett rolled onto his back and looked up at Rick, smiling. "Never better. Told you it'd be a piece of cake."

10

Bible camp wasted no time getting started, lest any teenager in town have a moment of unstructured supervision over the summer break, Rick lamented, now that he'd traded his textbooks for biblical ones. He even carried the same school bookbag to the church each morning. Each day was supposed to have its own activities. Bible study was supposed to be led by an instructor. Instead, old Beth Shoemaker would knit in her chair and insist on absolute silence while they all pretended to read. In consideration of her services, Rick's father would keep an eye on her. That way, her grandson wouldn't have to send her off to adult daycare.

On occasion, Rick observed old Mrs. Shoemaker in some twilight between awake and asleep, when she'd moan to herself from her chair about Jesus.

"She's calling for him," Garrett whispered in Rick's ear. "If he answers and comes down to get her, do you think your dad would let us go any earlier?"

Rick sighed. "Probably not. She wants out of here as much as we do, but I don't think my daddy's letting anyone leave."

Other days were worse, in Rick's estimation. The

activity was advertised in the church's brochure as a team-building exercise, but Rick just pulled up the same weeds in the church's back yard as he did every weekend—only with some extra hands who were duped into paying for the privilege to help.

Garrett dropped a trash bag filled with weeds in front of Rick and took off his gardening gloves. "Okay, that's it. No more. Water break."

Rick smiled. "May as well make it a lunch break."

The two boys took their lunches from the refrigerator in the church kitchen and went out back behind the church to the old swing set that had been there as long as Rick could remember. Rick flipped the morning-dew-covered black plastic swing seat over to reveal a dry side suitable for him to sit on. Garrett did the same.

Garrett took a bite of his ham sandwich. "It's gonna get up to ninety-five today."

Rick and Garrett casually swung back and forth, neither quite synchronized with the other.

"At some point, we'll run out of clothes we can take off," Rick joked.

Garrett looked ruefully at Rick. "I wouldn't complain."

Rick blushed.

Garrett leaned over to Rick and lowered his voice. "We need to find someplace to go."

Rick laughed. "Here? I mean, we should wait for Mrs. Shoemaker to fall asleep. Then again, I have a pretty good suspicion we'd wake her, regardless."

"What about your dad's office? Is he here today?"

"No, but he keeps that door locked. It's where the offerings are kept. I don't even have a key."

They each swung silently, momentarily in time with one another.

"There's the basement—we could make a little fort out of tables," Rick suggested.

"We could hide inside," Garrett said.

Rick looked around and watched kids of all ages walking around the yard behind the church. Some were playing tag. Others had spread a tattered quilt on the grass and were sharing their lunch. It wouldn't be long before the younger kids would rush over to play on the swings. It also wouldn't be long before they'd be missed if they were out of sight for too long. Rick thought the younger children were like small sentinels, eager to report any truancy or small infraction of a rule to Mrs. Shoemaker.

"Sucks it's so hard to find time with my boyfriend," Garrett mumbled with a smile, looking at Rick from the corner of his eye.

The word. *That* word. *Boyfriend*. Rick's body flushed with adrenaline. It was the word he dared not speak to himself, much less expect from Garrett. His deepest desire and all his fantasies now had a name. It was like he had been given the greatest gift.

"Boyfriend, huh?" Rick smirked, his voice as measured as possible.

Garrett looked ahead, not willing to read Rick's eyes. "Don't make a big deal out of it, but yeah."

Rick smiled. "Well, come on then, boyfriend. Let's take a quick trip to the basement."

"We won't have much time."

"We won't need it," Rick laughed.

The boys jumped off swings they had long since outgrown and jogged around the sentinels and off to the church entrance. Mrs. Shoemaker was sitting in her rocking chair in the church, head slumped to the side in sleep, her mouth open, snoring peacefully. It was her afternoon nap, which always began just after her morning nap ended.

Unseen, they made their way to the other end of the church and went down the stairwell. It would only be a short time before lunch was over and the work camp would resume. But Rick knew any moment alone with Garrett would last forever in his memory.

The basement had the damp smell of mold. Thick beige tarps hung over furniture deemed too nice to discard but too useless to remember. Dust collected on the tarps with each passing season. A foggy window let in some light, supplemented by the naked bulb on an exposed rafter, which Rick turned on by pulling a thin metal string. A pile of excess lumber from some unfinished renovation lay in one corner. A stack of tables rested in another. Bingo nights, the homecoming festival, and a seemingly endless succession of church meetings offered those enough use to be spared from the dust.

Rick and Garrett silently flipped over a table and snapped the legs into place. Another table leaned against its side, making the small fort, he imagined. Rick flipped a dusty tarp on its back and smoothed it out to make an improvised carpet on top of the cold concrete floor. Garrett ducked down and joined him under the table. Above the percussion of his own heartbeat, Rick could hear muffled sounds of the younger kids playing out back.

Garrett reached out and touched Rick's shoulder. Their eyes met, and Rick noticed Garrett's hand trembled. Garrett closed his eyes and met Rick's lips with his own. They moved tremulously toward one another. Rick remembered to breathe. Their hands quivered less. Their bodies moved closer to one another. One kiss evolved into a longer kiss. Garrett eventually leaned forward, gently leading Rick to lay on his back.

The weight of Garrett's body was its own embrace. Rick dared to slide a hand underneath Garrett's t-shirt. His skin was smooth and damp with sweat. Garrett moaned softly and rewarded the gesture with a deeper, more passionate kiss. After what felt to Rick like hours, Garrett slid his arm under his shirt, pulling it off as his hand caressed his chest. Their long kiss was interrupted only for a moment as Rick guided Garrett's shirt off. They resumed their embrace, and Rick surrendered completely to the sensation of his skin gliding over Garrett's.

Rick wanted to go further. It was as if his body compelled him by instinct to do things he never dared imagine. Rick fumbled open the button on his jeans. His zipper almost went down on its own, quickly met by Garrett's hand. Rick moaned and pulled Garrett closer.

"Boys!" Mrs. Shoemaker yelled from the top of the stairs. "What in creation are you doing down there?"

Startled, Garrett jumped up, bumping his head on the table.

"Mrs. Shoemaker, they're under the table. K-i-s-s-i-n-g!" one of the sentinels standing next to her proclaimed, pointing his stubby finger at the accused.

Garrett rolled out from under the table, shirt still off and hair tousled. Rick jumped up as well, fumbling at his pants.

"We weren't kissing! We were just wrestling!" Garrett pleaded.

"They were kissing, Mrs. Shoemaker. We saw them from the window," the sentinel said, laughing.

Mrs. Shoemaker's eyes were alert. Her expression was a mix of horror and concern. Rick managed to button his pants and groped for his shirt among the shadows on the floor. The shadows were once their ally. Now they betrayed him, frustrating his escape.

"Tim," Mrs. Shoemaker calmly explained with her eyes still locked on the boys, "they were just wrestling. That's all. The mind plays tricks. That old window barely lets light through. Sometimes we only see what we want to."

"But Mrs. Shoemaker—"

"Tim," she said, "go back out and finish your lunch. Don't make me tell you a second time."

Tim huffed, and his small shoulders sank to match his pouting expression. He folded his arms and stomped out behind her. As his footsteps faded up the stairs, Mrs. Shoemaker glanced behind her and then softly closed the door.

"Boys, I don't know what you were doing down here, but if Pastor Harris hears of this, it will be Hell to pay."

"Mrs. Shoemaker," Rick pleaded, nearly in tears,

"I promise—we were just wrestling. Trying to move some tables."

"Boys," she said, cutting him off, "I can only protect you just so much." She paused in thought. "You just need to be careful."

Garrett slipped his shirt back on. They all stood in silence for a moment before Mrs. Shoemaker turned for the door and hobbled back up the stairs. Her orthopedic shoes clomped against the wooden stairs with each step. Despite her promise, each footfall sounded to Rick like a judge's gavel slamming down after the issuance of a death sentence.

Garrett and Rick's eyes met, their faces white. What was elation a moment ago became a shame just as deep.

"We need to get out of here," Rick said.

Garrett nodded, and his voice quivered. "We'll pretend nothing happened. Just wrestling."

They bounded up the stairs, abandoning the discretion they'd sought to keep on the way down. Without making eye contact with Mrs. Shoemaker, they dashed through the church toward the door.

"No running," the older woman called out as she lowered herself back into her rocking chair. Once again, the boys didn't heed her warning.

Their efforts to pretend nothing happened were

betrayed by the children who gathered in small groups, whispering to one another, glancing back at Rick and Garrett from time to time. Rick heard soft giggles as he clamped the shearers in the bushes by the church's porch. Garrett wisely devoted himself to the task of sweeping the back porch. *Best not to be seen together*, Rick agreed.

As the afternoon wore on, Rick's stomach filled with dread. His father would be coming before long. Events had been set in motion, and he was powerless to stop them. Giving confirmation to his anxiety, he heard the rumbling of tires on gravel. He looked behind him and saw his father's old, green truck headed down the long road between the highway and the church.

Rick returned to the same bush he'd pruned earlier, pretending to work as he clipped mere centimeters from the top of the bush, his hands shaking.

The door slammed shut. Footsteps became closer.

"Your momma would be proud," the pastor said, observing the work as he made his way up the stairs to the church.

"Yes, sir. I learned from the best," Rick said as cheerfully as he could. A waft of bourbon followed behind the man as he passed the steps to the church. Most of the younger children were inside for the Bible lesson, all exhausted from their play. The older children had finished their chores and sat in their encampments with their friends around the grounds. The sun was going down, but it'd be daylight for a bit longer.

Rick cleaned up the cut branches, leaving no room in his handiwork for any criticism. Garrett walked around the side of the building and met eyes with Rick, face sunken.

"Rick!" the pastor's voice boomed as the church door swung wide open and banged against the side of the wall, chipping off splinters of wood. "Get over here!"

Rick's stomach dropped. He stood up to meet his father's enraged eyes. The elder Harris stomped down the stairs and lumbered over to his son. The man's waist had grown a bit larger with each passing year. His sermons made the old windows rattle in their chipped wooden frames that much more each time he'd drop a notch in his belt. His orations roared so loudly that no one had the chance to speak over him. He wouldn't have heard them if they tried. And Rick had a lifetime of experience to know the man never seemed to stop speaking.

"A boy told me that you and that Garrett boy were together in the basement!"

"Daddy, we were just wrestling. That's all," Rick pleaded.

"Bullshit. That's what Mrs. Shoemaker said."

"Pastor Harris," Garret said with a steadiness in his voice that Rick envied, "it was all my fault. I started it. We were just moving some tables and started to horseplay."

The pastor's eyes narrowed. "I know all about you, boy. I know your wicked tendencies!"

"Daddy!" Rick yelled as the man moved toward Garrett as if to strike him. Garrett stood still with a calmness that countered the pastor's rage.

The pastor spun around. "You defending this queer, son?"

"No, sir," Rick promised, unfamiliar with the slanderous word his father used. His own words burnt his tongue. With the lie came the acknowledgement of the slander. The vile word had no place in the love he felt for Garrett. His heart yearned to fight back, but his mind and frail body were paralyzed by fear.

Ignoring him, his father turned to face Rick. "This boy's parents came to me years ago. He confessed the sin of homosexuality. Did you know that? Did he tell you that?"

Rick's body shook in anticipation of the belt. "What?"

"We prayed with his family. Laid hands on that boy. Cast out that demon. His parents said it was a miracle. He was saved. Never believed it. Never did. Devil has a hold on that boy. Never wanted you to be around him. Your mother and I knew something like this would happen. Did he touch you? Did he kiss you?"

Rick repeated the lie so earnestly that he forgot it wasn't the truth. "No, sir. We were just wrestling. We didn't break anything. Didn't mean any harm."

The pastor studied his son's eyes. He furrowed his brow and then turned to face Garrett. "You touch my boy? You kiss him?"

"No, sir."

The pastor sighed. "Once a faggot, always a faggot. I never believed that sin could be cast out." He turned again to his son. "I've asked you twice. I'll ask you again, only once more. Do you deny—here, in the house of God and at the pain of his wrath—that this boy never touched you?"

"Sir, I promise. He never touched me."

His expression was stone-like, even though his eyes were filled with fire. "We'll see about that."

The pastor put both of the boys in his truck. They sat side by side in silence as they roared down the gravel road on the way to Garrett's home. After twenty minutes of silence, the pastor parked his dusty truck in the driveway. It stood in contrast to the nicer cars parked in the cul-de-sac of Garrett's neighborhood. He slammed the door on his way out and made his way toward the house. The boys followed behind in silence.

"Martha, is your husband home?" the pastor asked as she opened the glass storm door.

"Why, yes, Pastor Harris. Please come in. Is something the matter?"

"Martha, Gabe," Pastor Harris said, greeting the man who came from the living room. "Word is that your boy was kissing my son in the church today."

Garrett's parents exchanged concerned expressions.

"Boys say there were just wrestling. I don't believe it. Not one damn word of it. A boy saw them through the window doing God knows what. Mrs. Shoemaker found them. She denies it, of course. She would. But we prayed about this before. We knew the devil found his way into your son's heart, and sin follows."

Clutching a glass of chardonnay to her chest, Martha said, "Pastor Harris, Garrett has been good ever since he was younger. He never confessed any other impure thoughts to us."

Gabe looked on silently. His expression matched the cold, stony expression on the pastor's face.

Martha sought to move the stone, ever so little of her wine splashing as she took her husband's shoulder. "Gabe! Tell the pastor this is a misunderstanding. Garrett, you wouldn't do that, would you? Garrett? Gabe, tell him!"

Gabe looked at his son. "Martha, if Pastor Harris says it's so, then it's so."

"Gabe! He's talking about your son!"

"You baby that boy, Martha. You always have."

"Dammit, Gabe! I can't be his mother and his father. Where are you when he needs a male influence in his life? What baseball games have you been to this year? When have you helped him with his homework?"

"I work, Martha."

"You work? That's your excuse for everything! That's why we're getting a divorce, Gabe. Oh, it's fine. Why shouldn't the pastor know? Pastor Harris, I may baby him, but his father is absent in his life. In my life!"

The pastor's expression relaxed. Rick reasoned it was more down to patronage than sympathy. "Martha, I know you two both do the best you can. They say a boy needs a father in his life. Can't be smothered by his mother either. I just need you to know that your boy isn't permitted to see mine again. Not ever. You handle your son and I'll certainly handle mine."

"Pastor Harris is right, Martha. He's right," Gabe said, looking at his son, but perhaps not seeing him. "I should be more a part of Garrett's life. I know I'm letting him down. I know I let you down. But I won't let our son fall into this sin. I'll be out of this house in a week. He can come with me to Charlotte before he goes off to college. It'll be best for him. We both know he's gifted. Very gifted. Belongs in a better school in the city."

Martha's attempt to respond initially came only in the form of her resigned sobs. "You're taking everything from me. You're taking my everything!" she finally mustered.

The men stood and watched the woman cry, but neither tried to console her.

"Gabe, I think you're doing the right thing. The lord has us make hard choices, but he is righteous."

Rick was stricken but worked to stare unflinchingly ahead as his life and Garrett's continued to avalanche like stones falling from a mountain into an unforgiving ocean. Garrett stood by silently. If he felt anything, Rick couldn't read it on his face, which was cold and rigid—like the face of a man in his casket.

Whatever else was said was lost on Rick. He became numb. Soon, he was following his father back to the truck. Doors slammed. The engine rumbled to a start. The sun had set, and Rick just watched all the life passing by him through the window as the two men rode in silence. The truck eventually slowed, and Rick's thoughts returned to the present.

Rick's started to flush. "Why are we here?"

His father didn't answer.

The truck pulled into a parking spot at the bus station off Highway 321. Dim lights cast a yellow glow over the pavement as his father got out of the car. Rick opened his door. The air was hot, humid. Moths danced around the lights, getting as close as they could but bouncing off the casing on the light that attracted them. Unrelenting, they tried again. *Would they give up or die trying*?

"I have a hundred dollars," his father said, digging in his wallet. "It'll get you to Charlotte to be with that boy. Or D.C. Maybe as far as San Francisco to be with the other queers. I don't know."

"Daddy, I'm not gay—we were just wrestling!"

"I'll tell your momma you ran off. We won't look for you. You can do anything you want, but you can't call this home ever again."

"Daddy—I don't want to leave. I don't want to go. Don't make me go. I promise nothing happened. I swear it! I swear!"

His father reluctantly made eye contact with him. "I don't care what you did—if you're going to stay part of this family, you best never dare think of doing it again, you hear?"

"Yes, Daddy! I swear."

"God may punish you more than I ever could. I

hope for your soul that you're not lying to me! Not in my home. Not in my church! I'm the pastor for this community, dammit! You won't embarrass this family again. You would just kill your mother. You'd kill her! You hear?"

Rick sobbed and nodded his head, overcome with the thought of hurting his mother. "I promise, Daddy. I promise."

The pastor studied him. Satisfied with his contrition, the man nodded. "Fine. Find your own way home. Don't be late for dinner. Your momma will worry."

The dusty truck's tires shrieked against the pavement as if in a continuation of his father's admonishment. The truck fishtailed slightly as the revved engine briefly overpowered its driver. For a moment, the thing was too powerful for his father to control, but he quickly steadied it on the road with his firm grip, leaving Rick alone in the still summer night.

At last, Rick began to cry. Whimpering soon turned to sobs. He knelt on the asphalt as if to pray, still hot from the day's scorching abuse. Wails of agonizing pain marked the pain bottled inside him. His tears were water dousing his love's flame. Soon, the love that once burned was reduced to hot embers—still too hot to touch. No flame can burn without air. His heart would need to be buried deep within him—deep enough to keep him safe and stop the fire from spreading to hurt his mother. Deep enough to never let the fire return. Determined not to be the moth that kills itself in its futile pursuit, Rick started the long walk to a home he no longer knew.

11

Rick rubbed his temples. It was much too early for him to partake in another discussion circle. The buzz from the bottomless mimosas at brunch were giving way to fatigue. He needed a nap more than he needed to talk about his feelings with drag queens.

They said the room was fit for purpose. Matching shag pink carpet lined the walls and the floor. It reminded Rick of a padded cell for the insane. Was it, perhaps? Rick, Jimmy, Bob, and Father Henry were sitting in a circle with a few others in their cohort. As usual, the discussion was led by Eileen and Marilyn. The day's theme was Disney characters. Eileen wore purple makeup, and her Ursula tentacles kept brushing against Bob's shoulder, much to his obvious annoyance. Marilyn had managed to stuff her afro into a black Minnie Mouse hat. The red dots on her dress matched those painted on her cheeks.

Rick adjusted himself on his carpet square. They each had one to sit on. Except for Father Henry, who reminded everyone that he preferred to sit on the floor. Rick was grateful. He used the extra carpet square to lift himself ever so slightly above the pink jungle that threatened to grow over him like a weed.

"Ladies," Eileen began, "this afternoon's discussion topic pertains to our first sexual experiences. Lord, for me it feels like a lifetime ago. It wasn't particularly romantic. No candles. No lavender fields. Just a Ford Bronco with a back seat that never stayed up. It was all I could hope for in the parking lot of a Walmart."

Marilyn raised her hands. "Preach! For me, it was a one-time thing. We started talking online back when everyone was still using dial-up. But we randomly met up at a puppy-play night in the basement of the Eagle. Those were the days." Marilyn's eyes glazed over in nostalgia.

"I never knew you were into BDSM," Eileen observed with a casual curiosity.

"I didn't know either, until that night. Honey, I asked him for a safe word and he told me it would be when he said he was done."

"Queen!" Eileen yelled. "That must have been amazing."

Marilyn sighed. "It was! Sadly, all I have is the memory of that one amazing night in a leash and the co-pay for erythromycin and a shot of ceftriaxone."

"We've all been there, girl. You go to the clinic

on Forty-Second Street?" Eileen asked as if she were talking about her favorite restaurant.

"No. The one in Chelsea. I had a frequent-customer card. Every tenth visit came with the shame for free."

Eileen turned to Rick. "Pastor Harris, what about you? What was your first time like?"

Rick cleared his throat. "I've never lied with a woman. Not before marriage."

"How about a man?" Marilyn asked with a coy smile.

Rick glared at her. "Never lied with a man either."

Eileen whimpered with an expression no more authentic than her costume. "That must be hard. We all live in a world where sex is as common as a sitcom that gets cancelled in the first season. It ends before it has the chance to get good. How do you resist the temptation? Stay so virtuous all the damn time?"

"I just steer clear from the temptation. Women tempted Adam with the apple. They haven't stopped tempting men. I just steer clear. Maintain my flock."

"I guess you can't miss what you've never had. Ever get lonely, though?" Eileen asked.

"I have my momma. I have my church."

"Have you dated before?" Marilyn asked.

"Nope. Never had. First, you date. Then, you kiss. Then, she wants to go further. Once the devil starts to tempt, he gets more powerful. Harder to say no. I say, just don't start."

Eileen turned to broaden the conversation. "Bob, how do you feel about that?"

Bob shifted on his carpet square. "Oh, I don't know. I ran around with girls in high school. College. After college. I never saw much of a problem with it. I don't blame Rick though—women are a lot of trouble. Child support is even more trouble."

"Pastor Harris is right. Those of us who tend to a flock can't tend to the affections of women," Father Henry added, sipping his second cup of tea from the same tea bag. "After being celibate long enough, you never think about it."

Eileen shook her head, "God, you religious people. You deprive yourselves of the best things life has to offer. And why? So we can work to spend an eternity in heaven? I bet they don't have sex there either, do they?"

"Girl, it'd be like going to a boring club without a drink special, where the drag show never starts and you can't leave," Marilyn muttered.

"Better that than the hell and damnation that awaits your kind," Rick reminded them once again. His daily chastisements were so regular that Marilyn suggested they be included on Missy's daily itinerary.

"Look, Reverend," Marilyn began, "we get it. You don't like us. We don't particularly like your kind either. But there's something you should know."

Marilyn leaned in and narrowed her chestnut eyes. "My family had nothing growing up. Not a damn thing. We lived in a busted Cadillac for a few months. Me, my momma, and my younger sister. Our dad was incarcerated. Your church wasn't there for us. They'd send us to a pantry, but we couldn't cook nothing. Then my mom found out I was gay, and she disowned me! Do you know what that's like?"

Rick looked down. The weeds bent over the mats under him, as if they were straining to entangle him.

"They disowned me!" Marilyn said, pointing at Rick. "Where was your church then? In my church, people didn't even talk about gay people. It was a sin too grave to even speak in public. But I managed to get to New York. Drag saved me. Drag queens took me in. Taught me to perform. Fed me. Housed me. Clothed me. Where was your damn church then?"

"Marilyn," Eileen quietly warned, softly placing her hand on her thigh.

"No, Eileen—you came up hard too. They should know!" she pushed the hand off her leg. "They should know that they preach love; they preach forgiveness—but what would they do? Their own God should be ashamed."

"I didn't write the Bible. I just preach it," Rick said, washing his hands of the matter.

"Well, not all of it," Marilyn reminded him. A red-stained tear streaked down her painted face, "I don't imagine you preach about the New Revelation."

"I'm sure they left it out of the Bible for a reason. Just some ancient heresy."

"You only believe what you want to," Marilyn retorted.

"Sounds like we have something in common then, ma'am sir."

"No. Oh no. I know what I believe," Marilyn said as she pushed herself up on her knees. "I believe that people like you are a fraud. You scare people into thinking what they do is wrong and then pass around the collection plate to extort them. Always the money. For the rest of them, they pay and go home on a Sunday afternoon thinking they're good people—better than the other people who get condemned on your pulpit—better than weak and maligned people too few in number and low in courage to speak up and defend themselves! Well, no more. Not now. Times they are a-changin', Reverend. We speak. We vote. We marry.

Hell, now we sit in the White House. It's naming names, Reverend."

"You're any different?" Rick countered. "After they published that blasphemy, you gays had a summer of riots. Burned down that church in Topeka. Got everyone from the airlines down to local school boards kowtowing to your whims. Advancing your liberal agenda. Everyone's too scared to oppose you. Your power over them comes from manipulating them with the same fear of God, which is exactly what you accuse us of doing! Then, these camps. Oh, let's talk about this. You convince people to extort us and force us to come here so we can all apologize to you and beg for the privilege of living under your oppression!"

"I thought *we* were dramatic," Eileen quipped.

"It's true," Father Henry said. "We use the same weapons on opposing sides of the war. It's just a distraction from the life we're called to live."

"What is that?" Rick spat.

"Service. Devotion."

"You forgot hypocrisy," Marilyn mumbled.

Undeterred, the priest calmly explained, "The church is led by mankind. Mankind is flawed. We sin."

Marilyn leaned in like a snake about to strike. "Who holds you accountable? A church that would shuffle priests around after they molested children?"

Father Henry sighed and looked down at his tea, the fatal blow having missed its mark. "The church has reformed itself. Those days are gone. The pain remains, but the offense has ceased. What can we do but ask for forgiveness and accept our penance? I have."

All the heads jerked over to look at the weathered priest. Neatly dressed in his black shirt and frayed Roman collar, his wispy white hair hastily parted to one side, he embodied the forlorn expression that always seemed to adorn him.

The priest took their expressions as his invitation to continue. "I was a young priest. My first parish. I became friends with another priest at the same parish. Our friendship became something more. I committed the sin of homosexuality, and my bishop learned of my transgression. I was given a choice: leave the church or devote myself to works abroad. I chose the latter, and I eventually ended up at my mission in Cambodia, forgotten by all except those I serve."

Eileen shook her head in confusion. "After the New Revelation, your church relaxed all those rules. You could even marry a man now. Why didn't you come back?"

"It wasn't a lifestyle I wanted to perpetuate. I found a purpose in my mission greater than any carnal desire I would hope to satisfy in the flesh."

"Jesus," Eileen whispered. "You're still punishing yourself for that now?"

Father Henry stirred his tea. "No, son. God punishes. I seek forgiveness and seek to atone."

"God, Father," Jimmy said. "Don't you worry that one day you'll wake up and have regrets? Regret what could have been?"

"Son, people in this world are dying of hunger. Thirst. When clean water is a luxury, one doesn't have the privilege of regret. It's selfish."

"What's your biggest regret, Jimmy?" Marilyn asked, sizing up the young man. "Or have you just not lived long enough yet to have any?"

Jimmy leaned back on his hands. They disappeared in the tangled pink carpet. Rick took the opportunity to observe Jimmy's bare shoulders bulge in his tank top as they assumed the weight of his body. "I don't know," he sighed. "Probably, not telling someone how I felt before it was too late. Maybe not knowing what I wanted."

"What happened?" Rick asked instinctively, disappointed in himself for perpetuating the conversation.

Jimmy straightened up. "Maybe I don't want to talk about it."

"I don't believe in regret," Marilyn interrupted. "You never know where the other road might take you.

Maybe you go the other way and get hit by a bus. Regret is nothing more than the lament of an unknown path. We think it might be better, but that's just optimism finding its voice."

Bob rolled his eyes.

"What about you, Bob? Aren't you afraid of regrets?" Marilyn asked.

Bob casually rubbed the scratched lenses of his glasses with his shirt. "I've never regretted a thing in my life."

"What about your daughter?"

"I don't have one," he spat. "Just a son who's auditioning for the role of one."

Marilyn laughed. "Yes, but what will happen if you two grow apart because you won't accept her identity? What if it's not a fad or something that could be fixed like a car with a flat tire?"

Bob shook his head and muttered something under his breath to the floor.

Eileen brushed a tentacle away from Bob's cheek. "Well, we certainly have learned a lot today. Just in time for afternoon cocktails, I believe."

No sooner did Eileen make her announcement than two pool boys made their way into the room. Empty cocktail glasses rattled on a tray as another pool boy followed behind, pushing a cart filled with liquor and mixers. The group roused themselves and stretched.

In the commotion, Rick moved next to Father Henry. "We're still on for this afternoon?" he asked, now with some hesitance. To him, the priest had become a broken mirror—an imperfect reflection of himself with glass sharp enough to cut if he got too close. Rick's disgust at his reflection was tempered with gratitude that the man at least had the strength to avoid acting on his desires in some boastful way.

The priest nodded in confirmation of their plan.

Rick picked up his carpet square and returned it to the stack in the corner of the room. Jimmy stood nearby.

"Bob and Father Henry are in. Three o'clock, right after history class, during the intermission before happy hour?" Rick asked.

"I'll be there," Jimmy whispered.

Rick felt the heavy weight of the folded note in his pocket. Today was the designated day. He dared not leave the scrap of paper behind for fear of it being found. In private moments, he'd unfold and reread it. *What secret meaning could it hold?*

"If you boys are looking for something to do tonight, there's a Judy Garland movie at nine in the common area. Open bar. A dessert tray. Fabulous!" Eileen mentioned.

Rick suddenly looked up. "Judy Garland? Which movie?"

"*Till the Clouds Roll By*, I believe."

Rick shrieked, "With Angela Lansbury and Frank Sinatra!"

"You know it?"

"Oh, yes. Oh, my momma would sit me down—we'd watch all those classics. They just don't make movies like that anymore."

"Well, baby, I will see you there!"

Rick composed himself, and Eileen walked over to make conversation with the others.

"That's damn good thinking, son," Father Henry said. "That double agent routine could help her—I mean him—reveal more information to us."

Rick blushed and cleared his throat. "Of course."

Rick carried his spiked lemonade with him to the next class—part two of a three-part lecture: *From the Stonewall to the White House*. It would have been a perfect time for a nap, except the instructor assured everyone there'd be a quiz at the end of each session. The instructor regularly reminded the class that a passing grade was necessary to help earn the coveted 'participation certificate' Rick and the others needed to return to their lives.

12

Over the previous two days, Rick had used every moment of his unscheduled time to search the grounds
and any space he, Jimmy, Bob, and Father Henry could
access without a key card. They took note of any visible
cameras. They created a floor map on the back of a napkin. Jimmy signed up for morning yoga as an excuse to
see the rear of the building overlooking a small pond.
Bob suffered a meandering conversation with a pool
boy about how hard it was to leave Pokémon and an
internet connection behind to work at the camp, just
to learn that the mail room was kept unlocked and
located right behind the guard at the front desk near
the entrance.

A rush of adrenaline brought Rick back to sobriety.
He decided that today would be the day they fought
back against the system that held them. The system that
imprisoned them. The system that would try to indoc-
trinate them. Today, they began their rescue mission.

"Excuse me! Excuse me!" Rick called out as loudly
as he could, holding Father Henry by the arm as he
coughed and stumbled along. They were flanked by
Bob and Jimmy, all wearing concerned expressions.

Rick approached the bewildered guard at the front desk. "Excuse me, sir. This man is coughing and has chest pains. I think he needs help!"

The guard leaped up and circled around his desk to grab the priest's arm, and together they helped him into a chair. "What happened?" he asked, reaching for his radio.

"Glitter," the priest choked out before another coughing spell overcame him.

Jimmy urgently pointed to the craft room. "We were working on handmade letters for the kids at the children's hospital. Big vat of glitter on the shelf…"

"And I bumped it!" Bob said. "It crashed down on the table next to this priest—went everywhere!"

"It was like a cloud of glitter!" Jimmy said. "I don't know how much he must have inhaled."

Rick wondered how much glitter could kill a man. "We got to him as soon as we could, but we were blinded by the shimmering glitter vapor. Looked like a damn Liberace concert."

"That's awful—but I'm sure he just needs some fresh air," the guard said, eyeing the glitter-covered men. "Let me call someone down who can take him outside."

"No!" Jimmy said. "We have no idea how much of that stuff is in him—the man needs to go to the infirmary!"

"Glitter can kill," Bob said somberly, with a hand on the guard's shoulder—preventing him from taking out his radio.

"I shouldn't leave my post… I can call someone—my shift's about to end," the guard said, his panic growing.

"Dammit, son," Bob said. "Look at the man—he can't wait. Let's take him now!"

On cue, Father Henry gave another coughing fit.

"Okay, yeah—for sure. Um, just come with me. We can walk him over," the guard said, hoisting Father Henry up with Bob's help.

Rick watched the men hobble toward the door. "We need to go contain the glitter scene—we can't let anyone else go in there until the cloud settles."

"Right!" Jimmy affirmed.

The guard looked back at them as he and Bob made their way to the front door with Father Henry slumped over their shoulders, only hesitating until Father Henry started yet another coughing fit.

The automatic doors closed behind them. The front lobby was now silent.

"Quick!" Rick said as he and Jimmy dashed behind the front desk and pushed open the door to the mail room.

Rick tasted acrid adrenaline burning his tongue. Jimmy closed the door behind them. Florescent lights softly buzzed above their heads as the two explored the small room. Absent were the lavish decorations that made the lobby look like a luxury hotel. Instead they found cinder-block walls. A scratched table supported a well-used paper-cutter and every manner of office supply. Dozens of small wooden cubbies stood against the far wall.

Jimmy ran his finger over words penned onto the wooden cubbies. "They have our names on them."

Rick scanned the rows of boxes and quickly found his name. A small envelope rested inside the box. Rick snatched it out. Neat handwriting on the front of the envelope read DO NOT DELIVER. Rick hastily stuffed it in his pocket.

Jimmy pointed to a stack of boxes in the corner beneath a stopped clock. "What is that?" Rick walked over and knelt beside them for a closer inspection.

"Jesus" Rick said, flipping the box over. "It says it's a restraint system."

"This one is a harness," Jimmy said, dusting the top of the box with his hand. "What would they need that for? Animals?"

Rick studied them. "No clue what happens here. I haven't seen any animals. So many of them though."

Jimmy held a stack of mail in front of Rick. "Here, it's from Missy Bottom's box. Let's take it. She runs the place. Maybe we can find out more about what all goes on here."

Rick hesitated. He hadn't planned on taking anything. He was too focused on his own letter to consider reading anyone else's mail.

"Rick, do you want to learn more about this place or not? The note said she was involved somehow—we might learn something."

Rick snatched the mail out of his hand. "Okay, dammit. You're right."

Muffled voices drifted in from the lobby. Rick and Jimmy snuck over to the small window on the mail room's door. Two pool boys walked into the lobby.

"Can you believe Devon called me a twink?" a pool boy in a red speedo asked. "I can bench twenty-five pounds on *each* side of the bar, *and* I have to shave my chest. I'm not a twink still, am I?"

"Brad..." a pool boy in a pink speedos began consolingly, "don't worry about Devon—he's just jealous you slept with Casey."

"Probably pissed that he didn't douche before Mark fucked him," Brad said.

"Probably not as pissed as Mark was."

They laughed, and their voices trailed off as they walked down the hall, the sound of their sandals flopping against their feet.

Rick took his ear from the door. "Quick, now!"

Quietly, Jimmy opened the door just wide enough for them to pass through. They crawled around the front desk and jumped up into the lobby. Rick's mouth was dry with fear. Jimmy tucked pieces of mail and a manila folder marked CONFIDENTIAL into his waist, under his shirt.

Keeping with the plan, Rick concentrated on his breathing and forced himself to act naturally as they crossed the security camera's line of sight and continued on to the rendezvous spot in their room. Rick focused on calming his shaking hands as he took the room key card from his wallet and unlocked the door. He closed it softly behind himself, only remembering then to breathe.

Jimmy collapsed on Rick's bed. "Jesus, that was close."

Rick glared at him for his word choice but was too distracted by the thought of joining him to hold any more than a momentary judgment.

Rick sat down at the desk and took out the sealed envelope. His hands still quivering, he unsealed the envelope and pulled out the piece of paper inside. He read the secret message aloud:

"I couldn't risk having this delivered. Too risky. Might be intercepted. Missy has something that doesn't belong to

her. You can go to places I can't. Please find it. It will set you all free. Rick, you are Jonah."

"Huh?" Jimmy exclaimed.

"You got me."

"Like from the Bible?"

"I can only assume."

Jimmy looked embarrassed. "I should know this, but what exactly was that story about him and the whale all about?"

Rick sighed and rubbed his brow. "Basically, Jonah was told by God to go and preach against a wicked city. Except, Jonah didn't want to go. Instead, he tried to flee God and then all sorts of bad things happened to him. You actually read the Bible to those kids?"

"Well, no. The pastor does that. We just go on service trips and stuff," Jimmy admitted.

Rick gave him another critical look. "They wrote a whole book about it in the Bible. The Book of Jonah."

"Ah," Jimmy said as dim recollection seemed to find him, "so, then what happened?"

Rick explained, rolling his eyes: "Jonah was on a ship and people knew the terrible things were caused by Jonah's disobedience to God. So he sacrificed himself and asked to be thrown into the sea so God would pick on him, not the crew. They did what they were told and the seas calmed, but God had a big fish or a whale—no one really knows—swallow him up. After some time, the fish spit him back up, and he was saved. He went on to obey God after."

"So this place is like the whale?"

"I guess so," Rick said. "If it is, I must be here because I disobeyed God. I should have done more. I should have never agreed to leave my flock behind to come to this sinful place!"

Jimmy sat up and put his hand on Rick's shoulder. "You're a good pastor. Not many people preach like you do anymore. There are far worse deserving far more of God's punishment than you."

"But there's hope," Rick said. "Eventually, the whale spat him out. God then decided he suffered enough and spared his life. This will end, Jimmy. We'll be spit out. We'll go back—with our certificates of attendance—and speak the truth about this place. We'll share what we know and what we still have to learn."

A knock at the door interrupted them. Jimmy sprang up to open it. Bob and Father Henry made a silent procession in. The priest's hair was a bit disheveled, and glitter stubbornly clung to his shoulders, but he looked alive as ever.

Father Henry settled his weight into a chair. "Did it work?"

Rick helped him into the chair. "Yes. We got it. What happened when you got to the clinic?"

Bob laughed. "Nothing. They gave him a glass of water, and it did the trick. A medical miracle."

"They assured me the glitter is from a non-toxic source. Evidently it's organic," the priest said.

"And vegan," Bob noted.

Rick read the letter to the newcomers. Father Henry stood up and paced the room. "So, what do we know? There's a person here who knows your father. He's in trouble. Somehow he can send mail, and I presume he knows a fair amount about how this place works. Missy has something that appears to be both the thing he needs and the thing that will set us free of this place."

Bob stood as well. "You think he's someone on the inside—like the staff?"

"Or maybe he's part of that secret group that we can't even interact with—when they put us on lockdown to avoid having our paths cross," Jimmy suggested.

"Whoever this person is, he's relying on us to do what's right. To use our time here to learn a truth that will help us do the Lord's work. We should pray for him," Rick offered, and bowed his head.

Jimmy interrupted, holding forth the stack of mail. "There's more we might be able to learn. We took this from Missy's mailbox."

Jimmy passed around the letters. Rick opened an invoice from the janitorial company. "Looks like this compound has seventy bathrooms, two common areas, fifty-five rooms. It goes on."

Bob whistled. "It's huge. We haven't seen half of it."

"I've got a receipt for all kinds of crazy things," Father Henry said as he squinted at the paper, no doubt regretting his reading glasses were still in his room. "They bought a case of something called Rush. Sounding rods. Are they catheterizing people?"

Rick shook his head. "Wouldn't surprise me. We found boxes of restraint kits in the mail room. Harnesses as well."

Bob assumed an expression that married surprise with revulsion: "Good God."

"Torture," Father Henry said softy, his gaze distant. "Just like the early Christians being thrown to the lions, I bet. I'm prepared to die for my faith."

"Speak for yourself," Bob said as he took his turn reading the invoices.

Rick peered over the mail to look at Jimmy's lap. "What's in the confidential envelope?"

Jimmy took the brown envelope and uncoiled the red string tethering it closed. He pulled out a letter. "The return address is from someone named Simon Slump. It's from the Vatican in Rome."

Father Henry sat up higher, and the other leaned in. The paper looked heavier in Jimmy's hand as the gravity of the situation fell upon him. Rick decided that a letter from Rome was certainly more interesting than how many rolls of toilet paper the facility used last month.

"What's it say?" Bob asked.

Jimmy cleared his throat and read the letter out loud in a steady voice:

"Dearest Missy Bottom—I am relieved to hear that the artifact arrived safely at your facility for you to hold in trust for us in your office. Obviously, I don't need to impress upon you how important it is to execute this operation with profound secrecy and exactly as planned. Your council placed great faith in you—over my noted objections. I trust you will prove my misgivings unfounded. No doubt, your assistance in this regard will assure your appointment to the North American council seat you seek. Your council emissary will reach out to you at the appropriate time to facilitate the artifact's transfer."

"What the hell is going on here?" asked Bob, breaking the silence.

"Jesus, I feel like Humphrey Bogart in one of those crime movies I used to watch with my momma," Rick said.

"Who's Humphrey Bogart?" Jimmy asked.

"Never mind," Rick said with a dismissive glare.

"All I know is we need to find a way to get to her office and see what it is."

"This might make it easier," Bob said, smiling and holding out a key card. "I took it from the front desk guard when we were carrying Father Henry to the medics."

"Very, very nice work, Bob. I underestimated you," Rick said with a rueful smirk.

"It's still dangerous," Jimmy said. "Cameras everywhere. We don't even know where her office is."

Rick leaned back and thought for a moment. "True. There's that movie tonight in the common area. With the open bar, Eileen will be drunk. Just like usual. I can see what I can learn. It'll be late. If I can get a general idea of where her office is, I can sneak out."

"It'll be a short trip if the guard had his card deactivated," Jimmy added.

"The guard said he was headed home," Bob recalled. "I doubt he was coming back into the building. He seemed eager to leave."

"Can't blame him," Jimmy muttered under his breath.

"Then it must be tonight," the priest concluded.

Jimmy took the custodian's invoice and annotated the collection of napkins he'd smuggled from the dining hall to improve upon the rough map of the facility and its grounds. He took a few educated guesses based on the apparent symmetry of each building's architecture to extrapolate where more rooms would be. Rick silently read the letter from the Vatican again, scrutinizing the decree for more clues. Bob and Father Henry left for their respective rooms to get ready for happy hour.

Jimmy put down his napkin montage and leaned over the edge of the bed. "Rick?"

"Yeah, Jimmy?" Rick asked, flipping the paper over to look for any unseen messages.

"I've lied to you."

Rick put down the paper and turned to see Jimmy holding his head with his arms braced on his legs at the edge of Rick's bed.

Jimmy looked up to meet Rick's gaze. "Before, I told you I was sent here because I saw two boys doing sinful things on a trip."

"Yeah," Rick recalled.

"Well, I was one of them."

Rick raised his eyebrows and leaned in.

Jimmy cleared his throat, and his voice quivered. "See, there was this other camp counselor. We spent a lot of time together. We shared a room. One night, we gave in. I didn't mean to. I knew it was wrong. I didn't want to sin."

The revelation brought an excitement Rick detested

but couldn't suppress. A puff of air blew over the burned embers, making a hidden fire glow ever so faintly—proof that it had never completely burned to ash.

"It's okay, son. What happened?" Rick asked, forcing his voice to exude calmness.

Jimmy continued his confession. "I reported it to the pastor as soon as we got back from the camp. The other guy denied anything ever happened. Then the guy threatened to sue me and the church for slander if he lost his job. I didn't think he'd get in trouble. I took the blame. I started it."

Rick shook his head sympathetically. "Oh, Jimmy."

"The pastor sent me here. I don't know why. I think it had something to do with the lawsuit. I still have these urges, though. I pray. I read the Bible. I know it's wrong."

Rick moved next to Jimmy on the bed, their thighs touching. He could feel the hair on Jimmy's leg brushing against his own, his warm body radiating what Rick longed to feel next to him. Rick put his hand on Jimmy's back.

"It's okay, Jimmy. This place—the sin all around us. It's the worst place imaginable for someone to be when they're struggling with that."

Jimmy turned, and his blue eyes locked with Rick's. The room seemed to disappear in the intensity of

Jimmy's expression. Jimmy wrapped his arm around Rick's waist and pulled him into a kiss. Their lips met tenderly at first. Rick was powerless to resist. His lips again met Jimmy's. This time, the kiss lingered, Rick shaking. Impaired by inexperience combined with his sudden inability to control his body, his kiss felt awkward. The next kiss was done with abandon. Their lips met and departed again and again like waves crashing against rocks on the shore. Slow. Rhythmic.

But each kiss reached further than the last as the tide began to rise. Even the most immovable stones give no answer to the restless waves crashing against them, but over time, waves inevitably change the entire terrain—etching stone with its kiss. At that moment, time seemed to stop. Growing in confidence, Rick pulled Jimmy closer. Their tongues met.

Rick regained control over his shaking hands and began to breathe normally again. His face was flush and hot. Just as tenderly as it began, their kiss ended, and their lips receded back into the turbulent ocean from which they came. Only time would tell when that tide would rise again. Rick found himself still awkwardly holding Jimmy at the edge of the bunk bed.

"I'm sorry," Jimmy said, his soft breath on Rick's face rekindling the flame ever so slightly.

Rick swallowed. "Don't be… this place. It's probably

what they're trying to do… surround us with homo-sexuality and turn us gay. I'm just as much to blame."

"Have you ever kissed a guy before?" Jimmy asked, moving his hand from Rick's back to his leg.

Rick glanced down at Jimmy's hand but didn't move it away. "No," he said after a long pause.

"All I ever did was kiss that other guy. We never went further, I swear!"

"And neither should we," Rick decided. "Satan is tempting us here. We have to keep our focus."

Jimmy moved his hand back from Rick's leg. "I agree. I'll be stronger, I promise."

Rick looked at Jimmy and struggled to find words. His promise was alcohol on a wound—necessary but painful. If he was like Jonah from the Bible, this would no doubt be the storm. The waves of his unspoken de-sires hadn't pitched him so close to capsizing in such a long time. He looked at Jimmy's face and for the briefest moment saw Garrett. He was reminded of the guilt he felt when they were caught and Garrett was sent away; the fear of disappointing his mother and revealing himself as a fraud hiding behind an elaborate masquerade weighed heavier on his heart than his lust.

I must try harder, he reminded himself.

13

Rick and Jimmy barely spoke a word at happy hour or over dinner. Rick worked to suppress the awful sin and focus on the task at hand. Unfortunately, suppressing his desires toward Jimmy was like trying to sink a life jacket: no matter how earnestly he fought to hold it under, it would rise right back to the surface.

Father Henry retired early to pray. All the free alcohol at the camp wouldn't be enough to entice Bob to watch a musical. Jimmy seemed to try just as hard to avoid Rick and left for his room after dinner without a word. Conversation with Jimmy was the scab that might go away if he had the restraint to avoid picking at it. Or it could be the splinter that would need to come out before it became infected, however painful the process may be. Rick wasn't sure.

Disgusted by the sweet elixirs that seemed to only bring sin and hangovers, Rick made a concerted effort to avoid alcohol that night. Sobriety was necessary for what would come next.

The common area was sparsely populated when Rick arrived. Sofas abutted a wide-screen TV in the corner of the room. Pool boys were dutifully setting up a makeshift bar against the wall, and custodians wearing uniforms from the dining hall were arranging trays of chocolate cake slices and lady fingers. The smell of butter and oil was accompanied by the crescendo of popping from the machine working in a corner. Rick wasn't sure if it was more like a college dorm common area or a retirement home. He had more familiarity with the former, but it felt too much like the latter.

He was struck with a memory of his father spending the last months of his life on this earth in one such home. The common area was thick with men in wheelchairs staring at a TV that none of them watched. Rick had spent as little time there as possible, only visiting when guilt propelled him across town in that old truck. To live a full life only to spend one's last days in lonely solitude was a fate worse than death. His father's heart was failing, his voice had grown silent, too weak to fight.

Here, mahogany shelves lined the walls. They held books no one likely ever read. It was a collection that appeared built over time and at great expense, but for what purpose? Rick wondered. Faulkner, Hemingway, and King were found among the books in the fiction section. A treatise on the American Conservative Intellectual Movement in America and a well-worn copy of the DSM-IV caught his eye in the non-fiction section. The books stood in silent refute of the insanity around them. Rick took solace in the camaraderie they offered.

One other guest from another cohort sat by the TV, reading one of the books. Was he reading or merely staring at a page to avoid the burden of speaking to anyone? Another guest napped in a recliner, no doubt sleeping off afternoon cocktails, his dinner drink, the after-dinner dessert wine, or all of the above.

"You're early!" Eileen called, approaching him from behind. Rick turned and saw her dressed in a golden evening gown that sparkled when it caught the light from the chandelier.

"I didn't want to miss the beginning," Rick said. Despite the circumstances, he grudgingly admitted to himself that he was looking forward to the film. At least it was something normal in which he knew what to expect.

"Punctuality is a virtue, they say. Do they actually say that though, dear? Does God truly want people on time? I've always heard that, but I'm not religious. Not anymore. Lord knows—I'm a drag queen. We never start anything on time."

"First Corinthians, I believe," Rick said, mustering his long-perfected art of using a smile to camouflage disgust. For most, a smile is little more than a window dressing to distract from their true feelings. It may look pretty, but the searing light from the window still shines through. For Rick, he knew the trick was to lift the eyebrows. Laugh as he smiled. He suspected they were both disguised. Rick just didn't need makeup and a dress.

"Oh, I'm sure I'm going to hell anyway. I'll get there when I get there. No hurry though—despite what it appears from the cigarettes and booze. I'm sure all the most interesting people will be there."

"You seem uncommonly comfortable with that fate," Rick chided.

"Baby, fire and brimstone will just turn me into a diamond," Eileen said, tossing her hair over a shoulder and strutting her way to the drink cart.

Rick walked behind her, suppressing his desire to discuss her mortality.

"Tell me, ma'am sir—how did you end up here?"

Eileen downed a shot and gestured for the pool boy to make another. "Marilyn," she answered, pausing to burp. "I've known her since we were both in Manhattan learning about the scene. We met at a ball. She was with another drag mother that ran her house. A real bitch. We found our way and got day jobs to pay the bills. Eventually, anyway. Lived together for a while. But she got this job and invited me to come along. Better than working for damp dollars at a bar and staying out all night after work."

"What do you know about Messy Bottom—or whatever his or her name is? The person that runs the place."

"Missy!" Eileen corrected. "Trust me, you do not want to meet a messy bottom, am I right?" she laughed, winking at the pool boy who had the lamentable task of bartending that night. Even if Eileen were the only one there, Rick suspected the poor kid wouldn't have much time for a break.

"Oh, Missy," Eileen laughed. "Don't get me started, baby."

Rick looked at her, quizzically. Without asking, a pool boy handed Rick a vodka tonic. Somehow, he'd remembered it was Rick's drink of choice. His most sincere intentions to avoid the drink were immediately washed away with the siren song of vodka splashing over ice.

"Baby, there's two types of gay people you need to know about. There's people like me and Marilyn. People who had to work and struggle. People who got disowned by their family, by society, or both," she said, waving her drink in the air to illustrate the vast hordes of some unseen society.

"Then," she said, "you got people like Missy. She

comes from money. White. She never had to come out. Her parents were always so supportive. Gives money to charities. Sits on boards. Then she has the audacity to say she understands us. She doesn't give a shit. Just concerned about her image. You know what I mean?"

Rick nodded but took causal note of Eileen's own whiteness, elaborate makeup, and the shimmery dress that made her look like a cross between an Oscar trophy and a prostitute.

"Of course, she pays more than I've ever seen before," Eileen said. "Treats us well. Our rooms are a lot nicer than yours, I admit. Then again, when you look like this every day, you need some extra space. I'm wearing more latex under this dress than the guy with the biggest dick at prom who paid attention to the safe sex video in high school. Can I get an amen?"

"If you get paid so much, I can't imagine how my church could afford to send me here."

"They probably didn't," she said, absentmindedly. "All the atonement camps are funded by some cabal of wealthy gay donors around the world. Your sponsors probably only paid some token amount. Sliding scale. That sort of thing."

Rick took a quick sip of his drink and considered the enormity of wealth the donors must have accumulated for the camps, coughing as he swallowed. "If your room is nice, I'm sure Missy's room is a palace. Have you been to it?"

Eileen laughed as she headed for the couch. "Oh, hell no. She's not my type. Get one of those slices of cake—so good. Pick me up a slice. And a lady finger or two, but only if it has cream filling. No chocolate. Labor Day is right around the corner, and I'll be damned if I have to hide in a t-shirt again at Fire Island. Fuck it, I had a salad. Make it three."

Dutifully, Rick started to pick at the dessert tray. He contemplated the difficulty of teasing out information while only understanding half of anything Eileen said. Whether it was for good measure or spite, Rick added a few extra lady fingers to the plate.

"Hey, boyfriend!" Eileen said, motioning to him from the other side of the room. "Be a dear and have Trevor make me another Lemon Drop. Have one for yourself while you're at it."

Grudgingly, Rick balanced a plate on top of a drink and held his own drink in the other hand. Lacking Eileen's grace, he wobbled back to the couch like an amateur circus performer and delicately placed the plate and glasses on the table just as the film began.

"Thank you, baby girl," Eileen cooed.

Rick sat close enough to her to talk, but no closer. He gave into to the drink that sat in front of him with little reluctance. Tonight, it wasn't alcohol—it was medicine. The lights dimmed, but Eileen's dress still managed to reflect light from somewhere. Maybe there was no light at all. *It could just be a side effect of homosexuality*, Rick considered.

"Oh, look at Judy's dress. Gives me an idea for a Sunday!"

"Yes, it's nice. Very modest. People don't dress like that nowadays."

Eileen chuckled. "What must you think of us? It's got to be so much to handle. I know. You probably hate us. You hate us, right? Honey, I don't care if you hate me. People have hated me for as long as I can remember. It's nothing new."

"I don't hate you," Rick said, surprising himself.

"Well, good. Beneath that crass shell and behind that Bible, I think you're a good guy at heart. Handsome too. Just a tadpole out of the water, they say."

Rick ignored her and kept his attention on the film. The cake was truly good, he decided. Moist. Not too sweet. Eileen smiled and gave Rick the gift of silence until the first number. She sang along. Rick knew the song. Another night, he might have hummed along. Not tonight though. *She sang for him tonight*, he thought.

Eileen downed her Lemon Drop, and Rick saw her eyes dart over to the bar. Taking the cue, Rick offered to get them another. She smiled her approval. The man who took refuge to read must have excused himself, but the other was still sleeping peacefully as the circumstances would permit.

"Thank you, boyfriend," she said as she took off her heels and tucked her feet underneath her. Another less memorable song began.

"It's just this place is so mysterious," Rick said, breaking the silence.

Eileen kept her attention on the movie but hummed her acknowledgment.

Rick tried again. "If I wanted to ask Missy some questions, where would I find her office?"

"Oh, it's in the administrative building—the same one you were in for the pedicures," she offered sleepily. "But it's restricted space, and good luck trying to get anything out of her if you run into her. We all sign non-disclosure agreements. I want to get an annual contract here, so I have to keep my mouth shut. Don't worry though, baby. Another week suffering through our company and you'll be back home with your momma and that church."

Rick took a deep breath. His inquisition was a success. He nibbled on another lady finger and rubbed his hand over the key card tucked in his pocket to make sure it was still there. He knew had to be patient. He took a sip of his drink, which tasted better than before. Rick leaned back and enjoyed the simple indulgence.

"He likes you, you know," Eileen said, folding her hands on her lap.

"Who?"

"Jimmy."

Rick felt his face flush. "Oh, I don't think so. Jimmy's as straight as I am."

Eileen laughed. "Baby, this isn't my first time to the bar. I can spot a straight man across the room while I'm still at the coat check. It's truly a gift, I know. I can also spot a gay guy too scared to come out of the closet. Mark my words. Before the week is out, he'll be out and proud."

In one gulp, Rick finished his drink. "I think he's a good, Christian man. Just lonely and a little to himself."

Eileen pursed her lips and raised her eyebrow in rebuttal.

Rick stood abruptly. "Anyway, it's been a long night. I'm off to bed."

"With whom?" Eileen asked with a sly smile Rick was happy to ignore.

Rick's shock was tempered by the bricks weighing down his stomach. *How was she so sure? Was she truly so perceptive? Were there cameras in their rooms?* The fear subsided with the urgency he now felt. Tonight, he was going to find answers.

"You should at least stay until the end!"

"Not tonight, Eileen. I already know how this ends."

14

Rick casually walked to the lobby. The guard was reading a paper. Though a small television was on beside him, his eyes were focused on his paper. "Going out for a walk?"

"It's a nice night. Thought I'd get some exercise before bed," Rick said, hoping not to cross the invisible fence that kept him there.

"I'd suggest the trail by the lake. It's peaceful this time of night."

Rick thanked him and walked outside. A warm breeze greeted him. It was moist with the day's humidity, which quickly met with the budding sweat on his brow. Rick walked past the lit square and took refuge in the shadows away from the lights that lined the walkways. Once he was outside the view of any cameras, he pulled a ski mask over his face. He took a moment of self-congratulation for packing clothes for more than one season.

Rather than walking to the front door, where he knew he'd be met with both light and cameras, he took a wide, arching path across the lawn and around to the side of the building. Just as Jimmy had told him, he found a side entrance. It was a plain door, no windows. Only a dimly lit lamp with a yellow glow greeted him. Moths swarmed it, tapping against the casing in their relentless flurry. Unlike the last time he confronted them, he knew leaving wasn't an option. Aside from the chirping cicadas from the pine trees in the distance, his own breathing was the only other sound in the night air.

All of their planning rested on what came next. He pulled the badge from his pocket and took one last look around to confirm he was alone with the night. He felt like he was turning the key to his old truck, not certain what might happen next.

He placed the badge against the glowing red card reader by the door handle and held his breath. A moment later the sensor's light changed to green, and the door unlatched. Rick slowly turned the handle and slid inside, finding there a cinder-block hallway painted a dull lime green. Lights encased in wire cages emitted a soft buzz above him.

He crept down the hall leading to two swinging double doors ahead. Utility closets and a bathroom were the only other rooms off the hall. No light could be seen through the gaps in the doors ahead. Growing in confidence, he pushed open one of the doors and found himself in the lobby he remembered from the first day at the camp. To his relief, he was alone.

Based on his best recollection, he retraced his steps to the pedicure room. Passing the room, he went farther down the hall to find another locked door. Fortunately, his card worked. He expected to find another cinder-block hallway. Instead, hardwood floors met his shoe and painted drywall lined the walls with crown molding to match the paneling at the wall's base. Regretting not packing a flashlight, he could barely make out the gloss of oil paintings that hung in faint light along the wall. Landscapes, mostly. A few ornate portraits of people he didn't recognize caught his attention.

He opened each door along the way. In the first, he found a classroom not unlike the others in his building. Resisting the temptation to linger, he kept moving. The next room was a conference room with two flat-screen televisions mounted on opposite walls and about a dozen pleated leather chairs encircling a long, rectangular table—elegant in its simplicity.

A plaque was hung about halfway down the hall. Rick leaned in and squinted to read in the dark. It was a map directing him to the executive residences, where Missy lived. Directly ahead was the headmistress's office. Relieved, his pace quickened.

He chanced a glance down the corridor to the residences. Locked doors would have awaited him down that passageway. Light shone from the doors' windows. *Someone must be awake*, he thought. He shuffled back into the darkness and approached the door to Missy's office. Where most of the doors were slabs of gray metal, this one was a light brown wood. It seemed more suited for the interior of a nice home.

Rick hesitated with the key card. *Would this office have more restricted access than a security guard's card would permit?* Expecting alarms to sound, Rick quickly recalled his way back in case he'd need to run for it. It was calming to know that whomever pursued him would be slowed down if they wore heels. With a deep breath, Rick laid the card against the reader. A moment later, the door softly clicked open, and Rick walked in.

Windows lined the entire back wall of the room from the floor to its twelve-foot ceiling. Moonlight cast a dim illumination over the entire office. Rick was relieved to be able to see more clearly. Still not daring to turn on a light, he began to explore. His hands met the knob on a coat closet. He moved further into the lion's den.

The sheen of an ornate wooden desk reflected the pale moonlight. Papers were strewn about her otherwise tidy desk. Rick surmised the entire office could be featured in a magazine at any given moment. The desk rested on a boldly colored rug that splashed over half the room. Fresh flowers sat in a vase, awaiting the light of a new day. Their yearning was in vain, Rick thought. *They were dead anyway.*

In the corner, Rick immediately knew he'd found what he'd come for. A wooden crate lay broken open. Packing material and splintered wood defiled the otherwise pristine office. She had been in a hurry to open it, whatever it was, he surmised. Rick found the contents propped against the corner wall. A tightly bound scroll about a foot long, wrapped in thick layers of plastic. He reached out and touched it, but as soon as he did, he heard voices.

The acrid taste of fear flushed in his mouth. Instinctually, he dashed across the office and slid inside the coat closet. Squeezed between two full-length fur coats that tickled his cheeks, he crouched down as far back into the darkness as the closet's walls would permit.

The office door swung open.

"This isn't a time for questions, Sean. It's time for answers," Missy said.

Rick squinted through the furs and small slats in the closet door. Her wig was gone, but her makeup remained. At first, Rick thought she was naked, but once the light was turned on, he saw she was wearing nude pantyhose stretched over molded inserts that bestowed a woman's figure on a man's body. She was wearing a white t-shirt, and the breasts she carried were no longer there. The half man, half woman marched to her desk and sat down.

"We're all trying, Mistress. We only want to serve you," another voice pleaded. The man who followed behind her shocked Rick in his appearance. He was wearing a black leather harness over his bare chest. The contraption looked identical to the ones Rick found in the mail room. He had what appeared to be a diamond-studded dog collar secured tightly around his neck. A gold name tag on the collar bounced playfully as he walked. His face was hidden under a black mask that muffled his voice when he spoke. The mask's pointed ears and long snout gave the appearance of a dog. He wore black leather shorts and had some protrusion coming out of his rear. Rick squinted to see better. He discovered it was an upturned rubber tail.

"You can start by handling our problem with the priest," she said, sighing.

"There will be no more problems with him, Mistress," the dog man said.

"The emissary will arrive this week to pick up the artifact. If this doesn't go exactly as planned—if we miss any detail—the consequences will be too grave to even consider. You understand that, right?"

"Yes, Mistress. Every detail is planned out. I re-confirmed that the treatment will be applied and the shipping labels will be falsified to permit the shipment to arrive on time."

"No records?"

"None."

Unnervingly, the dog man's tail seemed to wag as he spoke.

Tucked between two fur coats, Rick felt the sweat on his face running down his cheek. Uncomfortable, he adjusted his body and accidentally jangled a hanger. *Shit*, he swore to himself. The dog man turned his head. His name tag on the collar flung up and bounced against his neck as he jerked his head toward the closet. Rick held his breath.

Missy looked alarmed. "What is it?"

The dog man's eyes settled on the closet door and Rick heard pulsing blood rushing in his ears. "Nothing, Mistress," he barked back to her after a long pause.

Missy sighed. "Fine. It sounds like you have everything accounted for."

"Yes, Mistress."

"You've been a good boy," she said, consolingly.

"You've earned the right to have some rest. It'll be a big day tomorrow. I want you showered and dressed in normal clothes."

"Yes, Mistress. Master takes care of me. Master likes it when I serve her?"

"Yes. Yes, I do."

"Would it please Master if I had dinner?"

"Shit, I forgot you didn't eat today. It's so late. Yes, of course. You may have dinner. Leftovers are in the lounge. I'll put something in your bowl. Let's call it a night."

Missy collected a few papers from her desk. She made her procession across the office, the dog man following dutifully behind. As soon as the lights were switched off and the door latched closed behind them, Rick took a deep breath and closed his eyes. He struggled to hear the footsteps trail off into silence. He dared not move.

After a few minutes, Rick was confident no one was coming back. Quietly, he opened the closet door and stepped back into the office. Whether it was fatigue or the alcohol impairing his judgment, he gave into his impulse. He walked back behind the desk and picked up the scroll, examining it as best he could in the dim light. Its mystery called to him, even though he feared exploring the tunnel too deep for fear of a sudden storm.

He carried the scroll at his side and traced now-familiar steps back down to the conference room in the hall, where he felt far enough from the residences to chance using the lights. Once there, he flipped a light switch and began to unwrap the object from its plastic layers. His eyes fought to adjust to the light. Just a quick look, he promised himself.

He paused as a door swung shut down the hall. Rick slapped the light switch, restoring darkness to the room. He peered out the door and down the hall. Missy's light was on again. Rick swore to himself, his way blocked.

With a rush of adrenaline, he tucked his prize under his arm, put the ski mask back on his face, and retraced his steps down the hall to the lobby and back down the service corridor. The janitor's room had every sort of cleaning supply. He rustled through the shelves and found a cloth bag that he thought would work. Carefully, he placed the object in the woven bag and slipped out the same door he'd used to enter.

The warm breeze welcomed him back to freedom. He took care to retrace his steps in the darkness, avoiding the amber lights that would betray him to the cameras. The bag in his hand felt suddenly heavier as doubts crept in. But he had crawled too deep in the tunnel to turn back now. The rain began, and forward was his only option.

A stone statue stood at his right. Emblazoned by lights in the night, he saw the New Revelation in its splendor. The blasphemy etched in stone glared down at him, as though judging him.

> *The homosexuals are blessed among God's children. Those who desire to enter the Kingdom of God must seek their companionship and atone.*

Rick passed through the lobby. The guard chuckled at his small television and gave no acknowledgment of Rick's return. Relieved, Rick took a deep breath as he turned the corner and headed back to his room. He was surprised to see light coming from under his door.

Jimmy darted up from his desk. "How'd it go?"

"I thought you'd be asleep," Rick remarked, softly closing the door behind him.

"Are you kidding? How could I? What's that?"

Rick gently laid the bag on the desk and slipped the artifact out.

"Jesus, Rick," Jimmy sighed as he moved the object around in its cover.

"If this is what I think it is, we may have a bigger problem on our hands," Rick said cautiously.

Rick carefully opened the bag and slid out the ancient document once again. Gently, he unrolled the scroll after removing the plastic once again. The paper felt more like animal skin than parchment. He wasn't sure. Weathered and yellow, faint purple ink took the shape of letters. Rick's stomach was bludgeoned with a jackhammer of throbbing pain.

Jimmy's fingers lightly glided over the text, as if in a caress. "What is it? Aramaic? Hebrew?"

"Greek," Rick corrected, his eyes reverent.

"The New Revelation? Why is it here? What the hell, Rick?" Jimmy said, panicking.

"Calm down. It's okay. I was there. In the room," Rick said, his voice shakily letting the words out. "Missy came in. I hid in a closet. She had some grotesque creature there with her."

"Creature?"

"No, it was a person. Dressed in leather, but like a dog. I think it was her slave. Called her his mistress. She was telling him someone would come for this. I don't know why."

"That's what the letter said—the letter from Rome," Jimmy recalled.

"He'll arrive for it this week."

"We need to get this back in her office," Jimmy said, shaking Rick's arm as if to wake him from a nightmare.

"I'm not about to go back in there!" Rick said, withdrawing his arm.

"Don't you think they'll notice that the most important document in the world right now is missing?"

Rick rubbed his temples and squinted in concentration. "We need to talk to Father Henry. He might be able to read it, I don't know."

"We can't keep it here," Jimmy said. "It's not easy to hide, and some pool boy is bound to find the damn thing when they come in to clean the room tomorrow!"

"You're right, you're right," Rick said. "I don't know what I was thinking! I should have just left it there. Let it rot for all I should care. We didn't sign up for this."

Jimmy looked stricken. "You're not going to destroy it, are you?"

"No, dammit. I don't know what we're going to do with it. But someone needs this—someone who knows my family. I trust that stranger more than Missy. It certainly doesn't belong to her."

"We can hide it."

"Hide it?"

"Well it can't stay here!" Jimmy said, raising his voice.

Rick thought for a moment. "The closet. Down the hall. With the cleaning supplies."

"You're going to put a priceless artifact behind a

stack of paper towels and hand soap?" Jimmy asked, incredulous.

"You have a better idea?"

Jimmy sat down on Rick's bed and collapsed on his back in frustration. Rick hoped Jimmy's scent would linger on his sheets. He resisted the urge to join him there.

"I guess not," Jimmy said, resigned.

Rick carefully slid the parchment back in the plastic sheath and then placed it back in the stolen tote bag. His adrenaline was tempered by creeping exhaustion. The prospect of handling a document that could have been transcribed by a biblical author bestowed a reverence for the artifact that competed with his revulsion, like holding an infant with a dirty diaper.

After consulting with Jimmy's napkin maps, they reassured themselves that no cameras would spot them as they went half the length down the hall to the janitor's closet. Rick tucked the bagged artifact onto the bottom shelf, behind a wall of toilet paper and economy-sized jugs of floor cleaner. Judging by the inventory, absent undercooked chicken in the dining hall or an Ebola outbreak, Rick felt confident it would rest in the tomb undiscovered for perhaps another two thousand years.

"I need a drink," Rick confessed when they got back to their room, his burden lifted.

"Do you think she has other slaves? Do you think

he was one of the guests who got brainwashed?" Jimmy asked as he raided the mini fridge for two small bottles of riesling.

"Could be. It could be anything," Rick pondered. "I couldn't even see his face. He had a mask on. He even had to ask her if he could eat. I think she fed him from a dog bowl. He seemed almost happy for the privilege. They did something terrible to his mind."

"Happy?"

"Yeah," Rick said, pausing to chug from the wine bottle. "I can't imagine what they must have done to him. The worse she treated him, the more grateful he seemed to be."

"Maybe he's the one that's been sending you notes. If they made me eat out of a dog bowl, I bet I'd be plotting my escape."

Rick sat down next to Jimmy on his bed. "This place is sick with an evil I've never seen." The blankets were ruffled from service as a makeshift couch.

Jimmy put his arm around Rick's waist and leaned into a side embrace. Rick's lust and exhaustion were too great to hold up the wall he built from bricks of denial painstakingly stacked over the years. Rick escalated the invitation and leaned in to have his lips meet Jimmy's.

Jimmy lay back on the bed and brought Rick with

him. Rick was no longer the teenager in the church basement, but he was just as nervous. *Will they know?*

"You and I are cut from the same cloth, Rick. Two guys held back by the same chains. My parents. Your mother. The lies we tell. Until now."

"Until now," Rick gently whispered in his ear as he settled the weight of his body on him.

Rick's hand explored under Jimmy's shirt. The terrain of his muscles started with stubbly hair on his abs, like saplings covering a new forest. It was no doubt recently shaven. This gave an answer as to why the shower drain in their bathroom looked like someone murdered a teddy bear every few days. His hand's journey made its way to his chest. He felt Jimmy's heartbeat as he caressed his soft nipple with the tip of his fingers.

Jimmy answered by lifting Rick's shirt off. He tossed it to the side, and Rick fumbled to take off his belt. By the time Rick had slid his pants off, Jimmy was already there. With only underwear separating them from a final consummation, Jimmy moved his lips and tongue to Rick's neck, their cocks pressing against one another in defiance of the thin fabric that kept them apart. Rick's moan ratified the act. This storm of passion tormented the seas of their lust. Waves crashed harder against the rocks on the shore than ever before. Stone on the shore was not merely etched by the water, but entire boulders fell, crashing into the ocean. Encouraged, Jimmy's mouth continued its journey over Rick's chest. His abs. Then, they met their last obstacle.

Paralyzed by pleasure, Rick offered no resistance. Yet he gave no invitation either. If Jimmy were to cross that last threshold, it would be his choice. Even as the ground seemed to rumble with the sound of Rick's wall collapsing, he knew that this final encroachment would be an act he was powerless to excuse as anything other than what it was.

15

"Lovelies, please take your seats. Yes, take them around the bar. Wherever you find them. There are a few in the corner at the high-top tables, by the stage," Marilyn instructed as the class filed into the room.

This was Rick's first time in the room. A strong smell of cleaning bleach lingered in the air, invoking the unmistakable feel of a dive bar. Rainbow flags and glossy photos advertising drag shows covered the walls. A worn wooden stage stood against the wall, a dark curtain framing its back. Scrapes and chips scarred the wood, no doubt the casualty of high-heeled shoes and countless spilled drinks. The lights were dim, but bottles behind the bar were illuminated with backlighting to make them glow like an oasis for thirsty patrons.

Marilyn ran her hand over a wooden piano near the stage with reverent approval.

"This is an exact recreation of Long John's. It was a gay bar that had its prime in nineteen eighty-five, but the bar closed more than a decade ago. Missy bought everything inside—from the posters on the wall to the toilets in the bathroom. We call it the gay-bar simulator. Honestly, it's more of a museum if you ask me."

Pool boys stood behind the bar, this occasion warranting them to wear shirts and jeans, apparently. Their white-washed denim and pastel pink and blue polo shirts certainly kept with the period of the time, Rick thought. Jimmy and Bob joined him at one of the high-top tables stage left.

"We're here for today's seminar, *Navigating Gay Spaces*. For many of you, this is probably the first time you've been to a gay bar. So, welcome. Some of you may be more familiar with them than you let on, but it's okay. It can be our secret," she said, winking.

The bartender walked a cocktail over to her before she climbed onto the stage. "Let me set the mood. What do you think of when I say nineteen eighty-five? The Reagan administration. The Cold War. You were probably at the theater seeing *Back to the Future* and playing games on Nintendo if you were young enough. But for the rest of us, we were in a parallel world. A world of fear and uncertainty. It was only that year that a test was developed to screen for H.I.V., but by that time, the virus had claimed thousands of lives and would claim millions more. No one knew who would be next. And that was all just the beginning."

Her words were met with sobering silence, only

interrupted by music playing softly in the background from a jukebox by the bathroom. Rick sighed and braced himself for another in the almost daily series of lectures on the plight of gays during the A.I.D.S. epidemic.

"People would die. Friends would die. They'd get sick. You'd visit them in the hospital and try to smile, never knowing exactly what to say. Sometimes they didn't even have family—well, not family that would talk to them or acknowledge them. Preachers on television would tell us we deserved it. Our suffering was God's plight. The forgiving, loving God somehow singled out gay people with this plague. God must have only had a mild distaste for abortion, adultery, pornography, murder, and everything else by comparison, I guess."

Rick rolled his eyes. He looked for Father Henry. He would take solace in the priest's stoic expression of unspoken judgment. But he wasn't there. He hadn't been at breakfast either. This wasn't uncommon. Father Henry would often forego his first meal—whether it was a hunger strike or merely a desire to make more time for prayer, Rick wasn't sure.

"Despite it all," Marilyn said, "it was the absolute best time to *ever* be gay."

Rick raised an eyebrow and exchanged surprised expressions with Bob and Jimmy. How her nostalgia for warm beer and dank bathrooms could overcome the tragedy she was recounting was lost on Rick.

"You see," she went on, "our oppression made us a community. Our ostracism made this a sacred, safe place. This was our church. Things are different now. Gay bars are far fewer in number. But we still have enough of them. Just understand the history before you ever step inside one. Respect this sacred ground—consecrated with the blood of our dead. That's what we're here to discuss today."

Rick leaned over the table. "Bob, have you seen Father Henry today?"

"No. Wasn't he at breakfast?"

"He wasn't. He's usually here. Jimmy and I need to talk to both of you after class. About last night."

Bob smiled. "I know. I tried to find you both this morning. I can't wait. Success?"

"More than you can imagine," Jimmy said with a smile, looking at Rick. Rick blushed but hoped to conceal his cards in the shadows, ever his ally.

"First things first," Marilyn said, pausing only briefly to take a sip of her drink. "We come here to get laid. If you end up coming here, fine. Maybe you got lost. Maybe you're with some drunk girls and they dragged you here. I don't know. Don't really care either. Bu, if a guy is so impaired in judgment as to try and flirt with you, don't be offended. If we're drunk enough, God knows who we'd try to flirt with. Hell, I remember going home with a six-foot-four polo player and woke up with five-foot-four guy who probably didn't even have a gym membership. I was so fucked up that night. Anyway, this is the one place where we're normal—where we can expect to have a shot at a guy. So don't get all indignant. You're the foreigner here, not us."

Someone raised his hand. "I was at a gay bar once in college. I was with some girls, like you said. I went to the bathroom. I was standing in line and some guy came up to me. He told me I was cute. Kissed my cheek and grabbed my ass."

Marilyn put her hands on her hips. "Your point? Honey, my ass is like a pincushion at this point. Just be glad you could still feel it."

Rick chuckled.

"Honestly though," she went on, "your first mistake was being alone. If you're straight, you should never, never be alone if you don't want shit like that to happen. Come with a gay guy. He can explain the situation. Better yet, you can be his wingman. Just because you don't wanna get laid doesn't mean he doesn't. Am I right, Trevor?"

The pool boy behind the bar looked back with a sheepish expression, perhaps more interested in keeping up with his drink orders than participating. It looked like he was pouring shots for everyone. Rick's stomach responded with equal trepidation.

"Want to know a secret incantation to say to make gays go away at a bar?" she asked. "Repeat after me: *I'm flattered, but I'm straight.*"

Murmured voices repeated the magic phrase.

"It's that simple," she said, raising her arms in surrender. "Which takes me to my next point: consent is sexy. No one should ever touch you when you don't want it. I know. But it happens. That said, if there's a drag show and you want to tip the drag queen, that's all it is. Don't grab her breasts. Don't touch her butt. Seriously, we'll kick your ass if you do. And… *do* tip us. Especially if you want to sit close to the bar like Pastor Rick and his cohorts over there," she said, hoisting her drink their way.

"Speaking of drag shows, here's a tip," she continued. "If the poster says the doors open at eight and the show starts at nine, just understand I'm probably still sleeping till like nine twenty. Then I have to go to the venue. At that point, I'll be in this latex body suit, but I won't have a wig on and my makeup will be a work in progress. I spend hundreds of dollars, and most nights, a drag queen doesn't have a chance to break even. So tip me, bitches. Anyway, you'd be lucky if the show starts at ten, so don't be impatient. Just drink more."

Looking up from his notes, the same guy raised his hand. "How much do we tip?"

"Depends on the city. Cheap-ass motherfuckers in most cities tip a dollar, but if you're in D.C., I know you have money and it best be at least five."

The guy nodded sympathetically. Rick gave passing consideration to what cash he had in his wallet—a thought interrupted by the shots delivered to the table. On his first day, he may have considered just what he was drinking. But by now, he only took fleeting notice of whether the poison was brown or clear. Today, it was brown. Grudgingly, he offered a half-hearted cheers to the table and downed it. Without a chaser, the burn lingered, but the sting revived him.

"Today's your lucky day. It's not in my contract to perform, but I figured it wouldn't be right if I didn't. So I invited Eileen to join me in a number we did back in Chelsea. Come on up, girlfriend!"

Eileen joined her on stage, and Trevor, with his head sunk low, dawdled over to the soundboard and cued up a song. Colored lights illuminated the stage, and the drag queens started to mouth the words for their routine.

Rick took the opportunity to lean in and catch Bob up on the artifact. His eyes widened with apprehension as Rick walked him through the heist, his encounter with the dog man, and Missy's covert plans.

Bob's eyes nearly popped out of his head. "You hid it behind toilet paper?"

"What the hell would you have done?" Rick asked.

Bob looked fleetingly at the bar as if to escape, then leaned in again. "Do you think Father Henry even knows how to read ancient Greek?"

Rick started to grind his teeth. "I don't know, but he's all we've got."

Looking up, Rick was momentarily captivated by the performance. Dramatically, Eileen took off her wig to reveal a second wig beneath. This one was long and purple. She tossed the long hair around with the momentum of her head rolling in time with the music. Marilyn left the stage and sashayed around the audience, collecting reluctant donations from the crowd, like a second collection plate passed around church after a sermon that droned on too long. Jimmy gave her five dollars without hesitation. She accepted the offering and left them alone.

"Even if he can read Greek, what are you going to do with it?" Bob asked.

Jimmy leaned in.

"We'll just keep it hidden until the person who sent the note asks for it," Rick said.

"I'm shocked they don't have the place on lockdown already. They must have noticed the thing was missing," Bob offered.

"The letter from the Vatican told her it'd be arriving. Surely they must have approved it," Jimmy reasoned.

"The dog person was saying that it needed to be treated somehow and then sent with some false shipping label somewhere to obscure that it was ever here," Rick said.

"That may explain it," Bob said. "Anyone who's trying to get away with something probably doesn't want too many people to know. If she called the police, she'd be admitting she had something she wasn't supposed to have. That might be our insurance policy."

Jimmy's expression darkened. "Unless she finds out who took it."

"They won't," Rick said, lightly touching Jimmy's shoulder. "I was careful. Avoided cameras. Wore a mask, just in case we missed one."

Their number ended with Marilyn landing in a split. A smattering of polite applause was offered in return. Marilyn got on her knees and frantically picked up the dollars scattered around the floor. Rick thought it strange that she even cared. With her unjustly high salary, why would she need to scavenge for the price of a latte? Old habit, perhaps. He wondered how much she earned, nonetheless. It reminded him of his burning desire to count the collections every Sunday as a measure of how well he gave his sermon. Perhaps he finally found something in common with her, he thought.

After another lecture on the proper way to wait for a drink at the bar and tipping etiquette for drinks, Marilyn brought out a dry-erase board and charted out the history of famous drag queens and their respective styles. By the end of her lecture, Rick was reasonably confident he could discern "camp" from "pageant" drag. Of the two, he quietly acknowledged his appreciation for the latter. Their shoes and glamour were more appealing to him.

They ended the presentation on the topic of recreational drugs, which had all been legalized by the new administration. Marilyn saw fit to hand out fliers on pharmacology, adverse effects, and dangerous combinations. She'd threatened to give a quiz on drug slang, so Rick took extra care to memorize as much as he could.

As the lecture ended, Marilyn invited them all to stay for the rest of the hour and have drinks before lunch. Rick paced himself. He needed to prepare for afternoon cocktails.

"Boys, come join the dance party—you all look so sullen by the bar," Marilyn said.

"I don't dance. Never have," Rick said.

"Never? Come baby," she said, pulling his arm.

Rick jerked his arm back. "I don't dance."

Marilyn studied him and frowned. "Suit yourself, but you might try it sometime. It's fun!"

Marilyn retreated to the crowd, and the loud music made cover for their conversation to continue.

Rick grabbed Jimmy's shoulder and leaned toward his ear. "We should talk about last night."

"Why?" Jimmy shrugged. "No big deal."

"No big deal? Jimmy, it was the biggest deal."

Jimmy rolled his eyes. "Don't freak out about it. It was fun. Let's just let it be what it was, right?"

Rick tried to compose himself. Perhaps there was a time and a place, but he decided this was neither. The tender innocence of the night before was matched by jarring indifference with the new day. Perhaps, it was just his way of dealing with it. *The young man with a nearly empty duffle bag is probably not one who likes to carry a lot of baggage,* he reasoned.

Rick seized the opportunity for a question as Marilyn walked by. "Father Henry wasn't at breakfast or in class today. Do you know if he's all right?"

Her smile faded. "Father Henry left this morning."

Jimmy put down his drink. "Left?"

"I think his church summoned him back to wherever he came from. Something about needing him back at the mission…"

The unsettled torment from Rick's gut reached his face. "He wouldn't just leave without saying goodbye. That doesn't make any sense."

She held up her hands as if in surrender. "Baby, that's all I was told."

"By whom?" Bob asked.

"Missy. She mentioned it at the team meeting this morning. I'll let you know if I hear anything else though. Meanwhile, you all should explore the bar a bit. Mingle! You three really should dance—make some new friends!"

She slipped over to join Eileen at the bar, and Rick's face went white.

"Good lord," Rick said. "Last night, I remember Missy said there was a problem with the priest, and the dog man said he'd handle it."

"You think they did something to him?" Bob asked.

Jimmy swirled what was left of his drink around his glass. "It's not like Father Henry. He may have left, but it doesn't make sense that he'd leave first thing in the morning. The man doesn't do anything quickly."

"His roommate might know something. Maybe he left something behind in his room, like a note or something," Rick said.

The three of them elected to be late for lunch in favor of investigating. When they arrived at Father Henry's door, they found it wedged open with a broom handle. A yellow bucket on wheels with a mop rested just outside. His room smelled of floor cleaner that hadn't quite dried. Bob gently pushed the door open. The room was vacant. Both bunk beds had been stripped of sheets. They filed in.

"His roommate is gone as well?" Jimmy asked.

"They certainly didn't wait long to clean it out. They took everything." Rick walked around the room, hoping it would offer answers.

"Not everything," Bob said, lifting the mattress on the bottom bunk. Jimmy and Rick walked over to look. Hidden between the mattress and the slats on the bed was Father Henry's open Bible.

Rick knelt down and picked up the well-read, leather-bound book, scrutinizing the pages.

Jimmy leaned in for closer inspection. "What was he reading?"

"The Book of Jonah," Rick said, skimming the pages.

"Just like the note?" Bob asked.

Rick nodded, flipping the pages to search for any other messages.

They jumped when the door opened. An alarmed janitor stood in the doorway.

"Oh, sorry," Bob said. "We were just looking for our friend, Father Henry, and his roommate. Do you know where they might have gone?"

"Sorry, sir. I was just told he left this morning," the janitor said. "But he didn't have a roommate. Not anymore, anyway. He did for the first few days, but the guy wanted his own room. Evidently, Father Henry kept him up praying all night."

"Did anyone say why he left?" Rick pressed.

The janitor shrugged. "No one tells me anything. I just clean the floors. Sorry."

Rick sighed. "We should head to lunch before any-one notices we're gone."

The others nodded their agreement. They made their somber procession down the corridor.

"I'm going to head back to my room. I need to check on… something," Rick said.

"Good idea," Bob said, knowingly. "We'll save a seat for you."

Rick's thoughts were racing. Clearly, Father Henry was trying to leave them a message. It seemed unlikely that Father Henry would have abandoned their search, especially without leaving a note. *Maybe he couldn't*, Rick thought. Perhaps he did the only thing circumstances would permit.

Rick turned the corner, and his heart nearly stopped. Missy was leaned up against the wall by his door. Her high-heeled red shoe rested against the wall to hold her weight. Her blood-red dress matched the expression on her face, her hair tangled in tightly twisted curls.

"Nice to see you, Pastor," she said, her voice even. "I think you have something that belongs to me."

16

The Vatican, Rome

F ather Simon Slump hustled past the morning crowds of tourists in St. Peter's Square. He started every day as early as he could, partly to avoid the tourists, not to mention the blistering summer heat. Today, his pace was especially brisk as he walked past the Swiss Guard. The majesty of St. Peter's Basilica was lost on him long ago. Cardinal Rodriguez was one man he wouldn't keep waiting.

Not surprisingly, he found the cardinal impatient, once escorted to his office. Cardinal Rodriguez was pacing back and forth, hands clasped behind his back. So recently appointed by the Holy Father, he was dressed in his full vestments. The pontificalia was no doubt intended to impress Father Slump as much as it was a commitment to the office.

"Good to see you, Simon," he said without sincerity. "I trust the artifact arrived, no?"

Father Slump cleared his throat. "It will. It's still

in transit. By the end of the week, it will be at the university."

"Two weeks to arrive?"

Father Slump commenced his rehearsed speech with measured disdain. "As you can certainly understand, extreme care was taken to transport the artifact from Rome to the United States. Next-day shipment isn't exactly feasible."

"I spoke to the Holy Father last night over dinner. The scroll was carbon dated when it was first discovered. Obviously, the parchment was as old as we suspected. I still don't understand why further testing was warranted."

"We spoke of this last year," Father Slump reminded him. "The parchment was tested, but the ink never was. A careful forgery could have applied ink to an ancient medium."

"Yes, I know, but that's not what I mean," the cardinal said, settling himself into a chair behind a desk that was more ornate than even the Holy Father's. "This isn't a time for doubt. You should understand this is bigger than any of us. Five years ago, you were a parish priest. Sex scandals, rising atheism, and dwindling parish attendance took such a toll on our faith in the West. Not to mention the internal corruption. Our worldwide mission was nearly bankrupt."

Father Slump clenched his jaw and assumed the invitation to sit on a chair across the desk. Father Slump committed the unspoken sin. The cardinal's expression confirmed the priest's assumption that the privilege was not extended to him.

"But look at how much has changed in just these few years," Cardinal Rodriguez argued, leaning forward. "The Holy Father and the College of Cardinals met and sanctioned the reinstatement of the sacrament of marriage for priests and bishops. Women are permitted to join the priesthood for the first time in our history. Now, record numbers of candidates are seeking the sacrament of holy orders. With the New Revelation, our faith is enriched. We can reach out to homosexuals around the world and welcome them to our faith in ways we never have before. The Holy Father's acknowledgment of his own sexuality was an unexpected gift for all of us. People aren't just coming back to the faith; scores of new Catholics are seeking the sacraments of baptism and confirmation."

Father Slump realized he was clenching his teeth so hard his jaw hurt. He relaxed and leaned back in the chair. These were not new arguments for him.

"I know this assignment is hard for you, Simon," the cardinal said, his voice softening. "But change was needed. Surely you wouldn't want Saint Peter's work to end under the weight of countless lawsuits and our own hypocrisy. Inevitably, the fruit of the last two thousand years would rot in the misery of our own sinful pride and hypocrisy. You're a pragmatic man. You must understand this."

"My agreement with this mission is subservient to my obligation of obedience, Cardinal Rodriguez."

"But you see, if this second round of tests are at all inconclusive or worse, what would happen next?"

Father Slump was tired of having the same conversation. As if he were reciting lines from a memorized script, he offered the position the cardinal always found most persuasive. "If we didn't consent to the independent testing, wouldn't the world think we have something to hide? Would that not bring the same doubt you fear in having it tested?"

Cardinal Rodriguez sighed. "Yes, I know. Fortunately for you, the Holy Father agrees with you. But that's why I have an insurance policy."

Father Slump swallowed and clenched his jaw again. A wicked grin revealed waves of wrinkles webbing the cardinal's face—a gruesome reminder of what lay hidden just beneath his otherwise stolid expression.

"This professor," the cardinal continued, "is far from unbiased. I met him years ago when he made the discovery. Naturally, we wanted to know more about the source and the messenger. We have a dossier on him." He produced a manila folder from a drawer and dropped it on his desk.

The priest eyed the stack of papers in front of him with revulsion.

"Pack your bags, Simon. I need you in D.C. Review the file, and then make it personally known to the professor that if his results show anything other than an unqualified affirmation of the document's authenticity, we will ruin his career."

"Blackmail?" the priest whispered, his words barely escaping the net in his throat.

"Insurance," the cardinal corrected. "He's an atheist, Simon. He's also having an affair. We have photos. Text messages. Much more. I'm sure he can be convinced that there's too much at stake, and we won't jeopardize our entire faith on his work."

Incensed, the priest stood up. "You can't expect me to do this. I'm a priest, not a mob boss!"

"You wish this cup would pass from you. I know. But as you said, your obedience must take precedence over your own will. This is too sensitive a matter to involve anyone else. Plus," he added, "there's another reason I need you there."

"What other reason?" Father Slump asked.

Cardinal Rodriguez leaned in. "This church has

many enemies. There's a society of homosexuals that has always taken positions contrary to our faith. Make no mistake, they will find any opportunity to thwart our plans—even if it's against their self-interests."

"What?" Father Slump asked, feigning his ignorance as best he could.

"They may have influence over this professor. You may encounter them. You must protect our mission."

Father Slump considered his position for a moment that felt like a lifetime. "Of course, Cardinal Rodriguez. I can leave tomorrow morning. I will be there before the document arrives."

The priest collected the documents the cardinal slid across his desk. The pages burned his hands as though with an unforgivable sin. His numb legs gave reluctant support to his weight as he stood up. Taking the file, he left the cardinal to attend to his busy schedule.

He strode through the maze of corridors and offices, heading back to his own. Ignoring his hunger and lamenting not having coffee or anything stronger, he made a detour. Father Ryan Kelly's office was as inconspicuous as the man who occupied it. A single office around a corner, with its name plate missing.

"Good morning, Simon," the priest said, inviting him to sit down. "Did you speak with Cardinal Rodriguez?"

"I did. We have a problem."

Father Kelly's smile faded as he closed the door. Muffled sounds of tourists gathering outside the building mixed in a chorus with distant sirens beyond the Vatican walls. The faint sounds were the only reminder of a world outside of the one they concocted for themselves.

"Our plan is in jeopardy. The cardinal gave me this," Father Slump said, holding a stack of documents in front of him. "It's dirt on the professor who's conducting the testing at the university in the United States. I'm to fly to D.C. immediately and coerce the man to deliver authenticating results, regardless of his testing."

Father Kelly rubbed his temples. "So, even if the Luminaries succeed in orchestrating this, the effort would be in vain?"

"I guess it depends on how persuasive I am," Father Slump said with a half-smile.

"You will share this development with the Luminaries? Who has the document now?"

Father Slump's forehead creased in consternation. "It's just outside D.C. The owner of one of the atonement camps has it now. She's not a Luminary, but she seeks to join their council. She calls herself Missy Bottom. She's rising in their ranks, and she volunteered for this role."

Father Kelly's expression turned to disgust. "How vile."

"I know. As I'm often reminded, they simply have resources we lack. They share our goals. Their representative will collect the document tomorrow. I spoke to Missy's representative just an hour ago. Everything is in place. They need not know of this development. It's critical that we stick with our plan," Father Slump said, letting his fist fall to the table.

Father Kelly rubbed his chin.

"It also came to my attention that the Cardinal may suspect their influence," Father Slump said. "I will need to personally oversee this."

Father Kelly pulled the drapes open to reveal the distant square. The light from the window made Father Slump squint. "Some days, I fear we're too late. Look at the crowds outside. They're here because of it. They're here because this church supplicated itself to the changing winds of society. Will they even turn back?"

"Have faith, Ryan. Our faith was built on a rock that does not change despite the passing times. It withstood the Dark Ages, the Inquisition, all of these petty sex scandals. Still it stands. No wind can topple it. No ocean can break it, no matter how relentless the waves. It's that rock that supports the foundation of our faith. Come what may. Let them leave. Did God not promise to spare Sodom even if only ten faithful could be found?"

"We'll certainly need more than ten of them to keep the lights on, Simon. But, your point is well taken."

17

"**C**ome in, won't you, dear?" Missy said, beckoning Rick into his room. Alarmed, Rick saw his suitcase open, his clothes indiscriminately strewn across the floor. Drawers were half open, and his and Jimmy's mattress were propped against the wall. Jimmy's duffle bag was turned inside out. His tank tops and jeans twinned with Rick's clothes on the floor, becoming one as their bodies had the night before. A few ceiling tiles had been slid aside to reveal anything that may rest above.

"Yes, Rick. We searched thoroughly this morning. Then, again. Where is it?"

Indignant, Rick said nothing. Instead, he surveyed the room and lamented how long it had taken him to carefully fold all the clothes.

"Our search wasn't completely wasted," Missy said, holding out a folded paper. "We did find a certain letter that was supposed to be delivered to me. How, exactly, did you come into possession of it?"

"I don't know what you're talking about," Rick spat, subtly patting his pocket to confirm the letters from the captive were still tucked inside.

"Don't fuck with me," she said, towering over him with the unnatural height bestowed upon her from her high-heeled shoes. "Did you think we'd not notice if it went missing? Did you think our very first step would be anything other than the security cameras?"

"What makes you think it was me?"

"You wore a mask. I'll give you credit for that. But you forgot your shoes. You're the only one at this camp who wears those same mud-colored loafers every day. They're just as offensive as the black belt you insist on pairing them with. Clearly, you were too busy plotting your heist to pay attention in the men's fashion seminar on your second day. We're gay. Did you honestly think we wouldn't notice?"

Rick was crestfallen. He had actually enjoyed that class. Then, a sick, souring cauldron of fear began to brew in his stomach. Fear gave way to fleeting confidence when he found the words to speak. "Why should I help you?"

Missy pounded her fist against the wall, the thud reverberating through the room, reminding Rick that her femininity was an illusion. "Who are you with? The Vatican? Did they send you here to steal it? To infiltrate this camp? If you don't tell me everything you know, I promise to end you! I will make your life an experience worse than the Hell you preach against!"

"I don't think you will," Rick said, surprising himself with his defiance. "You're not supposed to have it either. Who are you going to tell?"

Missy glared at him. Her eyes bore into his skull as though a proxy for her crimson nails. Then, she smiled, which gave way to a maddened chuckle. Rick watched her horrifying transfiguration in bewilderment. Instinctively, he took a few steps back.

"Pastor Harris, I owe you an apology. We're not so different after all—you and me."

"What do you mean?"

Her expression softened. "We want the same thing. At least you appear to. There's no one at this camp who probably hates the New Revelation more than you, no? You've hated every minute here. You'd like nothing more than to have this whole thing go away as if it never happened. Go back to the forgotten country town you came from and preach on about how much you hate us, no?"

If Rick didn't want that before, the idea was growing on him that morning. He glared at her in silence.

Missy leaned in and whispered, her breath hot against his cheek. "Well, I want the same thing, my dear."

"What?" Rick asked.

"Don't play so dumb, pastor. I admit, you do it well. But, the emissary will be here tomorrow, and I *need* to deliver that artifact! As I suspect you damn well know, I'm a Luminary. Or, I will be. They're counting on me to do this. When we succeed, the New Revelation will be deemed a fraud. This whole world will come crashing down, and you can help me make that happen!"

Rick's knees went soft. "How?"

"We've arranged to have new ink discretely applied to the first letter on the scroll—the one part of the artifact the Catholic Church sanctioned for radiocarbon date testing this week. When they do, the world will believe it to be a fraud. It doesn't matter if you know. No one will believe you. In fact, I suspect you already do. The Vatican warned that there were rumors this camp could be infiltrated."

"Why would you do that? What would happen to you? This place?"

Missy studied him. "You really have no idea, do you? The Luminaries are the governing council of gays around the world. They act in secret, but in plain sight. You think it's an accident when some pop star is plucked from obscurity and rises to fame and fortune? Of course not! It never was. Everything you watch on TV, listen to on the radio, or even wear on your ever-so homely body is because the *council* willed it!"

"Bullshit."

"Oh no. Don't play me. We've done this for

generations. Phase One took decades. Why do you think gay men take jobs as florists, baristas, stylists, and fashion designers? It's no accident. We sought to ingratiate ourselves with straight, white women to leverage their institutional power and earn civil rights. Tolerance. Marriage. We were doing just fine. Incrementalism. Then, this damned New Revelation!"

Rick's gaze settled on her enraged face, twisted in gnarled revulsion as she paced the room. "Ever since the New Revelation, people have gone from hating us to tolerating us, and now they practically worship us! They elect us to public office. They raise their kids with the slim hope they'll grow up to be one of us. Our gay bars have gone from a place of sanctuary to a damn tourist attraction. They think their salvation hinges on our approval. The walls that divided us gave us culture. Now, we're becoming homogenized. Plain. Normal. Worse, boring!"

"What about this place?" Rick asked. "If people don't believe in the New Revelation, I doubt they'd be tripping over themselves to send people here. You'd be bankrupt. Out of business."

"Honey, I've made enough off this place to retire several times over. The pool boys will eventually sober up and go on with their lives. I'll give the queens that work here something even better than a paycheck—I'll give them their *heritage* back."

"What makes you think they'd even want it? Isn't this better?" Rick asked.

"A friend of mine was in Philadelphia's last truly gay bar the other week. It's a leather bar, naturally. Sure, you may see rainbow flags outside most gay bars still, but they're just husks of what they used to be. Inside, you'll find more straight people than gay ones. Management caters to the new straight majority more than the gay minority these days. It's all about the money. They're infested with gangs of white women stumbling around in veils, celebrating their bachelorette parties and using us as their props—trying to make their eyes focus and walk straight as they suddenly realize two vodka clubs is the rough equivalent of eleven of the wine spritzers they sip every Wednesday after work. A guy came up to my friend. They hit it off, until he said he was straight. He just wanted to try out what it's like to be gay. Being gay isn't a choice. It's not some free trial period at a gym. It's an identity. They will thank us."

Exhausted, Rick slumped into a chair. His mind was a bee's nest. If he got too close to grasping what he wanted, he was in danger of being stung.

"Just tell me where it is, and I'll forget all about this. By the time you're released, this will all be done. You can go home. Back to whatever backwoods, ignorant congregation you must lead. They'd see you as a hero. Someone who went into the belly of the beast and came back to tell the tale."

"Like Jonah and the whale," Rick muttered in an almost silent exhale.

"What's it going to be, baby?"

Rick sighed. "It's in the closet. Down the hall," he said with resignation.

"Naturally, that'd be the first place you'd go if you needed to hide something. I should have figured," she said with a bemused smile. "Show me."

Rick stood and escorted his captor to the very room he'd hoped she wouldn't find. The light in the janitor's closet seemed dimmer than before, the smell of the solvents more pungent. Still, it did little to mask the molded, stale air of a room neglected. Perhaps it gave shelter to its secret too long, and the corroded parchment had created the stench. The room was a mirror. In it, Rick was reluctantly forced to see his own reflection.

"There. Behind the toilet paper. Second shelf," he confessed.

"You put the most valuable historical document in two thousand years behind toilet paper!" she shrieked. "It's poetic, I'll give you that."

Abandoning her dignified stature, she knelt down

on the shoe-scuffed floor and swiped dozens of rolls aside with her arm. They flew like shrapnel across the small room, rolling across the floor.

The shelf was empty.

Rick's eyes widened. He knelt beside her and shoved even more rolls aside. Nothing. His mind raced as he moved to the third shelf and hastily shoved his arm behind bottles of floor cleaner. They fell harmlessly on the floor, bouncing and rolling to rest. Still nothing. The stone was moved away, and the body was missing from the tomb.

"Where is it, Pastor? Where the *hell* is it?"

"I don't know, I don't know," he pleaded, still frantically searching for the object he'd hidden just the night before.

Missy at last stood up. She patted her dress down to smooth out the wrinkles. "As I said, you're not as dumb as you seem. I'm not sure who sent you. You may be acting alone. More likely, you're being used by one of your friends. We've detained Jimmy, Bob, and Father Henry. We'll get to the bottom of this. You'll need to come with me."

"Father Henry? I thought he left?"

"He did no such thing. He merely outed himself yesterday. The camp is divided into two. Those who have come out as gay and those who haven't," she said.

"We move them accordingly. Your groups don't mix. Those who come out need special care. They have their own classes."

Missy motioned to the door. Rick saw a security guard and two of the pool boys who looked like they actually spent time in the gym doing more than taking flattering selfies.

The guard stepped closer. "I need you to come with me." Missy grabbed his arms and fastened fluffy pink handcuffs tightly around his wrists.

"What the hell?" Rick asked, taking note of how tight the cuffs gripped his wrists, despite their comical effect.

"Initiate lockdown for transport," Missy directed.

The guard muttered something in his radio. Seconds later, Rick heard the same two-tone xylophone chime he recalled from his first day, followed by an automated announcement. "Ladies and gentleman, access to the east residence is temporarily restricted. All program doors are now locking."

The lights in the hall changed from white to a warm amber, guiding their way down the hall and out into the courtyard. They walked hurriedly. The guard muttered more commands into his radio as they burst through the doors to the adjacent building. Missy walked at the formation's head, leading the squad down a hall that was new to Rick. The walls were now the cold cinder block he had discovered before. They reminded him of a hospital, or a prison.

"We use this room for our advanced class, *Finding Your Fetish*. Seems appropriate. You'll be kept here until the emissary collects the deliverable. If you want out, you'll tell us where to find what we want," she said before grabbing the guard's radio and walking into the unseen distance.

Rick's fuzzy handcuffs were taken off by the guard, and he was pushed into the room. The door locked behind him.

"Rick!" Jimmy said, running to embrace him. Rick met Jimmy in his arms and held him tightly. He felt safe in his embrace, his arms engulfing his heart as much as his body. He grabbed Jimmy's cheeks and pulled him in to meet his lips with his own. Instinct and passion guided him. Acting with abandon, Rick no longer cared if Bob, Father Henry, or God himself saw. For the first time, Rick knew. *He knew.* He finally, finally knew.

"Rick? What the hell are you doing?" Bob asked, his voice drawing Rick back to the moment. Bob's face was stricken in disbelief. Mrs. Shoemaker's face looked down at Rick from the stairs. Rick was no longer the boy who hid in the basement, but he hadn't aged a day. Under the bright lights, there were no shadows for him to hide in.

"It's been right in front of me—my whole life," Rick said, his words tumbling out faster than he could hold them back. "I don't have the strength to hide it anymore. I'm so sorry. I'm so sorry,"

"I fought it so long, Rick. I just didn't want to see it either," Jimmy confessed, a tear cooling his reddened face.

"That's life, son," Father Henry said. "We only see what we choose to."

"As for me, I don't give a shit," Bob said testily. "I just want to get out of here. How are we gonna do it?"

Rick was reminded of his life in North Carolina's mountains. He would put on his winter gloves and a heavy coat. Prepared for the cold morning air, he nonetheless opened the door to walk into a biting wind that would pierce every layer. Instead, warm air followed behind winter's sudden retreat. He recalled how certain he was to expect bleak gray skies in the deep winter that would blanch the color from the trees and the frozen dew that made each blade of grass a prickly spear that would crunch under his feet and dampen his socks. His apprehension was rendered no more than a fiction on that first day of spring. The way things were was no promise of the way things would be in the splendor of a new day.

Instead, he smiled. He took off all the layers of fear he'd dressed himself in over the years since he'd seen Garrett for the last time. There was no wrath or judgment—only Bob's passing disinterest that reminded Rick that no one truly would ever care as much as he did. The moment quickly faded as Rick made a sober acknowledgment of a new captivity that found him just as he escaped from his own.

Rick surveyed the room like a witness to a car crash.

"My God, what is this place?"

The room was dimly lit. The walls were padded with a pleated pink fabric. Cables dangled from the walls. A wooden structure in the shape of a cross lay on its side. Every implement of paddle and rope hung from the rear wall. Four beds stripped of sheets were positioned inside, each appointed with their own set of ropes or cables. Metal rods of varying lengths and diameters reflected what dim light fell upon them.

"Torture. Crucifixions. That's our best guess," Father Henry speculated in calm exhaustion.

Rick recalled the letters tucked in his pocket. "Have you seen anyone else in any of these rooms?"

"No," Bob said. "They rounded us up at lunch. That

dog man you spoke of interrogated us about the artifact. They want it. Bad."

Jimmy gently let go of the hand Rick only then realized he was still holding. "We didn't tell them anything,"

"It's all about Missy," Rick began frantically. "She's part of a secret group of gay people called the Luminaries. They want to doctor the New Testament to make it look like a forgery!"

Father Henry's eyes were wild. "Look like? You mean it's real?"

The thought hadn't occurred to him. "Yes. Yes, I suppose so," Rick said, hairs tingling on his neck.

"Did you tell them where to find it?" Bob asked.

Rick concentrated, searching for the missing pieces to the puzzle. "I did, but it's not there."

Bob and Father Henry stood and walked over to him, both looking dumbfounded. Rick went on to describe the Luminaries and Missy's vague reference to the Vatican as best as he could recall. Father Henry listened intently, settling himself on the edge of one of the beds.

Father Henry rubbed his chin. "The Catholic Church is not as uniformly appreciative of the New Revelation as people may imagine. Traditionalists are slow to change. Perhaps some elements of the Vatican would support the Luminaries' goals, as evidenced by the officiate's letter to Missy. Others, they would certainly oppose it."

"She thinks we might be agents of the Vatican who want to take the New Revelation and thwart her plans," Rick added.

"We need to protect that document," Father Henry said decisively. "Not only is it authentic, but the Luminaries would do far more harm than they led you to believe, Rick."

"How so?" Rick asked.

"The secularists would use this as another nail in the cross to discredit Christianity itself. The Catholic Church would lose all its recent converts. With it, money. Vatican finances have long been clouded in mystery and scandal, but they're not as robust as most may believe. If that faith falters, so goes the rest of Christianity. Unopposed, there's no telling how far secularists in this group of Luminaries would go to pervert our society. A ship untethered to its mooring will drift aimlessly into the open ocean."

Bob and Jimmy nodded in agreement as the weight of Father Henry's assessment sank in. As of that moment, Rick was conscripted in a war he did not seek, but would do everything in his power to win.

ours passed. Jimmy and Rick were sitting on the floor, Jimmy resting his head in Rick's lap. Rick now acquiesced to his tender affection. The dog man silently left bottles of water and bowls of sticky rice taken from the buffet lunch they'd missed. Hunger found its way to them nonetheless. Conversation became difficult once their captors decided they needed entertainment. Pop songs blared over the room's speakers. Porn played on a TV by the wall, acting as an unwanted instruction manual for the implements surrounding them.

Startled, Rick jumped when the lock on the door buzzed, announcing someone's arrival. Jimmy rose from his lap, and they fixed their gaze on the door. Mercifully, the music in the room fell silent just as the door opened.

"I trust each of you have had some time to consider your next steps," Missy said upon entering. She had abandoned the red dress. In its place, she wore a black leather dress with short sleeves and a black belt around her waist. Buttons snugly grasped their holes from the collared neck to the bottom of the dress where her knees would have been. Tall black boots climbed her legs and reached to some unseen terminus under the dress. They were laced with intricate straps that left no part of the boot with air to breathe between leather and flesh. Her lipstick and eyeliner matched, giving her face a hint at the tormented soul within. Her straight blonde wig was the only color that escaped the vortex of darkness.

"You've had a lot more time than that, it seems," she said, smiling at Rick. "Apparently, you're full of surprises, Pastor. The room is on camera. We caught great footage of you making out with Jimmy. What would your mother say?" Her smile took a wicked form.

"I told you everything," Rick insisted, getting to his feet.

"Be that as it may, I see no harm in sending a few screenshots of the encounter home. Let her be the judge."

Rick saw himself once again at the train station with his father. He recalled the frightened child who knew he'd lose everything if he didn't betray the boy he loved and the person he was. The prospect of this world spilling like acid on his now-distant home burned a pit inside him.

"Don't you dare!"

"You know my price. In the meantime, perhaps Jimmy would like to learn how those sounding rods work. Could spice up your budding romance, no? Or perhaps Bob?"

Two larger men followed her into the room, each turning sideways to fit through the threshold. These weren't pool boys. Each wore an executioner's mask and carried with them the putrid scent of their unwashed musk. The odor was as brutal as the men looked, each burly and tall enough to tower over Missy.

"Who will it be?" she asked, taking an assortment of metal rods from the wall. "The other room is all set up. We just need a volunteer, preferably one who's verbal. Sam and Ash really like verbal play. Someone who can talk. Tell us things we need to learn."

Missy condemned their silence with her squinted eyes. "Pick, or I will."

Father Henry stood. "Let them be. Take me."

Missy smiled. Her eyes took measure of the man seated before her. "Trust me, Father. I can't wait. I've wanted to see just how far you truly will go to defend this faith of yours. Be careful what you ask for. Just tell me where it is. I don't even care who sent you. You would be the obvious choice for their spy, wouldn't you?"

Father Henry gave no response. His face was resigned as he casually walked to the door. The men followed, having no need to force him. Missy frowned, looking disappointed that she wouldn't have to drag him out.

"For his sake, you should act soon," she said before following the men and closing the door.

"Jesus," Bob said. "What the hell are they going to do to him?"

"He's gonna sue them out of business!" Jimmy insisted.

Rick sighed. "I think we're way beyond that now. Her entire world hinges on us giving her something we don't have."

Rick paced around the room, heart racing. The sound of Bob fruitlessly trying to pick the lock with two of the smaller rods was all they heard, the music still yet to return. Jimmy pressed his ear against the wall.

"I just hear some talking," Jimmy whispered. "They're asking him where it is. Rick, we need to stop this! Is there anywhere else it could be?"

Rick's frustration boiled over into anger. "No. I'm certain where we left it. We looked everywhere. Maybe someone saw us? I don't know. I just don't know!"

From the adjoining room, Rick heard a yell. The yell was followed by a scream. Not just any scream, but a mortal one. It was the scream of a battlefield amputation from some lost war. A scream whose agony was contagious, like a brushfire blowing over dead grass.

Father Henry was the first casualty in their war. He was no doubt contorted in pain behind the wall. There was no way to stop it, no way to end it. The fire spread quickly. Another scream followed. Then another.

"Dammit, let us out of here!" Rick cried, pounding on the wall. The plea went unanswered as the sadistic work continued. The unseen men laughed and taunted their victim. Someone demanded "the bigger one." Moments later, Father Henry's response came, this time in a weeping cry of surrendered agony.

Missy's voice was so loud it was like she was still in the room with him. "Where is it!?" she demanded again and again.

Of course there was no music, Rick thought. She wanted them to hear. She wanted them to hear everything.

Father Henry's voice found new strength, booming over her. "I don't have it! We don't have it!"

His plea was disregarded, and his voice turned to a shriek that cut through the walls and into Rick's heart. Crying, he kept pounding on the wall. "We'll do anything! Just let him go! Let him go!"

At last, the voices quieted. Then, silence. "I can't hear anything," Jimmy said, his voice quivering as he pressed his ear harder against the wall.

Sweating, Rick paced the floor, occasionally hitting the wall. Time seemed to slow, and even the agony in the room beyond became preferable to the silence of the unknown. There would be no patience. There would be no forgiveness. *The same needled rods could be employed against our enemy*, Rick thought. He chose the longest one on the wall as his weapon.

"If they come back, we'll fight them!" he demanded through gritted teeth.

Jimmy and Bob looked at Rick with shocked eyes.

The moment was interrupted as the door buzzed once again. Rick crouched, ready to strike. The door opened slowly, creaking on its worn hinges. Rick dropped the rod to support the man, now dressed in just his shirt and underwear as he slumped against the wall.

"Father Henry!" Jimmy said, running to the man and helping him up. The priest's pants fell from his hand to the floor as he gave his weight to the support Jimmy offered.

Bob rushed to help Jimmy settle him to the floor as the door closed. "Are you okay?"

"Okay? Are you kidding? It was wonderful," he said with an attempt at a smile. "I'd do it again, if they'd let me."

"Jesus," Rick said as the realization hit him that the priest wasn't joking.

"But it won't be me next time. They'll take another

of us in the night," Father Henry said. "They won't stop until they get what they want."

Rick knew the two most dangerous people in the world were those who stood to lose everything and those who had nothing left to lose. That night, a locked door was all that separated the two camps. If his father had known he was gay, the church would have never accepted him. He would have lost his livelihood, his mother's respect, and all of his coveted dignity. It was a fear so deep that his father would have abandoned his only son with a few dollars at the burning bush disguised as a train station rather than confront that reality. *Would Missy do any less?*

They sat in silence as hours passed. The porn started again, but without competition from the music, the maniacal laughter and taunting humiliation the dominant masters gave to their submissive captives was impossible to ignore. Every manner of bondage and torture was explored. Again and again. The line between pleasure and pain was blurred to the point of being indistinguishable. These were no actors. Rick couldn't understand the appeal, and no part of him was willing to suffer for another man's pleasure. Not anymore.

Jimmy looked pleadingly into Rick's eyes. Jimmy's helplessness gave Rick strength. This was his flock, and he would defend them with a newfound reserve of resolve that began to reverberate within him. Was this not his calling? Were Billy Martin and all the others who fought in the shadows of his willful ignorance any less deserving of his protection? His advocacy. His own sacrifice. His safety. What of his wealth? His comfort. His reputation. Were these so great a sacrifice as to justify inaction? *No*, he thought. They were all suddenly like pennies falling to the floor. Around others, he may pick up the coin for fear of being seen thriftless. Alone, he was so indifferent as to even reclaim a worthless cent. *What justifies holding onto what I don't value?*

Every choice he'd ever made was to follow his father in each step of his life. But he could go no further on that journey. His father's footsteps were washed away like the ocean reclaiming them from the sand on the shore. He could no longer see the well-worn path ahead of him—only a blank slate of fresh sand that stretched into the horizon. He would need to choose his own path.

"I was wrong," Bob said, breaking the silence and sliding his glasses over his ears. "All this time, I never understood my son. Eh, my daughter, that is. I've seen some crazy shit here. Drag queens. Learned about a history of oppression and misunderstanding. Honestly, Rick—if you're a man of God and fought so hard to embrace who you are and failed to change, I can't imagine my daughter would fare any better. My child shouldn't spend all her life in self-doubt and agony. That would be worse than any mistake she might make with hormone replacement. I just need to choose to be a part of her life and guide her through this nonsense as best I can, regardless of whether I'll ever understand any of it. I just want to be her dad."

"You miss her?" Rick asked.

"I'd do anything to be back with her right now," Bob said, his hands supporting the weight of his head and the regrets it held. With his glasses freshly polished, he could see. His sight was finally clear.

The door buzzed again. Rick lunged for his weapon, but stumbled. Jimmy and Bob leaped to their feet, and Father Henry raised his head to see his captors' return. Instead, it was neither Missy nor her minions. It was just Marilyn, followed by Eileen. They opened the door no more than necessary to slip inside the room.

"Boys," Marilyn whispered. "This is a prison break! We're getting you out of here—follow us!"

For their escape attempt, they wore matching black jumpsuits. Each appeared to make only a perfunctory attempt at tucking their wigs under black caps. Eileen's mantra was always, "Don't get ready, stay ready." It was evident that dire circumstances gave no excuse to slouch, since their makeup was still fresh. Like drag ninjas, they shuffled everyone out of the room.

For the first time, Rick was happy to see them. Dawn came as if by surprise after the long and cold night.

The lights were dim, and the hallway was quiet. Rick tried to ask a question but was quickly hushed. Marilyn and Eileen acted with an urgency that only barely covered a fear no makeup could fully conceal. Rick recognized the route they took—they were headed for the same exit he had taken in his heist. Once outside, Rick could barely contain his excitement to be free. The night air was never more alive to him.

"Stay in the shadows, little ones!" Marilyn said, her jog transitioning into a sprint. "We're headed for that dirt road by the lake. Car there."

Everyone did their best to keep up. Father Henry labored in his jog, nursing a hurt leg that limped behind him with each stride. Jimmy ran like a gazelle, graceful and with effortless speed. Rick was wheezing. Too many drinks and open buffets slowed him down as much as his long-neglected gym membership. Still, he did better than Bob, who likely hadn't run since high school.

"Girlfriend, you sober enough to drink—I mean drive?" Eileen asked.

Marilyn fumbled for the keys to the beaten blue

station wagon parked under the cover of a tree branch. "Oh, girl. I should be. I had two cocktails at dinner and only two more and a shot of whiskey after."

"I had three cocktails, but the first one shouldn't count. That pool boy with the crossed eyes made it. It was like seltzer water. I had a Long Island after dinner, but I nursed it," Eileen recounted.

Marilyn kept fumbling with the keys. Flood lights cracked on over the grounds behind them. Dim at first, they got steadily brighter with each precious second that passed.

"Dammit, they must have figured out we left!" Eileen cursed.

"Here, girl. You're the least drunk to drive," Marilyn said, handing the keys over in surrender.

Eileen swiftly unlocked the doors, and everyone dove inside. The engine started, but Eileen kept the lights off. Tires spun dirt from the ground, and the car lurched forward.

"You know where you're going?" Bob asked, panting.

"Absolutely," Eileen said in steady resolve as the car sped up, leaving a wake of dust on the trail.

Terrified, Rick pointed from the backseat. "There's a fence ahead!"

Eileen's acknowledgment came from the gas pedal. The engine roared out its defiance. They closed in on the gate. Undeterred, Eileen leaned forward and steadied the car toward the gate's center and the lock that held them captive. The car jolted on impact with the fence. The lock gave way to the barreling car. Tires screeched on impact with pavement as they caught traction in a sharp turn onto the highway. The car fishtailed for a moment before Eileen steadied the wheel.

"Missy is after us! They sent the original New Revelation here! To the camp! I took it. I don't know why, I just did—I wanted to find out what the hell was going on here. I'm so sorry—I didn't mean for any of this to happen," Rick sobbed.

"I know, baby," Eileen said. "I'm the one that should be sorry."

"Why?" Risk asked.

"That's a longer discussion, baby. Right now, we need to get you all to safety. Stay buckled in. It's gonna be a long drive."

"Wait, we're just leaving? What about our stuff?" Bob asked.

"Forget that now, honey. Leave everything behind," Marilyn said, consoling him as best she could.

Eileen pursed her lips. "I told you Missy was a bitch."

"More than that," Rick said. "She said she was working with a group she called the Luminaries. They're trying to turn that document into a forgery and bring things back to how they were before. She's crazy!"

Eileen and Marilyn exchanged glances.

"Someone is coming to take it to doctor it. Except, we can't find it—it's not where I put it. She'll chase us until she gets it," Rick went on.

"It's not missing, baby," Eileen said. "It's in the trunk."

19

"**F**ind them!" Missy said, her voice shrill and un-hinged. "I want every pool boy to be sent out. Search the grounds. They can't be far."

"Mistress," the dog man whined, "security reports that a car left from the lake and burst through the gate onto the highway!"

"What?" Missy gasped. "How? How the *hell* did they get a car?"

The dog man shrugged, his bewilderment hidden behind his mask.

"They must have had help from the inside. This place must be infiltrated by the Vatican. Dammit! We need that car—they must have the artifact!"

"I'll have your car pulled around, Mistress."

Missy sighed. "If they are from the Vatican, we know exactly where they're headed. We won't find them in the night. We won't have to."

The dog man crouched in a seated position beside her, awaiting orders.

"Organize a security sweep. I want to know every soul who's still here. Find out who's missing. We need to figure out who they're working with!"

"Yes, mistress," the dog man said, bounding to his feet and rushing out of her office.

Missy stood up and looked out the window onto the floodlight-illuminated grounds behind her. She uncorked a bottle of whiskey from the serving tray and poured a splash into a waiting glass. She swirled her drink thoughtfully, taking a moment to savor the aroma before downing it like a shot.

Sitting, she pulled her phone closer to her ear and made a call she had been hoping she could avoid. The call went directly to Father Slump's voice mail. Frustrated, she hung up. It would be five in the morning in the Vatican, she thought. He should be up by now. There was another call she knew she could make. *Too soon*, she thought. Letting the Luminaries know she failed would seal her fate. There was still hope. Quite a lot, in fact.

Missy hated waiting. She paced the room. Absentmindedly, she turned on the news. There she was, the president of the United States. Even with the sound muted, Missy could tell that President Stacey Macomb was lauding passage of her signature legislation for trans rights. Like all legislation, the Trans Identity and Rights Entitlement Act was only a patchwork of half-measures watered down by a congress too afraid to make the change the community actually needed.

TIRE was the perfect name for the legislation. Trans people would be given funding to cover reassignment surgery, but the paltry sum wouldn't cover the entire cost. Employment discrimination was forbidden, but it only applied to businesses that employed one hundred people or more. People would be left out.

The Luminaries' approach would have been different, she thought. Rather than being satisfied with a single piece of legislation and a photo op, they would have demanded more comprehensive change. Over time, certainly. Now, the voting majority was pacified, believing victory was won. Everyone always leaves the field when the game is over. Having settled on a winner and loser, spectators would leave the stadium with regular people left to pick up all their trash. All she could think about was how difficult it would be to raise money for the cause now that everyone believed the problem solved.

Certainly, there were times for radical change. Occasionally, a brick needed to be thrown through a window and a paddy wagon needed to be tipped over. The Luminaries didn't orchestrate Stonewall, but they foresaw it. It was the inevitable consequence of steam collecting under a lid. But Stonewall had given way to the modern gay-rights movement. It brought light to the victimized. If it weren't for H.I.V. and A.I.D.S.

decimating a generation of her leadership, who knows how much progress they would have made by now. Institutional change, on the other hand, was never foreseen. Like sex with the hottest guy who blows his load after only a few minutes, it was never satisfying. *It was too much and too soon,* she thought.

The door swung open, Sean forgetting to knock. Obediently, he strode over to Missy and squatted in front of her, holding out two folders.

"We conducted the search, Mistress. Two staff members are missing: Eileen Right and Marilyn Man Hoe."

Missy snatched the folders and sat at her desk. Even frozen with vials of Botox, her forehead still crinkled in consternation.

"I know Marilyn. I recruited her. But who is Eileen?" she asked herself, logging into her computer.

Sean silently awaited his next command as Missy searched the web while looking over Eileen's file. "It's strange, Sean. Says in her file that she worked in Manhattan and D.C., but I can't find her on the internet. No social media. No advertisements for her drag shows."

"She said that Marilyn brought her here. They were friends before."

"Her background check was clear," Missy confirmed. "We waived the letters of recommendation on account of Marilyn vouching for her, evidently."

"Is she the spy?" Sean asked eagerly.

Missy ignored the question. Instead of calling someone who may still be asleep, she picked up her phone and called someone who'd still be awake.

"Judy, good to hear your voice," Missy said, her smile warming her words. "My dear, we have a problem, and I need your help. You know the D.C. scene better than any queen in the district. Eileen Right. Ever work with her? Know who she is?"

Missy's smile faded at what Judy had to say.

"I suspected as much," Missy sighed. "Look, I need someone I can trust. Tonight, Eileen Right and Marilyn Man Hoe will be headed into D.C. They'll have four other men with them. One's a priest. He'll stand out. Then again, maybe not these days. In any event, I need to find them. Immediately. I know bars close at two. I need you and every queen you can recruit to look for them. They have something with them. It's of great importance to me. I so desperately need that back. It will mean so much to me personally, not to mention the Luminaries, if you can quietly arrange that."

Missy hummed her agreement as she listened, nodding. "Thank you, dear," she said, hanging up.

Missy took off her wig and ruffled her cropped brown hair. The wig covered a bald spot on his head. He wiped off a layer of lipstick with a tissue on the desk and started to pull chunks of latex padding from his chest and thighs.

"Bring my car around and book a suite for me at the usual hotel in D.C. I'm going down tonight. Be here in the morning when the emissary arrives," he said, his voice deepening.

"What shall I tell him, Master?"

"Stall. I'll be back with it before he leaves."

20

"**W**hat?" Rick gasped. "You put an original manuscript of the New Revelation in your trunk?"

"Better than a janitor's closet," Eileen retorted.

"How did you get it?" Bob asked.

"I saw you and Jimmy trying to hide it in there when I left the lounge after the movie you didn't finish watching," Eileen said. "Naturally, I was curious. I thought it would be safer with me. When you all went missing, the rest was easy to figure out. Plus, the pool boys gossip like old hens on a Sunday."

"You're all in our house now. A drag mother always protects her young," Marilyn added.

The car started to slow to a normal speed. Rick knew he'd feel safer with every mile that separated him from whatever Missy would do to them if they were caught, but he also acknowledged careful driving was preferable to being pulled over.

"So, where are we going?" Jimmy asked.

"Right now? We're going to get gas and an energy drink. I'm gonna fall out if I don't get some caffeine up in here, am I right?" Eileen said.

"Relax, Jimmy," Marilyn said. "Between the two

of us, we know the D.C. scene well. We can find protection there. We need to get this scroll safely to the professor at the university before Missy can rock the boat any more than she already has."

Rick realized that they were back in civilization. He had never been so thankful for the mundane billboards along the highway, advertising a familiar life. If his cell phone wasn't somewhere under a pile of clothes in his room, he'd no doubt have service here. Would his mamma have called? He longed to know. A creature of habit, he still carried his wallet. Fortunately, the well-worn leather wallet he'd had since childhood carried all he needed to restart his life. He wondered whether there'd be any sales at Macy's when he got back.

Breathlessly, Bob leaned toward the front seat. "We could just go to the police."

Marilyn chuckled. "And say what? 'Excuse me, Officer, we're two drag queens and have an ancient historical document that was stolen by another drag queen, and she's out to kill us if she doesn't get it back.' Honey, they'd be more likely to send us away for being crazy."

"Lord, they'd lock me up right away as soon as they saw all my parking tickets. Girl, those go back to the Obama administration," Eileen said.

The car rumbled to a stop at the gas station. A few people loitered in the parking lot. Suddenly, Rick became self-conscious of being seen with Marilyn and Eileen in the convenience store, but hunger persuaded him to ignore the embarrassment. Side glances from customers and their whispered conversations followed Eileen and Marilyn into the store. Whether blind or indifferent to the attention, they hastily plucked up bags of chips and bottles of energy drinks. By the time they left, they looked more prepared for a frat party than a pit stop. Rick envied the confidence he had yet to acquire, and maybe never would.

Having nearly forgotten the flavor of anything without alcohol, he greedily sipped a large soda and carried a hot dog back to the car, having already finished one before he even left the store. Chips and candy bounced alongside him in a plastic bag.

Once again, the car growled to life. With the tank full, their journey continued.

Rick's thoughts returned to Elder Monroe and the life he longed to have back. "I guess this means I won't get my certificate."

"Oh, child," Marilyn said, looking at Rick and Jimmy in the rearview mirror. "That camp wasn't about atoning to us—it was about atoning to yourselves. Always has been. All these people who come there, most of them are just like you—closeted. Angry. Scared, mostly. Don't love themselves—or haven't yet. Some figure it out. Some don't. Ones who don't just go home telling people about sensitivity training and pedicures. Ones who do go home to *live*. To live before it's so late that regrets are bigger than hope."

"If we survive this, I'll go home with you and tell your church elder myself that you passed the classes," Eileen promised.

"I'm ready to fight," Bob said. "My daughter deserves to live in a world where she's respected. Where she has rights. If that thing in the trunk is what we need to make that happen, I'm in. If I can't stand up for it, I can't stand up for her."

"It may take people a long time to understand its grace, but it's real, and we must be obedient in all things with our God," Father Henry added.

Jimmy sat in silence, watching the trees pass by. He seemed lost in his thoughts, so Rick didn't want to intrude with conversation. It was late. Fatigue waxed as the adrenaline from the escape started to wane. With another hour or so before they'd reach D.C., Rick settled in to sleep, jerking back to consciousness when his head started to droop too far. Eventually, he found a comfortable spot, one where he felt safe. With his head supported by Jimmy's shoulder, he drifted off.

The car's trunk slammed closed, waking Rick. Disoriented, he looked around. The city's lights illuminated the car's interior, revealing its torn leather seats and the crumbs on the floor. He could see specks of glitter, stray rhinestones, and strands of hair from dozens of wigs in the light's glare.

Rick rubbed his eyes. His mouth was dry, and his body ached for more sleep,

"Where are we?"

"Metropolis," Marilyn informed him. "It's a gay bar. We know one of the queens here."

With some hesitation, Rick followed Jimmy and the others out of the car. From the parking lot he saw a short line of people at the door having their ID's checked by the bouncer. From across the street he could hear the rhythmic bass from the dance club. The door was a foreboding portal into a world he was not yet prepared to explore.

Eileen anticipated Rick's question. "No, you can't stay here."

"You're taking it with you!" Rick said, alarmed. Eileen carried the tan tote bag beside her.

Eileen looked around, taking measure of her surroundings. "It's safer with us than in the car."

After passing through the security line and each paying a ten-dollar cover charge (which Rick deemed outlandishly high), they made their way into the main floor. The music was louder now. Lyrics were matched with the same beat he heard outside, but he couldn't follow them.

"What are we supposed to do?" Rick asked, feeling uncertain of where he should stand or how they'd meet anyone in the crowd of drunken patrons.

"Act natural, baby. Get a drink," Marilyn suggested. "Practice what you learned in class and you'll be fine."

Rick, Jimmy, Bob, and Father Henry found an open space at the main bar, each paying for their drinks for the first time since they'd arrived at the camp. Before Rick's Manhattan was poured, Marilyn spotted a friend.

"Bitch!" a drag queen screeched joyfully before embracing Marilyn and lightly kissing her cheek. "Damn, girl. I thought you was down being a camp counselor or some shit."

Marilyn motioned over to the only people in the bar not wearing drag, crop tops, or skinny jeans. "I'm bringing all the camp to the camp, baby. It's a field trip. I thought they'd like to see what a real gay bar was like."

"Looks like you still have a lot of work to do with them," she observed.

"Everyone, this Gertrude La Turd," Marilyn said, walking her over to the group. "This bitch taught me everything I know about drag. I haven't been sober or had a gag reflex since the night we met at a bathhouse in New York."

"Honey, you didn't have one to begin with. Boys, it's a pleasure," she said, offering her hand.

Bob reluctantly took it and mechanically answered, "I'm flattered, but I'm straight."

Gertrude frowned and looked at him quizzically before moving on with her introductions. She shook Rick's hand. He thought Gertrude's fleshy palm betrayed her masculinity as much as the unshaved chest hair. She was shackled in a pink dress several sizes too small to hold her waist or bosom. The flowing gown nudged against the legs of several bar patrons around her. Wispy light-pink wings fluttered behind her when she walked. Clasping her rainbow wand, she curtsied when her hand met Rick's.

"No one does camp better than Gert," Marilyn said.

Gertrude puffed out her already brimming chest. "Thank you, dear. Tonight, I'm doing my own arrangement. I don't lip sync, you know. I sing all my own songs."

With memories of bad karaoke, Rick cringed. Another performer was on the stage across the bar, no doubt less confident in her singing ability. She mouthed the words of some song he had never heard before. Christian pop was probably not a chart topper at this particular bar, he reasoned. Despite this, she attracted a sizable crowd of younger men waving money at her.

It was D.C., so Rick knew the crowd would likely be throwing fives and tens at them. He was relieved to have visited the ATM at the gas station, should circumstances require him to make an offering.

Gertrude tapped her long-nailed finger against her chin. "If you really want to give them the full experience, I could use some backup dancers. I need people to ring little bells and dance around behind me. You think they're up to the task?"

Eileen laughed. "Honey, I think they were born for it."

Father Henry rolled his eyes and turned to extend his condescending glare on the rest of the patrons he'd yet to silently condemn. Jimmy took an anxious gulp of his drink. If it was anything like Rick's, he thought it was probably vodka watered down with more vodka.

"I'm flattered, but I'm straight," Bob repeated with more urgency, drawing another confused expression from Gertrude.

Marilyn put her hands on her hips and laughed. "Oh, it will be fun, boys!"

"Come, come," Gertrude said, motioning with her wand, as if it were an enchantment.

"You can't be serious," Rick said.

"Boys," Eileen said, leaning in, "don't fight us on this."

Surmising that earnest suggestion carried a weight Rick couldn't appreciate, he finished his drink and stood. Overcoming his reluctance, he followed the queens to a back room. Hesitatingly, Jimmy followed. Bob and Father Henry obstinately kept watch from the bar.

The back room was as much of a chaotic circus as the main bar, just with fewer people. Drag queens darted around the room in a rush, borrowing every manner of makeup and helping one another zip dresses that resisted their most earnest efforts. Small bench tables with mismatched mirrors lined a wall. Bags, wigs, glitter, and eyelashes were like landmines Rick had to step around to make his way to Gertrude's station at the end of the room.

"This should fit," Gertrude said, handing Rick a simple black dress.

Rick inspected the dress, trying to discern the top from the bottom and the front from the back. Gertrude rustled through a bag of accessories to produce a costume-jewelry version of a pearl necklace best suited for a woman in her twilight years.

"I'm not taking off my clothes," Rick protested.

Gertrude considered for a moment. "You're a genius! Yes, it'll look even trashier if you don't. You'll serve us walk-of-shame glamour realness!"

She was speaking in tongues for all Rick could make of her. Still, he silently acquiesced.

Jimmy slipped his own costume over his tank top. White with red polka dots, it looked like a young woman's summer dress. Gertrude delicately tucked the thrift-store price tag underneath the collar.

She looked him up and down like an artist admiring her own painting. "Perfect. Don't change a thing."

Meanwhile, Eileen discreetly put the priceless tan bag under Gertrude's table and started to distribute tiny handbells to the recruits.

"Boys, the song is 'Ring My Bell' by the infamous Anita Ward. When the chorus comes up, just ring these bells and dance around in circles around me. But you gotta vogue it, babies. Vogue it! You can do that, right? Marilyn, they can vogue, can't they?"

"Oh, absolutely, girl!" Marilyn promised with confidence.

Satisfied with the assurance, Gertrude poured carefully measured shots of something from her repurposed water bottle into small red plastic cups. It was for "good luck," she asserted. Rick happily sipped whatever it was. Water mixed with a soapy bitterness stung his tongue. He winced as he swallowed.

Jimmy's face puckered with the sour taste. "What kind of alcohol is this?"

"It's not, honey. It's molly. I dissolved a bunch of it in my water to dose it out. If I did the math right, one ounce should be enough. It's medicine, baby," Gertrude explained.

Rick took a step back from the tainted cup. "You mean pure MDMA?"

"Damn. Someone was paying attention in the *Let's Get the Party Started* lecture. Nice job! It's wonderful, though. You'll see," Marilyn said.

Jimmy shrugged his shoulders and offered a cheers. Reluctantly, Rick raised his glass, and they both took the rest of the mix like a shot. Rick's face puckered again, and he winced until the taste subsided.

Over the next half hour, Rick and Jimmy submitted themselves to whatever makeup and accessories the queens subjected them to. Rick looked at the finished product in the mirror. Ultimately, their work resulted in him looking like a meth-addicted prostitute who'd learned makeup at a clown college.

"Oh, it's perfect!" Gertrude squealed.

Rick tried to wipe off a trail of lipstick that left his lips and climbed up his cheek, but Gertrude swatted his hand away, assuring him that was the way it was supposed to be. Still uncertain what he'd been poisoned with, Rick shivered, and his hands were sweating more than usual.

"I think I'm a little nauseous," Jimmy said.

Rick wasn't certain whether it was from the drug or his circumstances, but he was starting to feel the same way.

"Don't you worry about that," Gertrude said. "It'll pass. You'll be rolling just in time!"

She promised that they were up after two more numbers. Rick didn't account for the long introductions and the critiques after each song. He felt like he was being led to an execution that kept being stayed with long commercial breaks.

Jimmy wrapped his arm around Rick's shoulder. Instantly, Rick sighed and relaxed the shoulders he didn't realize he was tensing. It was better than being merely at ease. It was wonderful. Warmth radiated from Jimmy's hand, passing through the straps on the dress and under his shirt. A touch became a massage without Jimmy even moving his hand. Rick leaned closer to Jimmy, sharing body heat.

"Have you taken this before?" Rick asked.

"No, but I think I feel weird. Not bad, just weird."

"I know. Same."

Gertrude clapped her hands, and her wings danced behind her. "We're up, ladies!"

Rick and Jimmy stood. Walking was different. Rick's socks were damp with sweat, which somehow cushioned his feet with each step, like he was floating. Suddenly alert, he didn't mind moving. For that matter, he didn't mind the idea of dancing. He had Jimmy beside him, and nothing else mattered, he decided.

The audience roared with laughter and applause as they took the stage. Gertrude told fans more with her expression than words ever could. She seemed to carry as much trepidation of her entourage as they had of her.

Rick rang his bell as the song started. He was instructed to wait. He just wanted to hear the sound it made. Jimmy laughed. Rick smiled and kissed his cheek.

It was time to perform. The chorus began. Rick improvised his part, ringing his bell without regard for any particular beat other than his own. Jimmy laughed and tried to mimic him. Anyone in the audience would be right to condemn them both as being hopelessly white and tragically inexperienced. But Gertrude played into it to the audience's delight. She took wide-eyed measure of their awkward spins and waddling dance, doing her most exaggerated best to follow their lead. Cheers and crumpled bills rained down on them. A few in the audience did their earnest best to reprise their dance moves, be it in tribute or mockery. Rick and Jimmy laughed, picking up the cash off the stage.

Rick and Jimmy met on their knees as they

scrambled to collect the dollars. Their eyes met and faces widened into giddy smiles.

"You know I love you," Rick said, laughing.

Jimmy's eyes lit. "I love you too, babe."

Their lips met, and Rick was bathed in soaking warmth from a summer's midday sun on a golden coast of sand. It wasn't like their first kiss, so filled with apprehension and danger. It was sheer passion. It was hard for him to stop. Every contour of his lips needed to be appreciated. One kiss easily gave way to another. They came like waves once more, just without any rocks and stones to get in their way. After what felt like a prelude to the eternity to follow, Rick felt Jimmy's lips stretch into a smile. They pulled away, both laughing.

"Let's do another one!" Jimmy yelled to Gertrude as they hustled off stage.

Gertrude laughed. "Babies, you were wonderful! Absolutely wonderful! Better than I could have ever imagined!"

"I will take full credit for everything they know," Eileen said. She and Marilyn followed behind as they made their way back to more congratulations in the dressing room.

Rick pulled off his tangerine-colored wig, and Jimmy did the same to his own. A few attempts were made to wipe off the lipstick and makeup, but it just smeared it on their faces. Giving up their attempts, they each took off their dresses.

"We should go," Eileen whispered.

Rick was crestfallen. "But why? Let's get some drinks! I want to see the next act!"

Eileen looked stern. "It's time."

With reality forced back upon him, Rick agreed. He collected his things and (almost as an afterthought) searched the floor for the bag. It wasn't where he saw Eileen put it. It wasn't on her shoulder. Rick looked furtively around the room, a flash of anxiety intruding on his elation.

"Eileen—where's the bag?" he hissed.

She looked surprised. "The bag? I'm not sure. I left it…"

Eileen pointed to an empty corner. She started to look around in earnest.

"Gert," Eileen said. "A bag. A tan bag—did you see it? Do you know where it went?"

Gertrude looked puzzled. She lifted a few wigs and looked under a few dresses in a perfunctory search, but soon shrugged her shoulders. Rick and Jimmy were less discrete. They widened the search area, intruding on other performers and digging under piles of costumes. Nothing.

"Dammit," Rick said, looking around. "Where could it be?"

Eileen looked uncertain but not alarmed. "It couldn't be far. Let's find Marilyn with the boys. They must have it."

Quickly, they parted ways with Gertrude.

"Is it done?" Marilyn asked.

Her expression was resolute. Bob and Father Henry were as stoic and bored as they had been when Rick left them, no doubt eager to find some sleep.

Eileen smiled. "Yes. The boys put on quite the act."

Rick grabbed her arm. "What about the bag?"

"Boys, it's time to go. We have a safe house to get to tonight," Eileen said, ignoring Rick.

"Hey," Rick said, grabbing her arm once again, "we can't just leave it here. Where's the bag?"

Eileen sighed and turned a sour expression to Rick. "Ever read Sun Tzu's *The Art of War*?"

Rick shook his head.

"To paraphrase, one way to victory is to subdue your enemy without having to confront her in combat."

21

Missy, now more benignly known as Charles Erbland, scowled as he sped down the highway. His phone rang, and he pressed the answer button on the heated wheel of that year's newest five-series.

"Judy," he said, "good to hear from you. Please make my day and tell me you have news."

"Better than that, baby. They were spotted at Metropolis tonight. Gertrude was expecting them. She distracted them, and one of her queens took the bag. In fact, I have it right here in front of me."

"Oh, thank God," Charles sighed. "Where can I pick it up?"

"Can you meet Gertrude at two when Metropolis closes?"

"Absolutely—I'll be there right on time, in fact," he said, smiling. "Remind me to buy Gertrude a drink. Maybe a house."

Judy laughed. "She'll be just as delighted with either, I suspect."

Charles ended the call and smiled for the first time in what felt like days. He relaxed his grip on the wheel and stopped weaving maniacally through traffic on the road. The occasion warranted turning on the radio to help distract him from his thoughts. He figured that if he made it there by two, he could even drive back the same night. Better for him to be there when the emissary arrived than spend the night in the hotel.

His mind wandered to what his life would soon be like. The fantasy inspired deep reserves of energy to combat his fatigue. Oscar invitations. Board memberships. A voice and a vote on all the most significant decisions in the world. He could help decide everything from which films were made to which social causes were worthy of advancing. Fame. Riches. Respect. His hands gripped the wheel tighter, as if to hold on to all he would soon acquire. No one could take it from him.

By the time he arrived at Metropolis, the streets were nearly empty. A street-sweeping van slowly made its way down the road, cleaning away the last remnants of the night's festivities. Its stiff bristles methodically ground away at the curb, picking up discarded cans and other trash, leaving the street refreshed for the day yet to come. *Tonight will be the same for me*, Charles thought.

"Gert, it's so wonderful to see you!" Charles exclaimed, lightly hugging her and kissing each cheek.

Gertrude clasped her hands. "Honey, I made *bank*

tonight! Those Christian boys you have down there sure helped me put on a good show. I feel bad stealing from them. Was this all really necessary?"

Charles sighed. "You have no idea. Needless to say, the Luminaries have made this their highest priority. Not just in D.C., but the world. I can't wait to give you all the credit, dear."

She shrugged her shoulders and held out the bag. "Well, here it is."

Charles took the tan tote bag with and groped the thick blue plastic covering its priceless contents with satisfaction. The plastic crinkled in his hands. Like a parent reunited with a lost child, he breathed out all the stress he was carrying. Gently, he placed it on the passenger seat and headed back to the compound. This was a gift he was eager to give.

With only a few hours of sleep, Charles woke early. He was determined to have the emissary meet Missy at her finest. She took extra care with her makeup, trying her best to hide the bags under her sleepless eyes. She chose a tall, blonde afro-style wig that poofed out in every direction, like a storm cloud billowing into the sky before a storm. A simple green dress complemented it, with matching stiletto heels and nails. She would make a statement the emissary could not ignore. Missy Bottom was ready for her coronation.

"Good morning!" Missy announced. "I hope your ride here was pleasant."

The man waiting in her office was dressed in a slim-fitting terry-blue suit of European cut. A boldly colored handkerchief complimented an equally adventurous tie. The attention to detail was evinced by matching socks and neatly polished burnt-umber shoes. He was exactly what Missy had imagined: refined and on the bleeding edge of fashion and sophistication. An emissary of the Luminaries would be nothing less.

"I prefer the comforts of a metropolitan area, but I do see the wisdom of having it sent here where it's easier to obscure. The plan is simple," he began without introduction. "I will apply a treatment to the parchment. This will give a false reading and make the document's ink appear to be about a hundred years old. A forgery, but not a contemporary one. It may be suspicious to have it appear too young, no? Then, we will repackage it and place the falsified shipping labels on the crate. The university will think it arrived directly from the Vatican. I will then take it to a shipping facility where our agents are embedded. They will facilitate the delivery for tomorrow. Please present the document."

Missy was taken aback by his directness. She would have preferred a "thank you" if not a gold-plated membership card. Crestfallen, she laid the artifact in the scuffed tote bag on her desk. The emissary began to unroll the fabric containing the implements of his craft, each held meticulously in cloth pockets. In front of himself, he had organized what looked like an antique well of ink and a selection of small brushes in varying sizes. He put on a pair of latex gloves, snapping them against his well-manicured hands.

"In here?" he asked with no shortage of disdain as he motioned to the bag in front of him.

Missy eagerly nodded. She took a seat opposite him at her desk and watched as he gently pulled the crinkly plastic out of the bag, tossing the sack aside. Like a surgeon, he carefully peeled away layer after layer of plastic.

"What the hell is this?" The emissary's disdain was a sharp knife that cut jaggedly into Missy's soul.

"What?" Missy asked, leaning over the table. Before her was an object she hadn't expected. Ignoring any protocol for handling the object, she reached over and unrolled a car mat, filthy with glitter and chip crumbs.

Her gasp was muffled with a shriek.

"Is this a joke, Missy? I'm not amused. We haven't much time. The delivery must be made this morning!"

"No, no, no!" she wailed.

The emissary's voice was cold, accusing, and impatient. "Where is it, Missy?"

"It was taken," she spat. "Taken by some students and employees here. I don't know how they found it."

The emissary took off his thick-rimmed square glasses. "Students?"

"Well, not likely. I suspect they're agents from the Vatican. How else would they know where to find it and what to do with it?"

"Do with it?"

"Well, yes. They went to D.C. We know that. They must be trying to deliver it to the professor themselves."

"You had a simple job, Missy. You just had to accept delivery and wait for me. If we don't succeed here, I promise we won't be the only ones to fail. I don't know what fantasies you may have regarding your stature in this community, but that's all they'll be if you don't fix this. Immediately!" he said.

Missy's mind reeled. Had Gertrude swapped it, or the others? Where is it now? If there were agents from the Vatican, there was only one person she could reach out to for help. Panicked, she lunged for her phone and tried again to reach Father Slump. The line rang once, and Missy rested the speaker phone on the table before her. Another ring. They sat in breathless silence.

"Missy?" Father Slump answered.

"Yes, Father Slump—it's good to hear your

voice. I tried to reach you last night. We have an urgent problem."

The priest's voice crackled over the poor cell-phone connection. "I was on a flight from Rome to D.C. I arrived this morning. What's happening?"

"I fear my camp was infiltrated with the Vatican's agents! They stole the artifact. The emissary is here with me now. We need it. We need to treat it and send it immediately, except I have no trace on it. Dammit, it could be anywhere."

There was a pensive silence on the line before the priest spoke. "I can assure you, it wasn't the Vatican who sent these people. Regardless, my superior sent me to blackmail the professor performing the analysis as a fail-safe. I can just as easily use the same information to make sure the results deem it a forgery."

"It's not anywhere," the emissary contributed, almost casually. "You said it was in D.C. Likely going to the very place we know it needs to."

"I'll be at the university in a few minutes," Father Slump added.

"For your sake, you better hope the priest is more competent than you've proved to be," the emissary warned.

"Don't blame her," Father Slump offered with

reluctance. "If she's up against what I think she is, we have bigger problems than the Vatican."

22

Rick stopped in the middle of the street. "What the hell are you talking about?"

Eileen turned to him. "This isn't my first rodeo. Marilyn and I spent enough time in tough situations to know that you always carry a robbery wallet. Missy knows everyone. I'm sure her social-climbing spies are everywhere, eager to do her bidding for some scraps off her table. What better way to get them off our trail than to let them think they have what they want? The scroll is in my trunk. I swapped it out when we got here."

"Especially not that bitch," Marilyn added. "I never liked Gert. Cheap ho, thinking she can sing."

Rick's jaw dropped. The streets were still busy with people laughing and shouting on their way from one bar to the next. The group's voices contributed to the symphony of the night: cars driving by, horns honking in the distance. Rick's ears still hissed from the loud music inside. His footsteps were still lightened by the drug that dampened his fear. He shivered in the warm air and held close to Jimmy.

As promised, the New Revelation lay unceremoniously on top of old magazines and empty bags of chips in the trunk. Marilyn found a plastic bag for it, and Rick insisted on keeping it in his lap as they made their way to Arlington.

Eileen parked the car along the street in front of a completely unremarkable house with the lights still on inside. She sent a quick text message, and everyone followed her up the steps to number two-two-nine. Fresh flowers in window beds greeted them on the porch of the maroon brick house. It looked like a family neighborhood—people commuting to D.C. and then returning to an idyllic suburban home. The streets were quiet, encouraging hushed tones.

A portly man in his fifties opened the door. He wore reading glasses and a cardigan sweater with holes that betrayed both its age and the man's indifference to fashion. Still, Rick thought he looked kind. He embraced Eileen and smiled, inviting everyone in.

"I'm glad you all made it!" the man said. "Linda and I pulled out the couch bed. There's a full bath downstairs and another upstairs. We left out towels and toiletries for everyone. Someone can claim dibs on the guest room upstairs, and there are two air mattresses downstairs in the basement. Is anyone hungry?"

"Thank you, Professor Mike. I'm starved, actually. I ate once yesterday, but I guess I can suffer the extra calories," Eileen conceded.

Mike shook his head. "If I've learned one thing over the years, it's to afford you your self-deprivation, no matter how unnecessary it may be."

The living room was lined with bookshelves. Papers were neatly stacked in piles—the likely product of some organizational strategy that made sense only to the professor, Rick assumed.

Comforting smells of hot food reached Rick as he made his way to the kitchen. He reluctantly took a seat at the table after Mike insisted. He was hungry, but he didn't want to unduly intrude on the stranger's generosity. The professor ladled hot beef stew into a bowl for him. Eileen helped herself to a can of beer in the fridge. Graciously, she gave one to Rick as well.

"Where's Charlie?" she asked.

The professor's tone darkened, and his age betrayed itself in the shadows cast under his eyes. "We had to put him down last fall. The vet thought it was cancer. Naturally, Linda wanted to adopt another right away, but I got her to compromise and wait a few more months. Can't blame her. With the kids out of the house, it's nice to have some company when I'm gone."

"I'm so sorry to hear that. She's in bed by this hour, I'd assume. Thank you so much for letting us stay the night."

"Are you kidding? I would have stayed up all night for this. Do you have it with you?"

Eileen motioned to Rick. In turn, he offered the plastic bag and its contents to the professor.

"Some introductions may be in order," Eileen offered. "This is Professor Michael Donahue. He was my graduate adviser in my post-doc program."

"You have a PhD? And you're a drag queen?" Bob asked, just as surprised as everyone else.

The professor smiled and offered beers to Bob, Jimmy, and Father Henry. Each accepted without hesitation.

"Honey, there's a lot you don't know about me. It's a long story. Much too long for tonight. All that matters is that we safely delivered the artifact to the professor," Eileen said.

"Wait, *that's* the professor at the university? You know him!" Rick said.

"Quite well," Eileen confirmed. "I even lived here for the last two years of my program. I'm not very close to my family, and grad school is ever so expensive. Mike and Linda are like family to me."

Eileen and the professor took the scroll to the professor's study and examined it together in hushed conversation. The effects of the drug were starting to wear off, and Rick could feel fatigue return. The stew was surprisingly welcome. Father Henry and Bob excused themselves while Rick moved on to his second bowl. They volunteered to take the beds in the basement, leaving Rick and Jimmy to the couch. Marilyn went upstairs to begin her nightly routine of showering, moisturizing, leg shaving, and everything else she needed to maintain her art.

"Tired?" Jimmy asked.

Rick interpreted the question as a suggestion. "Exhausted. You?"

"Same. I guess it's time for bed?"

"Absolutely. Are you going to finish that roll?"

"All yours. So, mission accomplished, right? What now?" Jimmy asked.

"Honestly, I haven't thought that far ahead. We have unfinished business at the camp still. The person who sent those notes may still need help. I'm thinking about going back. I need my stuff, at least."

"Jesus, not me. No way I'm going back there. I could get a bus tomorrow. Head back home, maybe."

Rick took a long sip of his beer, trying to ignore the admission. "Are you going to finish your stew?"

"No," Jimmy said, pushing it away. "I wasn't as hungry as I thought. The drugs, probably."

Rick's mind was swirling, but he broke the silence with the only words that came to him. "Home already?"

"I've got to get back home. Explain everything to my church. A life to return to."

Rick's panic was subdued by the trailing effects of the drug, but his mind still raced, trying to find reasons to keep hold of the only part of this madness that made any sense to him.

Fatigue gave license to Rick's candor. "I want to be a part of that life."

Jimmy was silent. He absently stirred his stew with a spoon.

Rick took meaning from what was unspoken. "But you said…"

"I know what I said," Jimmy interjected. "I just can't stay here forever. What would you have me do? Move in and live with you and your mother? We just met and all. I mean, I want to keep in touch. See where things go."

Rick was at a loss for words. On one hand, he couldn't disagree with Jimmy's logic. It was all so impractical. The thought of explaining any of this to his mother was a mountain he was unprepared to climb. At the same time, why couldn't they just run away together? Start a new life. He'd tasted an apple from the tree and couldn't imagine going back to the way things were, as if they had never happened.

Jimmy stretched and excused himself to the shower. Rick resigned himself to the moment and cleaned their dishes. It would be one less thing for the professor or his wife to do. On his way to the pullout couch, Rick passed by Eileen in the dining room. She was reading through a stack of papers.

"Now's as good a time as any," Rick said. "Most of the drag queens I've met at the camp seem like they've barely finished high school. You have a PhD, and you called this place a safe house. Who the hell are you?"

Eileen laughed. "Fine, have a seat."

Rick took a seat at the table. The chairs were mismatched shades of wood, and the table looked as if it had survived years of children running into it, chipping and scraping its sides. Each scratch was a story and a memory for someone, growing older and scarred with time, just like those who sat before it.

"You're quite right, Rick. I've kept lots of things from you. I had to. For now, I can tell you that I'm not actually a drag queen. Well, I am now, naturally. Yes, I've known Marilyn for as long as I've said. We did do some amateur drag together what feels like a lifetime ago. But I went to college. Studied anthropology in grad school. I was working abroad in northern Syria as a part of some completely unrelated research. At that time, I was as closeted as I could be for obvious reasons, but I guess I wasn't as subtle about it as I thought."

"Syria? Jesus. Not the safest place," Rick observed.

"I've never really been too afraid of danger. It's part of the fun, isn't it?" Eileen said with a playful smile. "Anyway, I was recruited by a small group of people. They call themselves the Custodians. They explained the New Revelation to me. I was intrigued. Naturally, I didn't believe any of it."

"This was before it was discovered?"

"It was no accident that it was discovered, Rick," Eileen said, pulling her mug of coffee closer to her. "The Custodians have known about it for centuries. They were charged with the responsibility of keeping it safe. One day, they reasoned, society would be receptive enough to LGBT rights that it could be rediscovered. That day, as you know, came. Our dear professor was the one who was entrusted with it."

Rick leaned back and tried to absorb what he was hearing. His chair creaked a warning to not lean back much further, but he did anyway. "Like a secret society?"

"Essentially. The excerpt was removed from the Gospel sometime during the patristic period or perhaps as late as the Council of Chalcedon. No one really knows anymore. Not even the Custodians who protect it. I theorize that it was removed either because of evolving social objections or perhaps because no one knew what it meant. The word for homosexual didn't exist in the way it does today. The author wrote a word best understood as slang at the time. Its meaning was forgotten by the time it was excluded. But a group of people summarized its meaning and dedicated themselves to protecting it. The Custodians have a vested interest—they're all gay themselves. The New Revelation has always been their greatest hope for redemption and recognition in their faith."

"So you *are* with the Vatican?" Rick asked.

"No. I suspect the Vatican's leadership would be aligned with our goals these days, but the Custodians have always acted independently and in secret. The Vatican is a splintered group, Rick. Not everyone there shares the same goals. It's risky to involve ourselves with them. Too hard to discern friend from foe."

"So that explains why you helped us."

"Relax, Rick. It's not the only reason. But we have sources in the Vatican, for sure. We learned what some in the Vatican were going to do to falsify the New Revelation's legitimacy, so I was sent to infiltrate the camp and prevent the forgery. It made sense. I already knew Marilyn, so she was able to help me get a job there. Plus, naturally, I knew the professor who would perform the test."

Rick dug into his pockets to pull out the notes. "But there's so much more to know about that camp."

"Yes," she said, interrupting him sternly, "but that can wait until tomorrow. I need to finish reading, and you need sleep. Marilyn texted a few pool boys back at the camp. They've packed up all your things. Took them hours. But we can pick it all up at a safe drop spot."

Reluctantly, Rick tucked the notes back in his pocket and decided the answers he sought could wait until morning.

Any talk of what comes next with Jimmy could be left to the next day as well, Rick reasoned. They had that night. A night for them to hold each other one more time as they slept on the creaky pullout bed with soft pillows and lumpy springs. Any discomfort was easily forgiven as long as Rick could hold him—as long as Rick had him in his life just that much longer. Jimmy was his life raft in the stormiest of oceans.

Rick turned off the antique lamp by the couch, and with Jimmy in his arms, he gave in to sleep.

23

"**D**o you have an appointment?" the receptionist asked, scanning the calendar on her screen.

"No, just call him. Tell him I'm here to see him about the artifact," Father Slump insisted.

With a confused expression, the receptionist dialed Professor Mike's office and explained the situation.

"Room four-five-five. Fourth floor. The elevators are down the hall. To the left," she instructed.

Father Slump thanked the woman curtly and made his way down the hall, carrying a folder by his side. He was relieved the professor was an early starter, not some tenured professor who began the day when or if he felt like it.

He gave two solid knocks on the open door to the professor's office and stepped inside. Professor Mike looked up from his computer and turned around to greet the stranger, as much as one could to someone with such a rigid expression. Father Slump's eyes were cold. He felt like an assassin meeting his unarmed target. The professor looked so pitifully unprepared for the assault.

The priest closed the door behind him and took a

seat by the desk. "I'm here to talk to you about the New Revelation I expect you'll be receiving today," he said.

"Actually, I already received it. It's in my lab. Who are you? I assume from your attire you're from the Vatican?"

"Not exactly," the priest said slowly. "I'm here on my own accord."

Professor Mike raised an eyebrow.

"It's very important to me that those test results show that the document is a forgery," the priest explained.

"Why is that? Doesn't the Vatican want the results confirmed?"

Father slump grew irritated. "I don't care what the Vatican wants. I'm telling you what *I* want."

Professor Mike chuckled. "Well, Father, we'll run the tests, and I guess we'll see."

"You don't take my meaning," Father Slump insisted. "Do you know a woman by the name of Patricia Fisher? Perhaps the same Patricia Fisher who works in your department?"

The professor put down his pen and searched the priest's face with anxious eyes.

"That's right, Professor. We have photographs. Videos, even. Do you take my meaning now? As I said, I need those results to come out the right way."

"How dare you," the professor said. "Who the hell are you?"

"Who I am doesn't matter. What I need is all that matters."

The professor's eyes darted around the room, taking in the various degrees hanging on the walls. He leaned in as if the documents may overhear him. "You're asking me to risk my academic integrity to conspire with you on this."

"I'm not asking," the priest said, pushing the folder across the desk. Mike hastily slid on his reading glasses. The color in his face faded as he flipped through the stack of glossy photographs that lay his indiscretions bare.

"Dammit," Mike said. "I have a wife and kids! This would ruin me! Ruin my life…"

"Which is exactly why you'll do as you're told," the priest said, feeling his guilt swell, weakening his resolve.

Mike rubbed his temples. "Please don't do this," he begged. "Don't bring them into this."

"I'm sorry," Father Slump said consolingly. "There are forces at play bigger than either of us. I'm a pawn trapped in the same game you are. I have no choice. And, it appears, neither do you."

Mike was silent but looked up with eyes blurred red. Father Slump leaned in to meet the professor halfway across the desk. "Do this, and I'll make sure these pictures are destroyed. These are the only copies. You can go about your life. What does it matter to you? You're not even a Christian."

Steadying his resolve, Mike sat up straighter in his chair. "It may not matter to me, but it matters to people I care about. It matters to our society! When truth can be suppressed with fear, we all lose."

"Perhaps," Father Slump said, rubbing his chin. "Your oldest daughter is in college nearby at George Washington. I suspect she'll be getting back from class later today. Shall I tell her, or would you prefer to first? What about your wife? She volunteers at the public library in Arlington. Would she like a copy as well?"

Mike's courage was fleeting. He slumped back in his chair, having suffered the assassin's fatal blow.

"You see," the priest said. "We know everything about you. The choice is up to you."

Mike steadied himself. "Look, you made your point. I don't know what I'm going to do. I need to think about this. You need to get the hell off my campus before I call security."

Satisfied that he needed to do no more, Father Slump stood up and took his folder. "We'll be in touch soon. Here's a number. Text me when you have the results."

With that, he left the office and hurried to his rental car in the parking lot. He said a silent prayer that the right choice would be made and the whole memory could be forgotten. Better to have threatened him than have to make good on the blackmail.

"Father Kelly, it's done," Father Slump reported into his cell phone.

"Excellent work. Do you have confirmation?"

"Not yet. But the threat was convincing. I've seen men willing to do anything to preserve their pride. This professor is no different. The Cardinal will be irate when he learns I failed."

"Don't worry about Rodriguez. I anticipate his station in the Vatican will collapse before he can do anything to retaliate. Once the old order is reestablished, I imagine you'll have your pick of assignments."

"Father, I've committed a grave sin today. Promise me that the threat was the weapon and there will be no need to release this filth and cause further injury to this man."

"You're absolved of this sin, my son."

Father Slump raised his voice. "Forgive me father, but I can take no absolution from a coconspirator."

There was silence on the line. "I understand you had your reservations here. All that matters is that we save this church from its own greater sin. Keep that information on the professor—we need to make sure we have it at the ready in case the professor retracts whatever favorable report he may produce."

Father Kelly's assurances did little to assuage his guilt. His face burned hot with shame, like a flaring sunburn. A confession would be some small salve to reduce the pain. The Basilica was close. There, he could find a priest to confess his sin. He put his faith in the sacrament of reconciliation to lighten the burden of his crime against man and God.

24

Rick paced the study. The house was too quiet. Graciously, Linda had made breakfast before leaving to volunteer. Bob was still getting ready. He agreed with Jimmy to head to the bus station. Father Henry had a few more days before his flight, so he accepted Eileen's invitation to stay at the house until then. The only thing worse than Jimmy leaving was the anticipation of him doing so.

"Baby, you're going to wear away the carpet. Come sit down," Marilyn said.

Rick rolled his eyes and sat down at the kitchen table, nervous energy making him want to immediately stand back up. Instead, Marilyn pushed a glass of orange juice his way.

"Leave it to Eileen to escape from the camp on a moment's notice and still remember to pack an extra dress and two wigs. Girl, she's getting ready now. Looks like a damn model. I wish I had those cheekbones. Makeup can only do so much. Look at me," she said, waving to her wrinkled dress. "I look like a better rendition of your walk of shame outfit from last night. Damn."

"We're not at the camp anymore. You know you don't have to dress like a drag queen all day," Rick reminded her.

"Oh, I know, baby. I don't get ready though. I stay ready. Plus, our contract required being in drag the whole time. Yes, heels all day hurt, but I don't mind it so much."

"Why? What do you get out of it? You're not performing."

"But I am, child. Some people wear costumes to be other people. I wear this to be myself. Out of drag, I'm just an obnoxious and marginalized black man. In this? Well, I can be the same bitch and get away with it. Better for people to laugh at me than condemn me," she said, admiring the jeweled bracelets on her arm. "We all wear costumes. Don't you?"

Rick nodded. "My costume wasn't bedazzled in rhinestone. It just kept me from having to disappoint people who wouldn't accept me—people who'd never see me the same after my card castle of lies fell down."

"Baby, you're wearing a raincoat on a clear day. You'll find that the people who love you most will care the least."

Rick let her words sink in for a moment. "So you were in on this the whole time?"

"Never had a second thought. Eileen is family. Family sticks together."

Jimmy walked into the kitchen. Rick wanted to hug him and never see him again in equal measure. Rick felt possessed by two separate people at once with no bridge in between. Jimmy was too calm. *Was this even hard for him?* He considered that maybe pretending it didn't matter was the only way he could pull himself away. Locked between anger and love, Rick was powerless to hate him.

"It's that time," Jimmy said.

Bob and Father Henry walked in behind him. As if on cue, Eileen walked down the stairs dressed like she was ready to win a pageant. White boots and a dress to match. Golden-blonde hair teased her cheeks. And why wouldn't she save her best dress for last? Today, she would claim her victory.

"Are you sure you can't stay?" Eileen asked.

"Would if I could, Eileen," Bob said with a sigh. "But I've been away from my family long enough. They need me home to be the father I should have been from the start. I owe all of you so much for helping me see what I couldn't see before."

"I never expected to come here and find myself," Jimmy said, avoiding eye contact with Rick. "I don't know what life will bring me when I go home, but I know I get to live it as authentically as I want."

"Babies, I hate to see you go. I'm gonna love to watch that ass of yours leave, though," Marilyn said, pointing to Jimmy and making him blush.

"Just stay," Rick said, his gaze locked on Jimmy.

Jimmy's effort to smile collapsed like a bridge carrying too much weight, and he finally met Rick's gaze.

"I can't," he said, barely moving his mouth.

Rick stood up and grabbed Jimmy's cheeks, bringing him into a passionate kiss. *It may be his last*, he thought. It would have to be a kiss to tell Jimmy what mere words could not. The kiss grew into a hug—a deep hug that enveloped Rick—his tears soaking into Jimmy's shoulders.

"I can't," Rick sobbed. "I can't without you. I need you. I don't want you to go!"

Jimmy's own eyes welled with tears. "I will see you again. I promise." The words cut without mercy, as Rick knew them to be a lie.

Rick stood in the desolate valley between opposing peaks of expectations and reality—peaks he confused for the same mountain just earlier in his journey. "I don't understand—if you can love me, how can you leave me?"

Jimmy hesitated. "Rick, I've got my whole life ahead of me. I don't have answers to all the questions. I need to explore the world and learn more about myself. So do you."

"This was so much more to me," Rick begged, no longer able to see the trail that led him there.

Jimmy's stricken expression was his only reply.

"The car's here," Bob said.

The time had come. *What audacity*, Rick thought. Why now? Why could the car not arrive a moment later? A day later? Time was reduced once again to seconds Rick would never forget—seconds he longed to stretch into a forever.

Rick gave Jimmy one more hug. The first hug was a plea to stay. The last hug was a goodbye. Mournfully, the two men made their way outside to the waiting car. Once Jimmy closed the door, Rick could no longer hold back his tears. Sobbing, he collapsed back into the chair in the kitchen. Just like that, the man he loved was gone.

"That's it?" Rick cried. "He was my everything, and what was I? His hookup? His coming-out experiment? He told me he *loved* me. Doesn't that mean anything?"

"Baby, we don't cry because we lost something," Marilyn said, wrapping her costume-jeweled arm around his shoulder. "We cry because we realize we never had what we thought we did."

The house felt empty. Three souls in the kitchen were too few to help mend the one with a broken heart. Light from the early morning sun poured through the window. It warmed Rick's face and dried his tears, as though showing him the path of a new day.

Rick wiped his tears on his sleeve. There was still work to do, and his resolve returned to vanquish his self-pity.

"We have to go back," he announced, almost defiantly.

"Back? To the camp?" Father Henry asked.

Rick dug in his pocket and pulled out two worn notes, each folded in a tightly wrapped square with frayed edges. "There's someone who needs our help. Someone is still stuck at that camp. They sent me notes…"

"No one is trapped there, Rick," Eileen said. "You were the only one ever trapped there. Not in body, but in a prison you weren't ready to see until now."

"But look," Rick said. "Read them for yourself!"

Eileen gently pushed the notes away. "I don't have to. I wrote them."

"What?" Rick's gaze settled on Eileen. Father Henry lowered himself into a chair beside them.

"Oh shit," Marilyn said, smiling and watching with anticipation.

Eileen rolled her eyes at Marilyn. "When I saw you on the roster, I knew I needed you in my cohort. At first, I just wanted to give you a reason to stay and not take the first car back to the airport. Then you surprised us—though I shouldn't have been. You always seek the truth. When you took the bait and discovered the New Revelation, you made my job a lot easier. I couldn't risk blowing my cover before we had it back."

"So you used us?" Father Henry asked.

"Regrettably, yes. I never intended to get you so embroiled in a fight that wasn't yours."

"But that can't be. The first note said you knew my parents."

She looked over at Marilyn, who was intently listening to the drama unfold. "That part was true."

"How?" Rick demanded.

Eileen laughed. "Surely you don't forget your first kiss, do you?"

Rick looked at her, dumbfounded.

Seeing his confusion, she tugged at her wig and lifted it from her head. She tousled her hair and started to remove her makeup with wet napkins from the table. He looked up at Rick with a smile that was his own.

Startled, Rick's jaw went slack, and he dropped the notes to the table.

"*Garrett*," he whispered.

Garrett smiled back at him, his eyes glimmering with happy tears.

"Garrett?" Rick repeated, as if to convince himself that his eyes weren't deceiving him.

"It's been a long time, my friend," Garrett said, leaning over to embrace Rick in a hug.

Marilyn wiped her brow. "Girl, you may be amateur, but that's the best damn drag reveal of the century!"

Garrett silenced her with a glare. "You know, Rick—the things you say about me in those damn sermons are clearly not true. Never got H.I.V. and certainly never died."

"But they said…"

"People say a lot of things. Gossip. Stories evolve. People with too much time on their hands make up their own reality. Life is like drag, Rick. Sometimes, just an illusion that lets people see what they want to."

"Jesus, I had no idea," he said. "I can't tell you how many nights I lay awake, missing you. Hoping someday I'd see you again, but never daring to believe it."

Garrett's voice darkened. "What if I did? You'd just come out of the closet? Throw away your livelihood? I don't understand why you could be so concerned with your own livelihood when you were so callously indifferent to mine."

"What do you mean? I always cared about you," Rick pleaded.

"Did you?" he asked. "Did you care about me when I was homeless on the streets in New York after my father kicked me out for dating some guy when I was in high school? When I was jumped and beaten to an inch of my life by some stupid homophobes on the subway?"

"I had no idea!"

"But you did," he said, pushing the makeup-stained napkins across the table. "How many people—violent, evil people—took shelter in your words? Did it give them license to do this? Did it make them think that it's okay to fracture someone's skull and break their collarbone because they weren't doing anything worse than what God would do to them? Did they feel better about themselves after?"

Rick tried to speak, but the words were stuck in his throat. He just looked down at the smeared kaleidoscope of matted colors on the napkin.

"Love each other as I have loved you," Garrett quoted. "In what part of the Bible did Christ condemn those whom he believed to be sinners? Never. Instead, he forgave them their transgressions—even the very people who would drive spikes into his flesh and leave him to die. How dare you speak his name and claim to follow his path?"

"I-I'm so, so sorry," Rick pleaded.

Garrett's face softened, and he leaned in, resting his hand on Rick's.

"But I forgive you," he said. "I still love you as much as I did when we were young. I've changed, but never changed."

"I will never say those words again. Never!" Rick assured him. "I'm not the same person I was before. You helped me see that."

"Life will test you, baby," Marilyn said. "Those words are easy to say but hard to live."

Keeping with the tradition of morning cocktails, Marilyn produced a bottle of champagne as if from thin air and popped the cork. She generously poured some into Rick's orange juice, diluting it until it was nearly transparent. Rick's mind was spinning, but the drink helped.

"Excuse me," Garrett said, taking his vibrating cell phone to the study.

Marilyn raised her flute. "To family."

To family, Rick thought, clinking his glass to hers. Rick remembered his father's stern, unforgiving chastisement the day he was nearly exiled from his own home. The incident was never spoken of again, but it lingered thereafter in the air like over-boiled cabbage. It lingered for so long that he stopped noticing it. Seen but unseen. Marilyn was right, he decided; his costume had been elaborately stitched together with the lies he told himself—the most deceptive of all lies—his disguise so perfect that even he couldn't see the truth. Here he sat, the sum of all his choices, successes, and failures. They all led him here. To today.

"There's a problem," Garrett said, his phone clutched to his chest. "Mike needs us at the university. Right away."

25

Professor Mike ushered them into his office and closed the door. His desk was like his home: papers strewn upon papers. It was like its own archaeological dig—the deeper one dug, the older the papers became.

"I didn't want to discuss it on the phone," he said, gathering the men in close. "Linda. Was she still home? Did you see her?"

Garrett looked puzzled. "Linda? She left a little after you did, for the library."

"She can't know. She just can't," Mike said with unhinged exasperation.

"Mike," Garrett said, putting his arm on the professor's shoulder, "relax. What happened?"

Mike paced the room and leaned against the side of his desk, looking out the window. "Garrett, I've made mistakes. I've done things I regret. Things I don't want Linda to know about."

"What are you talking about?" Garrett asked, his voice tense.

"A priest came to see me this morning," Mike said, not daring to meet Garrett's gaze. "He has evidence of an affair I had. He knows everything. Everything about me. Had a folder with pictures, documents. Said he'd tell Linda and Eve if our test results affirmed the age of the document."

"What?" Garrett steadied himself against a chair he hoped could support a weight he could not bear on his own. "You cheated on Linda?"

Mike looked up, his stricken eyes bleeding his apology in tears. "Garrett, I'm so sorry. I lied to you. Lied to them. I can't let them know. Not like this."

Garrett walked over and hugged the broken man. No judgment or condemnation, just whatever love he was able to share. It was a hug that reminded Mike to breathe.

"Listen," Garrett said, "there will be other ways for us to get what we need without you having to pay this price. You didn't choose this. You don't deserve this."

"Wait, you're going to just give in to this asshole?" Rick asked.

Garrett looked pensive, then resigned. "I won't destroy my family to save it."

Marilyn confidently nodded her head. "Family sticks together."

"Tell me about this priest," Father Henry said, stepping more into the room. "What did he look like?"

Mike sat down and took off his glasses to rub his

eyes. "I don't know. About your height. Slight build. Gray hair but cut short."

"Icy blue eyes?"

Mike looked up. "Yes, actually. Strikingly so."

"You know him?" Rick asked.

"It's Slump," Father Henry said. "The same priest who sent the letter to Missy."

Rick struggled to find his words. "You never mentioned…"

"I hoped I'd never have to," Father Henry said.

The professor opened the desk drawer, the sound of wood scraping against wood.

"Here. I was given this number. I'm to text him when I have the results he wants."

"You realize what this means, Garrett," Rick interjected. "All you've worked for, that *generations* of people have worked for. It all fails if we give into his demands."

Marilyn stood up and tugged at her ever more wrinkled dress. "I imagine people will feel betrayed. To believe something and then be told it's not true. Atonement camps will be ghost towns. Heaven only knows what would happen to all the rights we've earned—not just recently, but ever since Stonewall."

"We've been hated before, Marilyn. I'm used to it," Garrett said, looking at Rick. "Still, nothing is a complete failure. We know the truth. We always will."

"Let me speak to him," Father Henry said. "Maybe I can persuade him."

All eyes turned to Professor Mike.

"Father Henry," the professor said, "I'm prepared to put my faith in you. If there's any way you can have him reconsider his threat, I'm willing to take that risk."

"Mike," Garrett cautioned.

"No, Garrett. Rick's right," the professor said. "We can't just surrender. We have to at least try. Testing is underway, and I won't have results until tomorrow. But I can draw up the falsified records today. We can give him those and be done with it."

Garrett rubbed his chin. "We could, but it wouldn't take too long before someone takes a close look at the results or someone in the lab notes the discrepancy and finds some type of experimental error. Mike, there's so much sensitivity here that I don't think your tenure could save you if this gets out."

The professor looked out the window. "Better to retire than lose my family. That's a cross I can't bear."

Rick impatiently shifted in his seat. "Truth will set you free, Mike. If you get ahead of this and tell your family first, they will forgive you."

"Sometimes," Garret said after a pause, "it's easier

to give advice than take it. You should know better than most how difficult the truth can be, Rick."

Rendered humbled and mute by his own hypocrisy, Rick resigned himself to whatever may come. Rick recalled the last time he saw his father. The man lay in the hospital bed, unable to speak, somewhere in the twilight between this life and the next. At that moment, Rick could have told him everything. He could have used that moment of solitude with only faintly beeping and whirring machines in audience to recount that event of his youth and repair the lie that tormented him. There would have been no shouting. No final condemnation. No disappointment. Instead, he'd remained silent. Love and compassion were the victors in their silent war. He hung onto the secrets that divided them as he acknowledged that the same secrets held them together in a conspiracy of silence. It was a balance that death itself dared not disturb. *How could I demand more from another?*

Rick, determined not to let Garrett down again, raised his gaze. "I have an idea—a way to help Mike."

Garrett gave the same bemused half-smile Rick recognized from the boy he used to know. "What do you have in mind?"

"Do you trust me?" Rick asked, recalling the words

once spoken to him to remedy his fear of the dark tunnel into the unknown.

"Implicitly," Garrett said, his smile widening.

"Good—a trick we learned at camp. Marilyn, tell me you have a bunch more of that makeup. And I'll need a dress. No, two."

"Honey," Marilyn said in a way that Rick knew he needn't have asked.

26

Forged documents in hand, Father Henry began his final mission. With a quick text, it was agreed that the professor would meet him at the Basilica of the National Shrine of the Immaculate Conception. Father Henry consecrated the lie with his insistence on going alone. As his cab rolled through the winding Washington streets, Father Henry heard the Basilica's bells toll. Were they a greeting or a warning? Father Henry considered it was nothing less than the beating heart of an entire faith, beginning long before these times, yet on the precipice of ending that very day. That very hour. They rang again, but louder as the cab drew ever closer. Today, Father Henry knew he would be tested. The faith itself would also confront this, its next crucible. *Once the elements of truth were dissolved in fire, would the faith take the worn path of its past, moving ever closer to a self–imposed execution? Or would a new era of life be born?* Father Henry stepped out of the car. The bells rang again, vibrating in his chest. In so doing, they shook out any vestiges of doubt Father Henry still carried with him.

He hobbled briskly through the grand doors. It

wasn't his first time there. He knew exactly where he was headed. Moving past crowds of tourists and masses being recited in small alcoves dedicated to Christian pilgrims, he moved forward. Not distracted by the art and sculpture that adorned the walls in a wealth of false idols to a God few truly worshiped, he moved to a deserted alcove, save one priest seated in the front pew before an empty altar. The altar shone with gold and silver, while not a block from the church, Father Henry had seen a homeless man collapsed on a stoop. Father Henry never met Christ, and if judged by his actions today, he questioned whether he ever would. Still, he shivered at the thought of Christ's revulsion toward those who buried their master's wealth in a hole dug into the ground.

"Father Slump," Father Henry said, startling the man.

Father Slump's face contorted into a mask of fear and shock. "Henry! What are you doing here?"

"It's been some time. I could ask you the same. You're a long way from Rome. A very long way, in fact."

Father Slump studied Father Henry's face for an answer to the riddle before him. Henry sat down next to him, papers in hand.

"I believe this is what you wanted," Father Henry

said, showing the lab results to the hollow man at his side.

"I thought the professor would be here with this," Father Slump said.

"How bold of you to stab the heart of this church from within. Delivering its death warrant in a house of worship," Father Henry mused with dark sarcasm.

"Quite the opposite," Father Slump insisted in an urgent whisper. "I'm here to save this church! Don't harbor compassion for those who would seek to have us sanction their lascivious designs."

"Have you learned nothing?" Father Henry asked. "Priests abused their callings and committed vile acts against the most innocent among us, and bishops hid the truth, becoming conspirators in the same sin. Does this wheel still spin? Are you here to kiss the cheek of the one you seek to betray? How many coins did they offer you? A promotion? A choice appointment?"

"You already have the blood on your own hands!" he roared, giving no reverence to the altar before him. "You would support their transgressions?"

"*Our* transgressions, Simon," Father Henry reminded him.

Father Slump's eyes darted side to side, confirming they were still alone. "That was a long time ago,

Henry. A sin for which I sought absolution and never surrendered to temptation again. Not with you and not with anyone else."

"How would your traitorous superiors land on the question of whether an affirmed homosexual could still lead in their ranks?"

"Blackmail? This is beneath you," Simon spat. "Do your best, old friend. I know too much. They stand more to lose by trying to silence me."

Father Henry bowed his head. "For what will it profit a man if he gains the whole world and forfeits his soul?"

"Ask yourself," Simon demanded, standing and snatching the report from Henry's hand. He folded it neatly in his wallet.

"What of that envelope in your hand? The evidence."

"This is not my burden and not mine to give you," Father Slump said, briskly walking away.

Father Henry took the borrowed cell phone from his pocket. "He's leaving with the blackmail evidence in a folder. You're up," he texted.

RICK OPENED THE TEXT and looked at Garrett. "Ready?"

Garrett chuckled and adjusted Rick's habit. "Sister, I got this. I'm more worried about you."

"I learned from the best, Sister Indulgence," Rick said, smiling.

Dressed in black tunics with their hair tucked neatly in habits, the men reflected on what Marilyn said was some of her best work: feminine, but understated. Her makeup make them look a generation older. She lamented to Rick that there was nothing she could do to make him look any wiser. Still, Rick marveled that she had created a masterpiece without even using lipstick or heels.

With feigned hunched backs and the measured steps of the aged, Rick and Garrett made their way into the church. Wafting incense rolled into an alcove from a nearby mass, causing Rick to cough just as Father Slump hurriedly approached the exit.

"Sister Persistence," Garrett shrieked with a shaky voice. "Just breathe. I have your inhaler in here somewhere."

Garrett frantically dug in his bag. Rick's cough became a wheeze. A few congregants passed by, giving them space but not stopping to help.

"Father!" Garrett said, grabbing Father Slump's arm. He looked shocked, like he had touched a hot pan. "Father, Sister needs our help."

"I can't…" Rick croaked, "I can't breathe… Help me, Father."

"What's this?" he asked, impatiently freeing his arm.

"Sister Persistence is allergic to incense. Always has been, and I can't find her inhaler. She can't breathe."

"Seems like she picked the wrong profession," Father Slump said, eyeing the door.

Rick took a moaning gulp of air, one so loud that it gave competition to the organ in the distance. A crowd started to gather. Father Slump glanced over to the door.

Garrett took the man's hand again. "Quickly, Father. I can't move her on my own. She's too heavy. Her penchant for all those unconsecrated bread wafers at night."

"Carbs!" Rick gasped, his hands around his neck, bent over and wheezing so loud his throat hurt.

"Good God," Father Slump said, eyeing the people rushing over. "Here, take this."

Garrett took the envelope filled with Mike's indiscretions, and the priest put Rick's arm around his shoulder.

"Sister Persistence, can you walk?" he asked, growing frantic.

Rick nodded and stumbled in his ill-fitting black pumps. "Not ready to meet Jesus today, Father—need fresh air!"

"Give us room," the priest shouted. The crowd made way for him to trudge to the door with Rick in his arms.

Rick amped up his coughing, on his way to a crescendo. "Hurry, Father."

An usher dashed ahead to push open the door, light cascading in. Rick squinted from the brightness, his eyes already wet with tears from his fit. After crossing the threshold into the sun, Rick carried his momentum and broke free from Father Slump, letting his weight slam against the railing outside.

"Sister, are you okay?" Father Slump asked, panting for air himself.

Rick stood erect and dusted off his dress. "Completely cured—an absolute miracle, Father Slump," he said in his own voice.

Father Slump's expression of bewilderment was a priceless gift to Rick. He gladly accepted it, smiled, and then hiked up his dress and bounded at full speed past the priest and back into the Basilica. Like a linebacker, he broke through the crowd by the door and ran as fast as he could to Garrett. "Got it?"

Garret held up the envelope, and with Rick at his side, raced down the aisle of the church toward a rear exit. Heads turned and watched the nuns escape, their black flats clapping against the ground and echoing through the Basilica. Rick heard shouting from behind but didn't care to look. Nothing would stop him now.

They turned a corner and plowed through an emergency exit, setting off a fire alarm in the building. Rick lost his shoes on the steps down to the road, where they found Mike, Marilyn, and Father Henry waiting for them in the professor's car. The door flung open. Garrett and Rick dove in, one after the other. Not waiting for the door to close, Mike sped away.

"We got the evidence for the blackmail, but he still has the falsified test results!" Rick yelled from the back seat.

"Child, you lost your shoes!" Marilyn said. "Still an amateur, so I'll let that slide."

"Thank God," Mike said. "I wished we could get that report back as well, but at least I have the chance to be the one that explains the affair to my family."

"No one should take away anyone's right to tell their own story," Rick said as Marilyn smiled and nodded her head.

"It's okay," Garrett said. "I have a plan to handle the problem with the test results. It'll take months to pull off, but I'm sure we can show experimental error."

"If Slump releases that report to the media, I don't know if it will help. A cloud of uncertainty will probably always linger," Mike said solemnly. "As an atheist, I can assure you that faith and doubt are not companions."

"You can always blame it on your research assistant," Garrett suggested with a coy smile.

"That's twice I pulled you out of a ditch, Garrett," Rick said. "You'll have to repay me, eventually."

Rick and Garrett looked at each other and laughed. Rick saw a spark in Garrett's eye. *A spark may be just enough to relight a fire*, he thought. He assured himself that all things meant to be will come in their own season.

27

A simple black pantsuit would do, Missy thought. All business today. Her heels clacked down the hall from her office to the conference room where the emissary sat, the sound bouncing off the walls. The camp was now nearly vacant, save a few pool boys who assisted a limited staff on what duties remained.

"Good morning, Emissary," she said, warmly grasping his hand. He wore a light-blue suit with a sprightful yellow pocket square neatly folded in his breast pocket.

To her surprise, he smiled broadly to match the Easter-like attire that announced his resurrection. She didn't know the man was capable of happiness.

"Thank you, dear. How was your night?"

"Just fine," she said, catching herself unprepared for small talk.

"Good, good," he said. "Clearly, you saw today's news?"

"How could I avoid it? Wall-to-wall coverage from D.C. to the Vatican and everywhere in between."

"When you told me of the priest's success, you'll forgive me for not believing you. It was truly quite an accomplishment; even though you strayed from the plan, ingenuity and luck found their way to win the day," the emissary said.

"I'll admit," Missy said, taking a seat beside him, "Father Slump truly saved our necks."

"Your neck," the emissary corrected with a raised finger.

Missy frowned.

"Don't rush to congratulate the man," the emissary continued. "That alliance was political. Rare that the wolf and the sheep should ever work together and rarer still for the arrangement to last. The wolf gets hungry, eventually."

"Naturally," Missy agreed. "We must not trust them."

The emissary's smile turned to a frown. "Well, dear, I rather think we're the wolves, no?"

Feeling like she was being critiqued for giving a wrong answer in class, she lowered her head in the face of rebuke.

"It would have been far better if we had possession of the New Revelation. Without it, our victory may be short-lived," the emissary said.

"We have allies in the media, government. I suspect they'll test it again and have conflicting results one day, but who will know what to believe?"

"Regardless, the Luminaries have taken note of your role in this enterprise and deem you worthy of a recognition that's commensurate to your contribution," he said with satisfaction.

"Oh?" Missy asked, giving every effort to appear both surprised and humbled when she was neither.

"The Luminaries also took note of Gertrude's role. You were wise to reach out to her. In fact, she'll be invited to join our council."

"Really?" Missy asked, gritting her teeth before she caught herself. "Naturally, Emissary, she was helpful, but she delivered us a decoy. Are you sure that's prudent?"

"We've had our eye on her for some time. People love her. Do you know she sings all her own songs in drag?"

Missy concentrated on her breathing.

"The council isn't done making new appointments," the emissary said, smiling.

Missy leaned in and drew a smile to match his.

"Sean? Is he still here?"

"Sean? My submissive?" she asked.

"Yes, that's right. Quite obedient. You trained him so well."

Missy struggled to connect her submissive's role in her appointment, but looked toward the door. "Sean! Sean, come!"

The dog man gingerly opened the door and stepped in from the hall. "Yes, Mistress? How may I serve you?"

"You've been summoned by the emissary," she said flatly.

"Dear Sean," he said, smiling and kneeling beside Sean, inspecting the name tag on his collar. "You've been such a good boy."

"Yes, your Emissary. I just want to please you," he said, bowing his head.

"I apologize for my informality, Sean. You can expect to receive your papers—membership papers, that is. The council saw fit to extend an invitation for you to join us on a provisional basis for the services and loyalty you've shown in this ordeal."

"Provisional membership in the council?" Missy squealed, unable to constrain her composure a moment longer. "Since when has the council offered provisional membership? And, to a submissive? What possible value would he bring to the Luminaries?"

The emissary studied her with fascinated eyes and a coy smile. "Surely, you don't question the wisdom of the council, dear?"

Missy swallowed her revulsion and made her best attempt at a weak smile. "Of course not, Emissary. I… only thought his mistress would be afforded advanced knowledge of the decision. I would have given him the reward myself."

The emissary turned again to the nearly prostrate

man in a harness and collar resting at his feet. "Loyalty is highly valued and rarely found. You honor us with your own, Sean. Will you serve us?"

Sean looked up at Missy, and she could see his wide eyes under the leather dog mask covering his face. His eyes seemed to plead permission from her. Before Missy could speak, Sean turned his head to look up at the emissary. "Yes, I will serve you, my master."

"Such a good boy," the emissary said as he gently unclasped the collar around Sean's neck. Missy leaned forward, indignant but silent.

The emissary took a new collar from his satchel, golden with diamond studs. The old collar dropped to the ground. Missy recognized the frayed black leather collar suddenly looked old and neglected in the splendor of his new gift. Carefully, the emissary fastened the new collar around Sean's expectant neck.

"Much better," the emissary said, taking estimation of the newly styled accessory. "I will be your new handler. We have a job for you."

"You're taking my submissive from me?" Missy asked, barely able to contain her spite.

The emissary chuckled. "I'm certain you can find a new one wherever you end up after all of this. Folsom Street Fair will be here before no time. I imagine they'll all be up for auction… or however one may acquire one."

Missy stared at Sean, but he didn't look back, his eyes fixed on his new master.

"Times will grow harsh for many of us," the emissary continued, standing up. "We are a culture formed not by faith, ethnicity, or race. No, we are forged by oppression and struggle. Without it, we're directionless. Luminaries are artists, writers, designers. Without pain, there is no art. Without suffering, no beauty. Conservative fundamentalist preachers will no doubt start condemning us to hell again, their voices so much louder now that they can say *I told you so*. But let them cast their stones."

Missy nodded in agreement.

"Anyway," the emissary said, "this, I believe, is yours."

He handed her a simple white envelope. She felt its weight in her hand, like a bar of gold pressed against her chest. The emissary excused himself with Sean tottering behind him and left Missy and her prize in the room's silence. Eagerly, she flicked her nails under the seal and opened the envelope, being careful not to rip the memento. Even scraps of paper commemorating the occasion would find their way to a display box in her imagined home, like a coveted piece of art to draw admiration from her social-climbing guests as they stalked her halls on trips to the bathroom, perhaps. In it, she withdrew a card.

"Thanks for the help—but, you still have a job to finish," the note read in a hastily handwritten scrawl. A twenty-five-dollar gift card dropped lifelessly to the table. Frantically, she flipped the envelope over and peered inside, looking for something else. She flipped the card over in an attempt to find the rest of what she was owed.

Dammit, she thought. She gritted her teeth and squinted, realizing the folly of her ill-invested faith, her rage turning inward. She then knew she was a victim of her own expectations. Everything was not lost, she assured herself in her effort to avoid hyperventilating. She took comfort in the small fortune she earned from the Luminaries in compensation for her role managing the camp. It would be more than enough for what would come next. A momentary setback, she thought. *If the Luminaries want their ultimate prize, they shall have it.* Her anger softened like the echo of a primal yell in a deep canyon. She took a deep breath and lifted her eyes to the news, which played muted on the television behind the table.

A reporter with a microphone stood outside a gay bar Missy didn't recognize in a city she'd never been to.

Vandals tear down pride flags, break window, the news ticker read. Angry young men with scarves masking their faces rioted through mists of smoke and tear gas. Flame-singed windows outside the bar made the glass opaque to what may be seen within—as they once were when gay bars hid down forgotten alleys, long before they found their prominence on the corner of every Main Street. Missy leaned back in her chair. Ignoring the torn envelope before her, she smiled. She smiled knowing she earned everything she fought for.

28

"Ricky? Ricky, is that you?" his mother called, trying without success to hold back Liberty as Rick fumbled with his keys at the door.

"Yes, Momma. It's me. I'm home!" he called, catching himself as the dog pounced on him with welcoming licks. "I brought you a gravy biscuit. How've you been?"

"Oh fine," she said, inching toward him with her walker and an oxygen tank in close escort. Her hair was not brushed, and dirty dishes were piled in the sink, overflowing to the counter behind her in the kitchen.

"Sam came by a few times to check on me," she said. "Best he could, anyway. Such a busy man. I made tea, come," she beckoned.

Rick brought in the last of the suitcases, grateful to the pool boys for reuniting him with his entire wardrobe. He joined his momma in the kitchen, sitting down at the table strewn with unopened mail.

"Did you have a good time at camp? Meet new friends?" she asked.

Rick stirred sugar into his tea. "I did."

"I'm so glad," she said. "You need new friends. I was so worried about you. They never called. At least

they sent some pictures," she said, pointing to the refrigerator.

There, Rick saw an enlarged photo of him embracing Jimmy. His cheeks turned scarlet red and words
dissolved like the sugar in his boiling-hot tea.

"I know, Ricky. I always have," she said.

"You knew?" he asked.

"Ever since you were young. Sitting with me when
your daddy would travel. Watching all those old movies. Then, that Garrett boy when you were young. A
mother always knows. Your father worked so hard to
cover that up, going so far as to spread false rumors
about that poor boy. His mother sold that house and
left town faster than the truth could ever come out."

Rick waited for the condemnation.

She took a sip of her tea. "You see, I've only ever
wanted you to be happy. Your father? We didn't always agree. He saw you for the son he wanted you to
be. Didn't want to see who you actually were. It's one
thing to love the idea of someone. Another thing to
love the person."

Rick's lower lip quivered. He soothed it with the
sweet tea. For as much as Jimmy broke his heart, the
event invited him to see his father with more empathy
than before. *Were we not guilty of the same crime?*

"Will I get to meet him? The young man in the photo?"

"I hope so," Rick said. "I hope you do."

"Sam left about a dozen messages for you, most of which were from today," his mother reported, rolling her eyes.

Elder Monroe was top of Rick's mind as well. Rick helped his mother with a few long-neglected chores, then shuffled to his office by the kitchen to take care of a few of his own. Half-written sermons and books surrounded him, all yearning to confirm biases he no longer harbored.

Face stern, he called the elder.

"Pastor! It's good to hear from you," Sam answered, his voice relieved.

"Likewise, Sam. We need to talk."

"First off," the elder said, "I need to apologize. Now, Rick, things the last few years have been all screwed up. Come to find out, you may have been right about a lot of things all this time. John Beck agrees. He called me this morning. He's all torn up about his son. Not sure what to do."

"You do need to apologize, Sam. First, for not having people look in on my momma," Rick said, as if reading from a list of grievances.

"Oh, now Rick—you know your momma," he

laughed. "She won't accept a hand from anyone, even if she was without a paddle in a boat in a storm. Stubborn. Always has been."

"And no one would have needed to if you didn't insist on sending me to that camp."

Sam paused. "I know, son. That's the thing. Everything will be different now, I imagine."

"It will," Rick concluded. "Starting with this: The church elders are dissolved. I control what I preach, how I handle my flock, what we spend, and how we raise it. Let me be clear—damn clear. I'm taking my church back."

"Well, now, son…" Sam said.

"It's not a request, Sam," Rick interjected. "I spoke to the other elders yesterday on my way home. We already took the vote. The bylaws are modified back to the way it was when my daddy ran things."

Sam tried to speak, but words only came out in stuttered syllables.

"And, I certainly will speak to John," Rick added before Sam could find his way back into the conversation. "I expect to see him on Sunday at church. If you'll excuse me, my momma has a kitchen full of dirty dishes and needs help with the laundry. I already did one load with this call and now I'll move onto the rest of it."

With that, Rick slammed the phone down and

pushed away the papers littering his desk. He decided it was time to draft a new sermon. *Garrett was right*. He truly was like Jonah, he thought—punished by God for not preaching the right message to the right people. The sea having settled from its fierce and tumultuous storm, Rick was given the gift of seeing far over a horizon made placid with his humility.

The week passed with Rick repairing the broken and neglected things in the home, writing as he found the time. He trimmed the bushes outside, each grown wild in the long summer days and storm-drenched by late afternoon rains. The shrubs reminded Rick that all things yearn to live. To grow. No matter how religiously one may return to trim the hedges, they will grow, whether in defiance of the sheers or perhaps just because they have no other choice.

Clouds rolled over the sky like the foam that waves leave behind as they rescind into the sea. A bubbled cloud would occasionally move between the heavens and the sun, cooling the breeze. Homecoming at the church had recently passed, but Rick knew this sermon would be the first he'd ever truly given.

"Today's sermon is about homosexuality," Rick began, looking out over the filled pews from his pulpit. This time, he knew the word needed no translation or explanation. It was perhaps the only word on anyone's mind. Nonstop news broadcasts gave the Vatican no veil to hide their shame. The same cameras reported on demands for accountability from politicians for their hasty support of policies predicated by mass deception. Mobs of angry young men were filmed burning pride flags in city streets, seeking accountability on their own brutal terms.

"If there is a gay person in this church, you should raise your hand!" he demanded. He looked out over the congregation. No hands were raised. His stern expression was unaffected by their silence.

Then, Rick gently raised his own.

Eyes lifted, and a few murmurs were heard over the gasps. Rick only raised his hand higher. But Rick was not alone. Another hand went up in the front pew. Garrett, seated next to his mother, smiled back. Marilyn, sitting next to him, did the same. Rick kept his hand high. Then, emboldened by numbers, another hand went up. John Beck's son. John looked to his son and back to Rick. Rick's gaze dared John to judge, dared him to speak. Dared him to do anything other than resign himself and his fears to the truth. John relaxed, and Rick slowly put his hand back down.

"Parents," Rick began, evenly, "if you have a gay son or a lesbian daughter, do you know what the Bible tells you to do? Do you know what your God tells you to do?"

Rick paused to let the people answer the question for themselves—or at least try to.

"You love them. That's what you do. When my daddy led this congregation, there was this boy. Let me tell you a story about him. He was gay. Instead of loving that young man, he was sent away and told his authenticity was mutually exclusive with God's love. That lie grew like a cancer that led his own parents to believe him just as unworthy of their love. Abandoned and lost, that young man was alone. He formed a new life for himself. Despite all the odds, he found his own family. With their love and support, he managed to go to college. Then grad school. That young man is here today," Rick said, pointing to Garrett in the pew. His mother smiled and reached over to touch Garrett's knee.

"For if we forsake our children, do we love them?" Rick asked.

Silence.

"For if we don't love our children, can we expect God to love us?" Rick asked.

"Amen," came John Beck's lone response. He smiled and wrapped his arm around his son's shoulder.

"Amen," others in the church said.

"Amen!" Rick said louder, inspiring still others to offer the refrain.

"I know there has been much said about the New

Revelation. Brothers and sisters, I know in my heart and with my own witness that it is, in fact, the authentic word of God. Time will be its judge. But even if you disagree, could it not have been? In what part of the Bible did our Lord condemn anyone? He, the only one without sin, invited anyone who had never sinned to cast the first stone. No one did. Not even him. Why now would we expect God to reserve a wrath of judgment for anyone else?" Rick asked, wiping the sweat from his brow.

"If anyone is to be judged, let it be ourselves for the way we treat people in this community. Two weeks ago, this church threatened me with the loss of my job if I didn't go to an atonement camp to repent to the gay community, and now I stopped counting how many of you came to apologize to me this week. Be warned, brothers and sisters. A person certain in his convictions is a person unable to see the error in his ways. But if you think religion's pursuit must lead to certainty, then that certainty is love," Rick said with tears welling in his eyes. Tears that he wished he could share in his father's witness.

"Just love one another," Rick concluded in his impassioned commandment.

The congregation's thunderous applause made Rick take a step back. He gave no thought of the collection

or any ticket revenue. He spoke to make a point, un-
concerned with how it would be received.

After all the handshakes and hugs, small talk and
laughter, everyone headed outside to enjoy the gift of a
warm afternoon in the waning days of summer. Another
year had come and passed. Rick heard the squeaky
swing creaking forward and back amidst their riders'
laughter. He remembered being on the same swing with
Garrett all those years ago. All things were cyclical,
really. People left his life and came back into it. That
cycle, just like the seasons, gave him hope. Hope that
nothing was truly over, not even life itself. Hope that
one day, the truth would be rediscovered.

Rick made a beeline past all those who wished him
congratulations and offered to shake his hand in search
of the one he knew wouldn't. Ryan was out by the old
pine trees near the parking lot, kicking pebbles with
his shoe, waiting for his parents by their car.

"Ryan, I owe you an apology," Rick said, approaching him with caution.

Ryan looked up and Rick took his silence as permission to continue. "I was never saying those things
about you—those were all the things I was just telling
myself since I was your age—all lies to trick me into
believing something other than the truth. You didn't
deserve it."

Ryan smirked and took his weight off the tree. "Pastor, you didn't deserve it either. All those years you spent lying to yourself. Do you regret what your life could have been if you had just figured it all out sooner?"

Rick looked across the field to see Garrett and his mother by the church front porch. They were talking next to the same shrubs he fought to tame every summer. "A wise person recently told me that regrets are just optimism finding its voice."

Ryan creased his brow.

"I didn't understand it at the time either," Rick said, chuckling. "I think I do now. We can look back over our lives and think of the path not taken. It's an illusion. Who's to say anything would be better when everything—good and bad—makes us the people we are today? We can't change the past, and we can't rely on the future, but we have today. Today, I want to start earning your forgiveness."

Ryan thought for a moment. "I think forgiveness is sorta like love. If it were something you earned, like getting paid for chores, it wouldn't make it special. So yes, I'll forgive you, even though I know I don't have to."

Rick's lips quivered as he wiped a tear from his eye. "Thank you, son. Thank you so much."

Marveling at the young man's wisdom, he found a new appreciation for the parents who were raising him.

People trickled from the church to their cars to go home; Garrett was the last one to leave. "Marilyn is headed back to the hotel—she's convinced she'll have diabetes and a heart attack if she eats a single other thing down here," Garrett said.

"She's probably right," Rick said. "This place isn't made for someone like her. I can't imagine how much she'd need to spend for all those new dresses if she outgrows them."

"This place," Garret said, looking at the aging church and overgrown lawn, "is it still made for someone like you?"

Rick smiled and took note of the honeydew bush wafting its nectar by the church and saw the old swings in the back—gently swinging in the breeze as if ghosts from his past still sat upon them. "I have my momma to take care of—not to mention this community. I've atoned to myself, and now I need to atone to them. But one day…"

"One day," Garrett said, embracing him. "And when that day comes, you'll know where to find me. I'm not done with you yet."

"Me either," Rick said, tightening his embrace.

THE END

Dedication

Dedicated to the middle school boys who would whisper *faggot* in the halls just loud enough for us to hear as we passed by. Dedicated to their teachers for not intervening. Dedicated to their parents for teaching them. Dedicated to the priests who lectured us about our sins while they perfected their own. Dedicated to the elected leaders who would deny us our rights in exchange for their offices. Dedicated to those who looked the other way in the A.I.D.S. crisis and hoped we would just go away.

Without your tireless support, this work would not have been possible.

Thank you for reading!

I hope you enjoyed my debut novel. There's no better way to support this work and help others find it than to leave a review online at Amazon. I will be eternally thankful if you would take a moment to do that.

If you'd like to stay in touch, please visit me at www.atonementbook.com. There, you can join my mailing list or reach out directly.

Author Bio

First-time author and Philadelphia resident, Evan is a playboy socialite who works in his spare time and enjoys the company of his friends and vodka. His hobbies include travel, dabbling in writing, and making questionable life choices that always lead to good memories.

Made in the USA
Middletown, DE
20 May 2021